TOLCARNE MEROCK

To Jean
with Best Wishes
Geoffrey Rawlings
(Pete)

TOLCARNE MEROCK

Geoffrey Rawlings

UNITED WRITERS
Cornwall

UNITED WRITERS PUBLICATIONS LTD
Ailsa, Castle Gate, Penzance, Cornwall.

British Library Cataloguing in Publication Data:
A catalogue record for this book is
available from the British Library.

ISBN 1 85200 097 X

Printed in Great Britain by
United Writers Publications Ltd
Cornwall.

To my wife Elizabeth.

Chapter One

I was sat beside the footbridge that spanned the River Menahyl, enjoying the view of the flowing river as it wound its lazy way through the Lanhearne valley in the parish of St Mawgan in Cornwall. After another half mile or so it would spread itself out along the beach and join forces with the Atlantic Ocean. It was always so peaceful down here away from the road and traffic. Every now and then I would hear the splash of a trout as it leapt out of the water to feast on an unsuspecting fly. I lit my pipe and settled back into my seat with a contented sigh, relishing the glorious surroundings.

Looking up at the far hillside, I could see 'Tolcarne Merock' nestling in the folds of the sloping fields. The men of old who had built the farmhouse and outbuildings had tucked them neatly in — just far enough back to escape the wild winter storms that howl up through the valley on their way inland from the Atlantic. In its hundreds of years of existence its weathered stonework must have seen much of men's triumphs and disappointments, but it is one particular episode in its long history that relentlessly pervades my thoughts today. It began in the spring of 1942. The war with Germany was in full swing, and every farm in the country was being pressed for more home-grown food to feed the hard-up population. These were difficult times, with most of the young men away fighting for King and country. Even young women were being called up to help work the farms. With their brown breeches, green jerseys and brown felt slouch-hats, they soon became a common sight in rural districts. They were known as the 'Land Army Girls'.

Tolcarne Merock was being farmed at that time by an old bachelor by the name of Reuben Gutheridge, aided by a young chap from the village called Norman Innis. Norman, like several others, had been exempted from the armed forces because of the important agricultural work he was engaged in. The two men worked well together, although side by side they made an unlikely couple. Reuben was short and thickset. His weather-beaten features were deeply rutted by the passing of time, and his hair — once a luscious black forest — was now an almost white halo encircling a brown shiny crown.

The younger man was much taller, and quite handsome in a rugged sort of way. His fair hair, closely cropped around his ears, fell waywardly over his forehead and pointed down to a pair of twinkling, honest blue eyes. His face was tanned but smooth. Time had yet still to do its work upon him. He loved his work at Tolcarne Merock, even though farming in this hilly region was always precarious, much best suited to sheep.

Apart from his many sheep, Reuben also kept twenty cows, a bull, and a scattering of hens which enjoyed life running freely around the farm. They were joined by several cats and a mangy-looking collie who answered to the name of William. William was in charge of rounding up all the creatures of this outpost which, much to his delight, included the cats as well.

On one particular morning the two men had just finished cleaning out the cowshed and were standing in the warm spring sunshine while Reuben enjoyed a well-earned pipe of tobacco. Both were clad in heavy hobnailed boots and leather gaiters which protected the legs of their thick corduroy trousers. These, in turn, were held up by wide, well-worn, leather belts. Their striped shirts were collarless. The collars would be carefully stored away in a drawer, then studded back on when needed for Sunday best. They both glanced round in surprise when a motor-car joggled its way into the bumpy yard and stopped with a shudder some twenty paces away from them. The car door was pushed open by a pompous-looking man who peered down and studied the ground very carefully before choosing an unsullied spot on which to rest his shiny black brogues. He alighted holding a clipboard in one hand, and with the other, carefully brushed some imaginary dust from his very smart dark pinstripe suit. Satisfied that all was perfect, he glanced up disdainfully at Reuben and Norman. In a rather posh voice, he said, 'I am seeking a Mr Reuben Gutheridge, of Tolcarne Merock farm.'

There was a stony silence while the two farmers weighed up their distinguished visitor.

'Come along now!' the gentleman said impatiently, 'I don't have all day. There is a war on, you know. Which of you is Reuben Gutheridge?'

'And who might you be?' retorted Reuben.

The visitor was getting ruffled. 'I will have you know, my man, that I am an official of His Majesty's Government, here on important business.'

'I thought you might be,' drawled Reuben with an exasperated sigh, followed by another seemingly infuriating silence.

Airing his annoyance with an exaggerated snort, the dark-suited visitor promptly turned away and opened the rear door of his car, whereupon to the farmers' amazement out stepped two young ladies, each with a heavy-looking suitcase.

Norman's face had surprised delight written all over it. 'They be Land Army girls,' he spluttered to Reuben.

Reuben looked flustered. 'I can see that, you fool, but what be they doing 'ere? That's what I want to know.'

His Majesty's pompous official clearly gained a perverse satisfaction from informing Reuben that the two girls had been allotted to his farm and that they would be billeted in the farmhouse. Reuben opened his mouth to protest but the man was already back in his car and roaring out of the farmyard.

The girls were left standing in the yard, clutching their cases and fawn overcoats as they nervously eyed their new boss.

Reuben coughed awkwardly and said, 'I'm a bachelor . . . I can't 'ave two maids staying in me 'ouse.'

Norman remained silent, engrossed in admiring the view. The girls did look smart in their uniforms, but his eyes rested longer on the smaller one of the two. Her cute little face peered nervously back at him from under her broad-rimmed hat as he prayed fervently that Reuben would let them stay.

The taller of the two girls suddenly moved towards Reuben with her hand outstretched to shake his hand. 'I'm Marcia Evans from North Wales, and my friend is Ruby Swabey from London. We promise not to annoy you, sir, if you'll let us stay here. We only want to help.'

Reuben, flustered and taken by surprise, asked her what she knew about farming.

9

'We have both had a little training,' Marcia answered. 'And I was brought up on my parents smallholding, so I do have some experience.'

'If Ruby's down from London,' Norman butted in quickly, 'she won't know anything much about farming, but I can soon show her, can't I, boss?'

Reuben threw him a despairing glance. 'Just go and get the cows' 'ay in the racks.' Returning his attention to the girls, he said, 'You'd better come inside and we'll 'ave some tay.'

Giving each other a knowing look, they picked up their cases and followed him towards the granite-walled farmhouse. The back door was open but Reuben raised his hand for them to wait while he ordered William to go in first. The dog did not need to be told twice; he bounded inside and raced around the slippery flagstone floor, barking and yelping like mad. The girls watched in astonishment as several terrified hens came flying out through the doorway amidst a cloud of airborne feathers. Not until a satisfied William sat panting and content in front of his master were the girls allowed in. They walked tentatively through the back kitchen, then paused as Reuben opened the creaky latch of the main kitchen door.

They followed him in and breathed in the warm, stuffy air of the gloomy kitchen for the very first time. Everything seemed miserably dark after coming in from the bright sunshine outside, but as their eyes grew accustomed to the shadowy darkness they were able to take in their new surroundings. The room was quite large with thick black beams supporting the ceiling. Several wicked-looking hooks hung from these timbers, each one supporting an odd-shaped, grimy package of some kind. A huge wooden table dominated the far end of the room, with six matching high-backed chairs placed untidily around it. The light from a solitary window struggled to reach inside through panes made opaque by years of dust and grime. A further cloud of dust rose to settle and stick happily on the greasy overhead beams as Reuben poked the fire in a cumbersome, black, coal-fired range. He brought a heavy iron kettle closer to the heat and gestured the girls to be seated.

There were two rather more comfortable-looking chairs, with arms and a curved, spoked back and well-flattened cushions, adjacent to the stove, but Marcia and Ruby chose those by the table, not wanting to upset the master of the house by unwittingly taking his favourite chair.

Reuben took down a tin from the mantelpiece and measured three heaped spoonfuls of tea into a cracked teapot before filling the pot to the brim with scalding hot water from an ancient kettle. Allowing the tea to brew, he then produced three enamel mugs from a cupboard built into the wall on the opposite side of the room and plonked them onto the table with a loud clatter that made both girls jump. He then disappeared through a side door, only to reappear almost at once with a jug of creamy milk.

'That must be the dairy,' Marcia whispered to Ruby.

Reuben swished a helping of milk into each of the chipped and tea-stained mugs, then filled them to the brim with strong dark-brown tea. The girls shuddered as their lips encountered the rough rims of the mugs, and their throats threatened to prevent the potent brew from slipping down. But aware of Reuben's watchful gaze, they both forced it down, trying not to grimace.

The old farmer retreated to his favourite chair by the fire and, with both hands wrapped around the steaming mug, cautiously studied the girls from under his bushy eyebrows. Both of 'em good-lookers, he reckoned. The one with the long dark hair Marcia, wasn't it? – now she was able to stand up fer 'erself by the look of her. Better be watching me P's and Q's where she's concerned, he decided. Now the other one – Ruby – with 'er short, mousy brown curls and coy little face, she might need a little more looking after. She was going to find life on the farm hard. Mustn't go upsetting 'er if I can help it.

In the far corner of the room stood a grandfather clock. It, too, had not escaped the constant daily ration of dust and grease. Its monotonous ticking took over the silence of the room as the girls fidgeted uneasily in their seats, not knowing what to say. They both started as Reuben suddenly sat up straight with his hands gripping the arms of the chair. Running his tongue over his lips, he said, 'What I want to know is who will be paying you two maids? – I certainly can't afford to!'

Here we go, Marcia thought to herself, farmers don't change much, whatever part of the country they come from. She gave Reuben a sweet smile. 'I think the government will pay, boss, and we are permitted one week's holiday as well.'

Reuben's expression brightened a little. 'Well that's all right

11

then,' he remarked, inwardly delighted at the new idea of cheap labour. After gulping down the last of his tea, he rose stiffly from his chair and moved towards the door. 'Right then, crib-times over. I'll show ee a room that you two can share while you be under me roof.'

The girls picked up their cases and followed him out into a poky hallway flanked by yet more doors and leading to a steep and narrow staircase. Reuben was already halfway up as they struggled with their heavy suitcases. His hobnailed boots clattered on the worn lino that swept down the stairs from top to bottom. It was just wide enough to accommodate both of his feet. Either side of the strip of lino was an inch or two of bare wood, camouflaged somewhat by its liberal covering of cotton wool dust. Manhandling the heavy cases with some difficulty in the confined space, they were both panting heavily when they reached the first floor landing. They made to drop the cases with great relief, only to find that Reuben had gone striding ahead along the gloomy, dark-painted landing, oblivious to their obvious discomfort. Passing the first door, he said, 'That be my room; don't ee go in that one mind.' He glared at them. 'That one be private.'

The girls exchanged a nervous glance, convinced they would never cross the threshold of that particular door. They followed Reuben to the end of the landing where he pushed open another door, this one stubborn and creaky.

'This can be yer room . . . ye can 'ave the rest of the day to put it to rights.' His eyes scanned the room as if he was seeing it for the first time, then he turned to the girls with an apologetic grin. 'See, me dears, nobody 'ave bin in 'ere for ages. I s'pose it's not too bad considering!' He stepped aside for them to enter.

Lost for words, they each succumbed to a barely strangled gasp. The bedroom was thick with dust and grime; a huge black spider scurried across one of the many huge cobwebs. The old fashioned bed had seen better days. Long ago it may have graced the bedroom with its ornate wrought ironwork and shiny brass orbs sitting atop each of the four posts. Now it stood lifeless and dull, with a faded striped mattress rolled up on its bare dusty springs.

Ruby and Marcia deposited their cases in front of the substantial wardrobe, wondering what further horrors lay in wait behind its closed doors.

Reuben's voice interrupted their scary thoughts. He was pointing to an unpolished, worm-ridden chest of drawers. 'Plenty of room to store yer stuff. And there's yer washing facilities.' Now his finger pointed to a low table with a large jug and basin resting on top. 'You get yer water from the well out in the back yard.'

The two girls looked at each other, dumbstruck as the old farmer cleared his throat and told them he had to get back to his farming duties. They remained rooted to the spot as they listened to his clumping footfalls receding along the landing. Then the footsteps stopped for a moment and Reuben's voice bellowed back to them: 'If yer wants hot water there be always plenty in the kettle on the stove.' Then, as an afterthought, he shouted, 'The privy be outside — just past the wash-'ouse!'

The look on the girls' faces mirrored the surrounding gloom as the sound of Reuben's boots faded into the distance.

Chapter Two

Ruby sat down on the hard bedsprings and buried her head in her hands. 'We can't stay here,' she whispered miserably, 'it's horrible. I want to go home.'

Marcia noted the tremor in her voice and moved to comfort her. 'Come on, Ruby,' she said, putting her arms around her, 'it will look a different place in an hour or two, you'll see. It's surprising what a little soap and water can do. We'll have it spick and span in no time, you see if we don't.' Easing Ruby to her feet, Marcia led her over to the window. 'First we must get some fresh air in here. All this dust makes me want to sneeze.'

Marcia opened the window and they both breathed in a lungful of the fresh country air. Below them was the front garden — a wilderness of wayward shrubs and trees.

Here and there a brave daffodil struggled to peep through, determined to enjoy its fair share of the warm spring sunshine. The girls leant back on the window ledge and despondently let their eyes wander back around the musty bedroom. Ruby gave a hopeless sigh. 'Where do we begin?'

'With soap and hot water,' Marcia replied firmly. Come on, Rube, the quicker we start the sooner we'll finish. Mr farmer Gutheridge won't know this place by the time we've finished with it.'

Ruby looked anything but convinced, but nevertheless followed meekly along behind Marcia back downstairs to the kitchen, where they soon found a bucket and a scrubbing brush. The brush had seen better days and had acquired several bald patches, but it would serve their purpose for now. Next to a metal bowl which was half-full of dirty water the girls found a large bar of yellow soap. Leaving Ruby to search around for some cleaning cloths, Marcia went to fill her bucket with hot water from the kettle. She was just refilling the kettle from the big pitcher in the dairy when Ruby came out with her arms full of rags which looked suspiciously like some of Reuben's old vests. Never mind, they had to use something. Armed with their newly-acquired supplies, they started on their daunting task.

After a couple of hours the bedroom had been transformed. It looked and smelt like an entirely different place. In an old linen chest out on the landing they had unearthed some half-decent but deeply creased bedding. After more searching they eventually found an iron which they heated on the kitchen stove. This took up valuable time as it would quickly cool and had to be frequently returned to the stove for reheating. With the job finally done, Marcia made a mental note to get another iron. While one was in use, the other could be on the stove heating up, which would certainly save a lot of time. The jug and basin was now well scrubbed and looked quite pretty with its pattern of tiny pink flowers. It had lost a chunk of its pouring lip somewhere along the way, but was still quite usable. The wardrobe and chest of drawers had been cleaned and the contents of the girls' suitcases neatly stacked away, and not a cobweb in sight. The girls stood back to admire the results of their handiwork, their eyes squinting against the bright sunlight that now found a way through the clean window panes and bounced brightly on the brass orbs of the bed. They both wore satisfied smiles as they slowly closed the door behind them before resolutely descending the stairs to make a determined start on the kitchen.

They tidied it up as best they could, making sure the teapot and mugs had a thoroughly good wash. Their new home suddenly looked far less uninviting. Ruby paused and rubbed her stomach. 'I'm really starving; it must be all this country air.'

Marcia agreed. 'Me too, and no doubt Reuben will expect his tea on the table the minute he comes in; he looks that sort. See if you can find some eggs. You shouldn't have to go far,' she laughed. 'The hens seem to favour the back kitchen . . . oh, and we'll need some potatoes – have a look in the sheds while you're outside.'

Having dispatched Ruby on her way, Marcia turned her attention to the packages hanging from the beams. Intrigued, she decided on a closer examination; it might be something they

15

could eat. Stepping up on to a chair, she carefully unhooked one of the packages, wobbling a bit as the weight of it took her by surprise. Stepping back down, she placed the package on the table and peeled back the yellowed muslin. It was indeed something to eat – a fine joint of ham, but it wasn't cooked. Bother, she thought to herself, that would have done nicely. She carefully covered the ham with its greasy muslin wrapper before turning her attention to the door of the dairy. Hopefully I'll have more luck in there, she thought, as she shakily replaced the ham on the beam.

It was a treat to step inside the cool dairy after the stuffy heat of the kitchen. The room was long and narrow, with a window at the far end. Stout metal gauze took the place of glass panes, which was ideal for letting cool air and daylight into the building. The dairy was purposely situated on the northern side of the house in order to escape the fierce sunshine that often favoured the rest of the farmhouse. As her eyes swept across the wide marble shelf which ran down one side of the room, Marcia spotted what she came for. Part of a large cooked ham stood alongside a sizeable pan which was filled to the brim with rich creamy milk. When she moved to pick up the ham, she spotted a bowl of crusty clotted cream standing nearby. Before she knew what she was doing, her finger had plunged into the depths of the bowl and had scooped up a rather large dollop of its contents. Before thrusting it into her mouth, she instinctively glanced over her shoulder to ensure that the coast was clear. She felt like a naughty schoolgirl as the delicious cream slowly melted in her mouth. Life here in Cornwall was perhaps not *all* bad after all, she resolved to tell Ruby as she picked up the ham and scooted back through to the kitchen.

The ham smelt delicious and was already making her mouth water. The next thing was a carving knife. She hunted around until she found what she wanted in one of the drawers, then set to work. Soon, with her mouth stuffed full of the tender meat, she had expertly sliced off enough generous portions for their evening meal, not forgetting an extra thick slice for Ruby to taste upon her return. She then returned the remainder of the meat to the dairy, this time resisting temptation as she passed daringly close to the bowl of cream.

Ruby duly returned with some large brown eggs. 'There's a bag of potatoes by the door of the back-kitchen,' she said, as her eyes fell lovingly on the freshly-sliced ham. 'Umm, that looks good.'

Marcia passed her the specially reserved slice, then handed her an enamel bowl. 'That's for the potatoes,' she said.

Reuben appeared just after five. He paused in the doorway, unable to believe his eyes. The kitchen looked clean and bright. The table was nicely laid and there was no denying the wonderful aroma of cooked ham. His look of amazement gave way to a wry smile. 'I see ee've found summin for us to eat then.'

'I hope you like it,' Marcia told him with a grin.

He sat down and picked up his knife and fork, impatient to begin. 'I see you maids 'ave cleaned up the place a bit as well!' His eyes never strayed from the food which was being heaped onto his plate.

Marcia suddenly turned on him, her black eyes flashing. 'Yes, we have! Because the bloody place is filthy, as right you know!' The colour started to rise in her cheeks. 'We can't live in these conditions . . . it's disgusting!'

Completely taken aback by her outburst, Reuben dropped his knife and fork on the table, rose from his chair and rounded the table to confront her. Placing his hands on her shoulders, he looked her squarely in the eye and said, 'Quite right, me girl . . . I should 'ave me ass kicked for letting it deteriorate so. You can 'ave another hour in 'ere tomorrow to clean it up some more.'

Ruby, still clutching her serving spoon in one hand and a pan of boiled potatoes in the other, looked from one to the other in astonished disbelief. Good old Marcey, she thought, I could do with some of her nerve.

Reuben returned to his chair and wasted no time in retrieving his knife and fork. His eyes feasted on the laden plate that Marcia placed in front of him. Without looking up, he mumbled, 'I be going to St Columb market in the morning – mebbe one of you maids could come along with me and fetch a few things fer the kitchen cupboard and such like.'

The girls exchanged a knowing look which said: Give us time, boss-man, you'll soon learn which side your bread is buttered on.

All three of them tucked heartily into the meal.

Halfway through, Reuben said, 'I see ee found the 'amm.'

17

Marcia, with her mouth full, just nodded.

Reuben grunted his approval and carried on eating.

Later, when the sun had set, Reuben fetched an oil lamp from its resting place on the window sill, gave it a swift shake to make sure it contained enough paraffin to see them through the evening, then removed the globe and told the girls to draw the curtains on both of the windows as he struck a match. 'Can't 'ave no light showing outside,' he gravely informed them. He waited until the windows were completely covered, then quickly lit the wick before the match burnt down to his fingers. As he replaced the globe the room was suddenly bathed in a soft shadowy light. 'There, that be better,' he remarked contentedly as the grandfather clock's pendulum struck six doleful notes. 'Ah, just in time for the news,' he added. He turned the switch on the scratched and well-worn wireless set, then sat down with a heavy sigh in his chair by the fire. He lit his pipe and rested his head back on the chair to listen to the news, which proved singularly depressing. An English cargo ship carrying vital military components from America had been torpedoed some ten miles off the Isles of Scilly. The brief excitement they all felt when they heard that British naval and commando forces had carried out a successful attack on the German dry-dock at St Naziare soon turned to despair as they next learnt that nearly half of our men had died, and several more had been taken prisoner. What a terrible price to pay!

Reuben finished his pipe in silence before going out to see to his sheep, and that was the last the girls saw of him on that, their first night at the farm. As they washed the dishes in a large enamel bowl on the kitchen table, Ruby said, 'I will end up with muscles like my Dad if I stay here for long. I feel completely worn out; I ache all over. What I could do with is a nice hot bath.'

Marcia smiled. 'I think I noticed a tin bath hanging outside the wash-house when we came in. We'll ask Reuben about it tomorrow. It looked pretty new.'

They looked at each other and giggled. From what they had seen of Reuben, a hardly used bath was a cert!

'At least it's nice and warm here,' Marcia said, the washing up over as they drew two chairs closer to the fire. 'It won't be too bad once we've got everything cleaned up.'

Ruby tried to put on a brave smile, but remained far from convinced that she would ever get used to this hard life.

Seeing that Reuben had offered to take one of them to the market in the morning, they decided to make a list of the provisions they needed. Marcia crossed to the window and, careful not to disturb the drawn curtains, reached round and felt for a candle she had noticed when she had cleaned and dusted the window sill earlier. The writing materials she had thoughtfully brought along with her were now neatly stashed away in one of the small drawers in the chest in their bedroom, but she would need a candle to light her way upstairs. She left the kitchen door open wide as she stepped out into the front hallway, so the light from the oil lamp provided a modicum of light around her. She lit the candle and held it high as she looked up the stairs. It was pitch black at the top. Within the boundaries of the flickering candlelight, grotesque shadows danced along the walls beside her. She felt her skin tighten. A cold knot of fear, somewhere deep inside, threatened to root her feet firmly to the spot. She gave an involuntary shudder, willing herself not to be so silly. If she carried on like this she would soon be as jumpy as Ruby. She took a deep breath and forced her heavy legs up the creaky staircase, telling herself that it was only the spooky candlelight causing all this trouble. She wouldn't take any notice of the shadows when she became used to them. Or so she fervently hoped.

On reaching the bedroom door, she placed the flickering candle on the floor of the landing. It was still daylight when they had finished cleaning the room, so the curtains were not yet drawn. She paused for a moment at the window and looked out at the blackness of the night. Away in the distance she saw the lights of an aeroplane as it rose into a starless sky. She remembered, then, that there was an aerodrome close by. She yawned, wondering whether the noise of the planes would keep her awake. She drew the curtains, then fetched the candle and placed it on the chest. After retrieving her pen and note-pad from the drawer and placing them in the deep pocket of her slacks, she raised the candle and glanced for a moment or two at the room. What a difference, she thought. That bed looks quite inviting now. Then her growing contentment was promptly shattered by a shrill scream!

Ruby!

Marcia raced along the landing and hurtled down the stairs. In her haste the flame of the candle had blown out, but the glow from the oil-lamp served to light her way much better on the way down. Skidding to a halt, she stood gasping in the doorway.

The embarrassed faces of Norman and Ruby looked guiltily back at her.

'I'm sorry,' Ruby stammered, raking her lip with her teeth. 'Norman scared the life out of me when he came in.'

Marcia managed a weak smile before flopping gratefully into one of the chairs. Her legs felt like jelly.

Ruby looked back shyly at Norman. 'I think I must have started to doze off, when I was startled by a scuttling noise over by the back door. When I turned to look, all I saw was a big, dark, shadowy figure looming over me . . . I almost fainted. That's when I screamed.'

'You scared me half to death,' Marcia declared, still feeling shaky.

'I know, I'm sorry. Then Norman spoke to me. I think I must have frightened him as much as he frightened me.'

'I've brought some eggs for your breakfast.' Norman sounded apologetic. Looking directly at Ruby, he went on, 'If you come over to the cowshed early in the morning, you can 'ave some milk . . . make yer own cream and butter.'

'Thanks, Norman, I'll be there,' Ruby told him happily.

As Norman was leaving, Marcia asked him whether they should lock the door. 'But Reuben's not in yet — we wouldn't want to lock him out of his own home.' Marcia glanced at the clock. 'He's been gone for ages.'

Norman looked back with a knowing grin as he opened the back door. 'You won't be having too much of boss's company in the evenings. He sees to 'is sheep, then it's off down to the Falcon pub for 'im most nights, as sure as me name is Norman. No, don't bother locking up,' he called over his shoulder, 'yer safe here; there's nothing to steal.'

The door slammed shut and the girls listened to Norman's receding footsteps before busying themselves with the morning's shopping list. Then it was time for bed. After turning the oil-lamp down to leave just the dimmest of light for Reuben when he returned, Marcia re-lit the candle and they made their way up to the unfamiliar bedroom. In spite of a lumpy mattress and the loud roar of the aeroplanes as they circled above the farm, they were both soon fast asleep.

They had survived their first day at Tolcarne Merock.

Chapter Three

In the weeks following, Ruby and Marcia became seasoned Land Army girls. Reuben and Norman proved to be good teachers; they certainly knew all about farming. Even Ruby had amazed herself. A while back she would have run a mile if a cow had so much as looked at her, now she could milk them and, if they were sick, could give them a drench, which was the name for animal medicine in a bottle. That in itself was no easy task. One girl would hold the cow by its nostrils and pull its head back, while the other would put the neck of the bottle into the corner of the beast's mouth and quickly pour the contents down its throat. It wasn't easy but the girls soon realised that if they were going to get any cooperation from the animals they first had to show them who was boss. Most of all, however, they enjoyed working with the horses. They had learnt how to harness them and were soon able to drive the wagons around the farm. Sometimes, when Reuben was in a good mood, he would let them take the horses for a canter across the fields. Both Ruby and Marcia loved these outings. They would ride up to the top field and look down at Mawgan Porth beach. The view was stunningly picturesque as they scanned it from their lofty perch. On sunny days the sea would be a beautiful postcard blue and they would hear the excited scream of the gulls as they wheeled and dived above the golden sands. On bad weather days, when the Atlantic was troubled by a heavy low, the ocean would change its mood to an angry dark grey or muddy green, and the gulls' cries would be drowned out by the roar and crash of the mighty waves as they pounded the towering cliffs. But whatever the sea's mood, the girls loved it. Each exciting new day left them feeling more at home in their different and old fashioned surroundings.

Sometimes they would opt for an evening walk through the nearby woods, or down one of the many narrow lanes. One of their favourite walks took them alongside a convent. It was hidden from the outside world by a tall stone wall which, in turn, also gave privacy to the Carmenite nuns who, because of the austere nature of their order, rarely ventured beyond it. Every so often outsiders would hear the melancholy tolling of the convent's bell, which only served to intensify the crypt-like silence that normally enshrouded the moss-covered stone barricade and the convent within. Only after they had passed it by would the two girls stop speaking in whispers. Such was the power of its strange aura. A little further on, the lane began to rise quite steeply and when they reached the top of the hill they would see the village of St Mawgan nestling in the valley below. Their eyes would be drawn first to the lofty church spire, peeping out from between the sprawling tall dark trees. Then they would wander across the way to see the cosy thatched roof of the post office. Next to it, in the centre of a shiny black playground, stood the compact village school, its summoning bell gracing one end of the apex of its tiled roof. The narrow humpbacked footbridge that straddled the very same river that flowed past Reuben's farm gave children access to their school, but carts and the occasional car would have to pick a way through the adjacent stony ford. More often than not the water was shallow, but when St Mawgan suffered several days of heavy rain the river would swell, and the vehicles would be marooned on either side until the level dropped back to normal.

Sometimes, from their elevated vantage point, they would spot Reuben scuttling along in his shiny brown boots, best breeches and gaiters, heading as fast as his legs could carry him to his favourite retreat, the Falcon pub. William, his faithful collie, would invariably be padding along behind, sometimes stopping to sniff something special in the hedgerow, then spurting quickly after his master in case he got left behind.

As the girls slowly made their way back to the farm they would wonder whether Reuben would return in the same polished way. Quite often he would stagger through the kitchen door as drunk as an unguided hand-cart. He was never any trouble. The girls would just leave him sitting on one of the kitchen chairs with his top half sprawled across the table, snoring away like a contented pig. Next morning he would be up as bright and early as always, and when he came in for his usual hearty breakfast not a word of his drunken escapade would be mentioned.

In the early summer months Reuben's one hundred and fifty sheep all had to be sheared. Ruby and Marcia had already had a few sleepless nights with some of these creatures when their cute and cuddly lambs had been born. They had both marvelled at how, after such a ludicrously short time, the baby lambs would stand drunkenly on their spindly little legs and begin to face the world. Some of them were born into a biting Atlantic wind, which made the girls wonder if the tiny mites would ever make it. But most of them did, providing their mothers were kept close at hand to give them the vital warmth and milk.

On the day of the shearing, all the sheep would be penned in the yard. Norman would sit each animal between his legs and deftly remove its thick woolly coat in one complete piece with his clipping shears. The sheep's contented expressions and quiet attitude seemed to suggest that the animals enjoyed their visit to the barber, and gave no indication of the trouble it had taken to get them there. It was the girls' job to catch the sheep and bring them to Norman. They soon discovered that the sheep were a lot faster than they looked. With footwork to match a prize boxer, they would sidestep the girls' outstretched arms and race to the farthest corner of the yard. A panting Ruby and Marcia were eyeing each other with expressions of utter helplessness, while Norman looked on in amusement, when Reuben appeared on the scene. He took one look at the evasive sheep, then shouted fiercely at a now red-faced Norman for not showing the two new girls how it should be done.

Without more ado, he strode over and picked up a small gate that was leaning against one of the cowsheds. 'Now watch me!' he called, his eyes boring into the girls from under his bushy eyebrows. Using the gate as a shield, he gradually drove one of the sheep into a corner. 'Now one of you maids come in round the side of the gate and grab 'im,' he ordered.

It was easy. After trapping a few more to show it was no fluke, he left them to get on with it while he busied himself rolling the sheep-wool into tight packages and then stuffing them well down into large hessian sacks. These would be crudely stitched along the top, then await collection by lorry to take them to the woollen mills.

When the last fleece had been stuffed into the bulging sack, they straightened their aching backs and gave a sigh of relief. It was hard work. They were all thankful that it was at last over for another year.

As the summer drew to a close, the harvesting began in earnest. First the hay, then the corn, and lastly the potatoes and turnips. Reuben relied on helpers who came up from the village. At these busy times they would often work from dawn to dusk to gather in the crops before the winter mists and biting winds blew in from the Atlantic Ocean. Ruby and Marcia had never worked so hard. But they both coped extremely well, and by the looks of their rosy cheeks and cheerful manner they were both very happy and healthy.

Each year when all was safely gathered in, Reuben would reward his helpers by giving them a slap-up farmhouse supper. This particular year was no exception and the old farmer was more than pleased to be able to hand over the food preparation and cooking to Ruby and Marcia. Because of the wartime rationing, food was scarce. But thanks to the farm, the kitchen table gradually filled with cooked hams, roosters, and the biggest joint of beef the girls had ever seen. Other little luxuries that weren't so readily available, Reuben would mysteriously supply. The 'goodies' were placed in the kitchen with not a word mentioned as to their source of origin. A single direct look from the old farmer told them: 'Don't ask!'

On the day of the party, Reuben sent Norman home an hour early to get changed and spruced up for the special 'do' that night.

Ruby and Marcia had almost finished laying the huge table, and were stood back admiring their handiwork when they heard a noise coming from the kitchen doorway. Both girls turned round in amazement. All they saw was a large barrel with a pair of stumpy, booted legs just visible underneath. The legs moved forward a little, then Reuben's face appeared round the side, as red as a beetroot, and puffing and panting like a wind-broken snail. They watched, intrigued, as with notable difficulty he manoeuvred himself and the barrel to the nearest spindle-backed chair. Having deposited the precious barrel squarely on the seat, he walked somewhat stiffly to his own chair and slumped down exhausted. He closed his eyes as little beads of sweat trickled down from his forehead and puddled together in the grey stubble of his unshaven chin.

The girls exchanged a worried glance, unsure what to do. Then Reuben opened his eyes, sat upright and, perky as anything, said, 'You two maids 'ave done an 'ansome job getting this lot ready.' Then, as his eyes scanned the barrel: 'I 'ope the authorities don't pay us a visit tonight!'

The two girls went upstairs to change, leaving Reuben to sample the ale and to make sure it was worth all his strenuous effort. It must have been good because he was on his second glass when Norman arrived shortly afterwards.

'I see you've got the ale then, boss.'

Reuben glanced furtively around. 'Shh! Keep yer voice down, boy . . . else everyone from the village will be up 'ere in a minute.'

Norman looked longingly at the frothing liquid. 'It certainly looks good, boss.'

Reuben took another large swig, smacked his lips appreciatively, then begrudgingly replied, 'I s'pose ee 'ad better fetch a glass and try a drop then.'

Quick to comply, Norman bent down and held his glass under the wooden tap. Just as the sparkling liquid began to trickle into his glass, Ruby and Marcia came down from upstairs. Norman looked up and was unable to believe his eyes. Two young ladies!

He hadn't really thought of them in that way before – more like workmates, really. But now, in their pretty flowered frocks and with their hair all fluffy and different . . . phew, he had come over all queer! Even Reuben gave them an appraising glance after wiping the froth from his lips. 'Wish I was forty years younger,' he declared ruefully.

The two men were brought back to earth by the sound of good ale splashing onto the hard slate floor. 'You idiot!' Reuben roared at Norman, horrified at the sight of his precious nectar going to waste. 'Turn the bloody tap off! Quick! – yer wasting me beer all over the floor!'

Norman glanced sheepishly at the girls, then hastily bent down and stopped the flow from the barrel. He felt really embarrassed. 'Sorry, boss,' he groaned, as his eyes strayed back to Ruby. Still

25

nursing his glass, he walked over to her and took her hand. 'You look beautiful, Ruby.'

'Why thank you, Norman,' she replied, the colour rising in her cheeks, 'you look quite dashing yourself.'

Reuben, still feeling peeved and perhaps a bit left out, grumpily said, 'Don't be telling the boy things like that . . . ee's big-headed enough as it is!'

The girls' forced laughter was interrupted by the unfamiliar sound of a car drawing up in the yard. It was usually only a ministry man who would bring a car to Reuben's door, which was the very last thing he wanted on this particular evening. Without uttering a word, he hid his glass behind a potted plant, then grabbed an overall from behind the kitchen door. With all the magnificent flair of a matador wielding his cape in front of the bull, he flung the garment over the beer barrel and stood in front of it with an expression of pure innocence written all over his gnarled old features.

Norman nervously peeked through the kitchen curtains, then glanced at Reuben with obvious relief. 'It be Mr Grenville, yer lawyer from St Columb, boss.'

Reuben dropped his unnatural pose, retrieved his glass from its hiding place, and returned the overalls to the back of the door. 'What's ee after? . . . coming up 'ere this late in the day,' he grumbled to himself.

There was a light tap on the door, and Mr Grenville entered. He was a tall, thin man in his mid-sixties, with a face that was hawk-like yet intelligent. He was bald, except for two frizzy black and white tufts of hair which topped either ear and probably helped to keep the rather large Homburg hat he always wore when out of doors from slipping down over his crafty, dark and bird-like eyes. With his navy blue serge suit and shiny black shoes, he looked ludicrously out of place standing in the humble farmhouse kitchen. His jacket was unbuttoned just enough to reveal a heavy gold watch-chain which hung imposingly across the front of his waistcoat. He stood there silently for a few moments while his eyes darted around the room and came finally to rest on the heavily-laden table. All eyes were upon him as his tongue slowly licked over his top lip, almost as if he was already tasting the appetising spread that lay before him. With great will power he tore his eyes away from the lavish feast and turned to face an amused but curious Reuben. 'Ah, my friend, I have just dropped by to see you about your will.'

'What will? I 'aven't got one!' Reuben replied warily.

'Quite so,' smiled the lawyer. 'I think the time has come to discuss the matter.' He gave a polite little cough as his eyes strayed back to the kitchen table. 'I seem to have stumbled in on your harvest supper . . . how rude of me,' he said, knowing full well that Reuben would invite him to stay, as he always did whenever Mr Grenville, in one way or another, would accidentally drop into the farmhouse at the most inopportune times. 'Ah!' he exclaimed, turning towards the girls, 'I suppose you two beauties are Reuben's Land Army girls?'

Before they could open their mouths to reply, Reuben butted in. 'They are indeed me own two farm maids,' he asserted proudly, puffing out his chest as if he were showing off the best livestock his farm had to offer.

'Then put down your glass and introduce me,' Mr Grenville countered, smoothing back some imaginary hair on his bald head before shaking hands with the two pleasing intakes.

Reuben opened his mouth to do the honours but Norman was quicker. 'This be Marcia from Wales, and this one . . .' His face took on a dreamy look. 'This is Ruby, and she 'ave come all the way down from London.'

Reuben gave a disgruntled look, but it was wasted on Norman; he only had eyes for the sweet Londoner.

Mr Grenville held Marcia's slender hand in his own tight and clammy grip as Norman did the introducing. He seemed loath to let go of it and, before relinquishing it, brought it up to his lips and planted a noisy kiss on the back of her palm. His lecherous gaze caught and held Marcia's eyes as he breathlessly asserted, 'The pleasure is *all* mine, me dear, and I do hope you will be very happy here.'

The girls soon realised that the lawyer had been a bit of a lad in his day.

Reuben, meanwhile, had fished out a bottle of fine port from the back of a dusty cupboard and magnanimously poured a large one for his uninvited guest. Having spent many after-hours drinking sessions with him in the pub, he knew exactly what his favourite tipples were. Reuben raised the glass and studied the contents in the light of the oil lamp before handing it over. 'I

27

reckon this be a good un . . . rich, 'ansome colour, 'tiz.' He passed the glass to Grenville. 'Ye might as well take a seat now ee be 'ere. There's plenty nuff grub, so that be all right.'

A look of delighted satisfaction spread across the lawyer's features as he eagerly accepted Reuben's hospitality. After quickly making himself comfortable in one of the fireside chairs, he took a large sip of the ruby red port. 'An excellent vintage, Reuben,' he commented appreciatively. 'I can see the gentlemen of the coast (smugglers) are still at work, even if there is a war on.'

'Don't know nuthin' 'bout that!' Reuben countered swiftly, managing to achieve a look of childlike innocence as he cut off a plug of tobacco and diligently rolled it in the palm of his hand before stuffing it into his pipe.

The girls, glad to have some respite from Grenville's unwanted attention, busied themselves at the table. But the respite was short-lived. Ruby was busily slicing a large ham and laying it neatly on a sizeable platter when the lawyer was again suddenly at her side, his gaze drawn hungrily back to the impending feast. 'That's a fine looking ham you have there, me dear.'

Ruby gave him a sweet smile. 'Would you care for a slice, Mr lawyer?'

'Oscar to my friends,' he said, returning her smile. 'Yes, you must call me Oscar . . . and perhaps a small slice wouldn't go amiss, me dear, with a spot of bread and butter.' He watched her closely as the carving knife started to slice through the succulent meat. 'Not *too* small, thank you, me dear.'

Reuben shook his head knowingly and turned away muttering to himself: '*Not too small, me dear!* The cunning old sod – that man 'ave got the appetite of a 'orse!'

Oscar appeared not to notice Reuben's rude mimicry. 'Real farm butter,' he said, stuffing another huge portion into his mouth. When his plate was cleared of the last crumb, and he had swallowed the remainder of the port, he sat back in his chair and with a long-suffering sigh said, 'How cruel this war has been to us.'

His companions were spared the inevitable long speech that was sure to have followed, by the arrival of the first of the invited guests.

28

Chapter Four

It wasn't long before the kitchen was filled to bursting point with all of the farm helpers, and many more had spilled over into the front room where Reuben had lit a fire, and which now looked warm and inviting after all the 'elbow grease' expended by Ruby and Marcia. Reuben and the girls did their guests proud; the glasses and plates were never empty. To give Reuben his due, he truly appreciated the way these loyal people had toiled on his behalf. He knew full well that life would prove much harder if their help wasn't forthcoming.

As the evening wore on, several of the younger guests had filtered out to the courtyard. The evening was balmy and still, and a big harvest moon hung low in the night sky, its magical light glimmering on the farmhouse and outbuildings and casting dark shadows beneath the trees, giving the farm a shimmering aura of excitement and mystery. Joe Trevains − the owner of Gluvian Flamank Farm, and Reuben's nearest neighbour − had brought along his accordion. And now, sitting on a bundle of hay provided by Norman, and with a pint glass of Reuben's ale to keep him lubricated, he was playing with all the gusto and finesse of a seasoned maestro. The young ones were delighted and were soon dancing and jitterbugging feverishly to all the latest hit-tunes. After Joe had rendered *Chattanooga Choo Choo* for what seemed the umpteenth time, he wiped the sweat from his brow and demanded a liquid break. But the good-natured moans soon changed to delighted cheering when he assured them all that he would continue with the music as soon he was rested.

The large kitchen table was now almost laid bare. The dancers kept strolling in and helping themselves, naturally feeling decidedly peckish after all their exertions, and anxious to refuel before the next hectic session.

Marcia was left on her own to wash the mountain of glasses and plates, which seemed to grow bigger each time she turned her back. It was some time now since she had spotted Ruby and Norman sneaking out of the kitchen door, but she did not begrudge them their time together. Dirty dishes will be the last thing on her mind right now, she thought. She smiled to herself as she recalled Ruby's first day at the farm, and marvelled at how things had changed for her. She glanced across to where Reuben was sitting with Oscar, deep in conversation with their heads close together. From their furtive looks and hushed tones, any observer would immediately assume that they were up to no good, and perhaps they were. Every so often the wily old lawyer would catch Marcia's eye and give her a knowing wink. When the poor girl had to pass close by to reheat the big black kettle, he always managed to touch her. It almost certainly never entered his head that she had to muster all her will power to stop herself from emptying the kettle's contents all over him, each time his sweaty hand made contact. When at last she caught up for a moment with the flood of dishes, Marcia thankfully found time to venture outside and join in the fun. For a while at least, she was safely out of reach of Oscar's roving hands.

Joe, having fortified himself, was strapping on his accordion in readiness for his next eagerly awaited rendition. Suddenly, a voice called out from the shadows, 'Where's Norman? . . . we haven't had a song from him yet!'

Other voices joined in: 'Come on, Norman . . .we want you to sing for us.'

It was only when someone shouted, 'Let's go and look for him!' that Norman appeared, walking back from the hay barn, hand-in-hand with Ruby. Sheepishly, he led her over to stand beside Joe while he whispered a few words in the musician's ear. An expectant hush settled over the assembled guests.

The first notes of the accordion broke the brief silence, and the exquisite tenor voice of Norman swept around the old farm buildings and spiralled round and through the dark, leafy trees and upward to the topmost branches, from where it was borne on the gentle breeze to the world outside. He was looking down at Ruby while he sang. They were lost in their own special world, oblivious to the audience and indeed even their own surroundings. *The Rose of Tralee* was just for her.

Reuben came outside to listen, closely followed by a slightly unsteady Mr Grenville whose hand was tightly clasped around yet another full glass of port. They stood beside Marcia in silence to hear Norman's singing, and it wasn't long before tears, shining like diamonds in the moonlight, trickled down the cheeks of both of these hardened old-timers.

The song ended amid a chorus of loud cheers and clapping, but when Norman bent forward and kissed Ruby on the lips, his audience went mad, cheering wildly and clapping even louder until they almost drowned out the mighty roar of the low-flying Spitfire that suddenly streaked over their heads, its wheels down ready for a safe landing at the St Mawgan aerodrome.

Marcia turned to Reuben. Smiling, she said, 'I think I have just lost my friend, boss.'

Reuben, his eyes still suspiciously shiny, slurred, 'The maid could do worse – Norman's a good lad, even if I do give 'im 'ell sometimes.'

Joe was now playing the *Hoky Coky* and everyone was joining in. Oscar, now much the worse for wear, slid his arm around Reuben's shoulder. 'You were saying you had a bottle of whiskey hidden away somewhere . . .' He waved his now empty glass under the old farmer's nose.

'Did I say that?' That ale must 'ave been good stuff, Reuben thought wryly, to 'ave loosened me tongue in such a way!

'You did indeed,' the lawyer assured him, taking him by the arm and ushering him back to the farmhouse.

By midnight the guests were thinning out; some making their way to their nearby homes, while some who had enjoyed more than their fair share of liquid refreshment had simply curled up in the warmth of the sweet-smelling hay. Others were just glad to lie down and rest the weary limbs that had danced the party night away so enthusiastically .

Marcia returned to the kitchen to tidy up and wash the last of the dishes. Thankfully, Reuben and Oscar were in the front room, no doubt still enjoying the covert bottle of whiskey. Ruby was missing, so after leaving everything tidy, Marcia wearily made her way up to her bedroom.

As she lay in bed thinking of the great evening everyone had enjoyed, her thoughts wandered back to her home in

Pembrokeshire. To her mother and father, and the rest of her family with their loyal and loving ways – very much like the Cornish folk really. Yes, they were almost one clan – the kind of people who will help to beat Mr Hitler one day. She smiled contentedly as she drifted off into a deep slumber.

Early next morning, just before five, Marcia dressed and went downstairs. To her surprise, Reuben was already up and outside milking the cows. How he could go to work so early after drinking all night with Mr Grenville, she would never know. He was a mystery and no mistake. She sighed as she poked some life into the fire, then put the faithful old kettle on to boil. No sign yet of Ruby.

What was that? An unfamiliar sound from the direction of the front room startled her. Too loud for mice, that was for sure. Her heart was beating nineteen to the dozen as she stealthily crept out into the front hallway. She studied the door in front of her for a second or two, then, with trembling fingers, quietly turned the well-worn door knob.

As the door inched open, her eyes swept over the gloomy confines of the curtained room and fell on the prostrate form of Oscar Grenville. He was sprawled out along the sofa with his large, black-shoed feet dangling from over the arm. He was fully dressed except for his white starched collar, which had been tugged off and unceremoniously thrown down on to the floor, next to the now discarded empty port glass.

Marcia took one more fleeting glance at the snoring, red-faced lawyer, then hastily backed-out through the door, closing it silently as she did so. She breathed a sigh of relief as she crossed the hall to the kitchen door. She did not fancy her chances if he had suddenly awoke to find her standing in his room.

As the dawn light gathered momentum, Marcia looked out of the window on to the now drab and empty courtyard. Her eyes were drawn to the big hay barn a few yards further on; there seemed to be movement in the hay. She stared in disbelief as the figure of a young woman suddenly popped out. The girl rubbed her eyes, brushed the dried grass from her skirt, then sped off down the lane as fast as her legs could carry her.

Marcia watched, fascinated, as a dozen or more of last night's guests sleepily emerged from the barn over the next few minutes. One or two of them made a hasty retreat, following the young

32

woman's route hot-foot down the lane, but the rest of them were clearly in no hurry whatsoever. They were chatting and laughing together as if the party was still in full swing . . . and Ruby was amongst them!

So that's where she got to, the rascal, Marcia thought, smiling to herself. Then a polite cough from right behind her made her jump half out of her skin. She spun round, and there stood the lawyer, starched collar and all. She was flabbergasted. Not more than five minutes ago he was out cold, dead to the world.

'Ah, my charming Marcia,' he smiled artfully, 'could you rustle up a bacon sandwich for me? I fear my work will suffer if I don't have any morning sustenance.'

Marcia fetched the bacon from the dairy and plonked the large, greasy package on the kitchen table. That man certainly knows how to get me worked up, she thought with annoyance, and it was then that she heard a commotion outside. In the next instant the kitchen door was flung open and Reuben, Norman, and William the dog came bustling in.

'Bacon sandwiches!' Reuben exclaimed as his eyes swept over the table. 'Yes, that be just the thing – can ee make a few dozen, me dear? Can't be sending these folk 'ome 'ungry . . . t'will never do.'

Marcia did not answer. It was a good thing that Ruby decided to make an appearance at that moment.

The kitchen was soon filled with an aromatic blue smoke. Norman kept running outside with plates piled high, and even Reuben did his bit by carrying steaming mugs of strong tea to his grateful visitors. The poor dog was sitting patiently beside Oscar, his eyes following each movement from plate to mouth with longing desire, but not a crumb was forthcoming. His only reward was a hesitant pat on his scruffy head when the lawyer rose stiffly from his chair and carefully wiped the last traces of shiny grease off his chin. The luckless collie eyed him with a look of hopeless frustration and then sauntered over to try his luck with the two busy cooks.

'Well, duty calls – I must be away now,' Oscar called to Reuben as he contentedly patted his own well-filled stomach. 'I'll probably see you at the Merlins farm harvest supper next week. They're a little behind you this year, Reuben.'

'I s'pect so,' grunted Reuben. 'But what wuz ee saying 'bout me will last night?'

'Oh that!' The lawyer looked slightly embarrassed. 'With all the excitement going on, it completely went from my mind. Never mind, I'll call on you one evening quite soon.' He gave a stately half-bow to the ladies and left briskly by the kitchen door.

When the last of the merry-makers had finally departed, Marcia and Ruby set about putting the house in order. It took them the best part of the morning before everything was looking shipshape and clean, and they both admitted they would rather take things a little easier that afternoon, but there was to be no respite. Reuben seemed to have the energy of a giant, and expected others to remain just as busy.

Later that day, Marcia made her way to the cowshed to put fresh hay in the mangers in readiness for the animals when they were brought in to be milked. As she was crossing the yard she spotted Reuben with his shoulder pressed tightly to one of the field gates. He was swearing and puffing, and pushing with all his might to close the gate. But there was a large obstacle in the shape of 'Benjie the bull' pushing even harder on the other side. Benjie urgently wanted to come into the yard, where he knew his girlfriends would soon be arriving, and he didn't want to miss out on anything.

Marcia watched for several moments as Reuben fought to get a foothold on the slippery cobblestones. He would just about manage to close the gate ready to fasten it, when the bull would charge again, forcing his hobnailed boots to slide back a few inches, and leaving the gate just short of the gatepost. Realising his difficulty, Marcia ran over and tried to help by pushing with all her might alongside Reuben, but to no avail. The bull was most determined.

'Git a rope . . . quick!' hissed Reuben.

Marcia soon found a strong piece of rope in an adjacent shed and hurried back to help.

'When I gits the gate closed, tie the rope round the two posts . . . quick mind!' Reuben was finding it hard to breathe, let alone talk. He took a deep breath and pushed with all his strength, and the gate closed. Marcia wound the rope firmly around the posts and it was secure at last.

'Thankee, me 'ansome, that ole varmit nearly had me beat that time,' Reuben panted. 'Ee knows I'm getting older . . . ee

34

wouldn't 'ave tried that on a few years back.'

Marcia just looked at him in amazement. 'Boss, you're the limit, competing with Benjie and after the hectic night you just spent. It was a wonder he didn't knock you flat!'

Old Reuben just smiled.

Chapter Five

As autumn approached, and the trees had started to shed their summer gowns, the news from the war front was far from good. Most evenings when the girls were sat snugly in the warm kitchen, they would hear the bombers taking off from the aerodrome. The farmhouse would shake with the vibrating rumble as they flew directly over the farm. And sometimes, if the planes were late coming back, the girls would see them, as they brought in the cows for early milking. Those planes which were luckily unscathed would circle the valley several times to enable their badly shot-up pals and machines to land first. It made the girls realise that war was a terrible reality. It was all too easy to forget the dreadful things that were happening around them when they were busy with the demanding work of the farm.

On one particular Saturday morning, Reuben told the girls to take a couple of bags of potatoes down to St Mawgan Church for the next day's harvest festival. After breakfast they harnessed up the farm's friendly horse, Star, to the two wheeled cart, for the short trip down the valley to the village. The girls were grateful to have this job. It was a pleasant change for them to get out of the farm for a while, and not to have Reuben breathing down their necks every few minutes. Star was a gentle mare, and she trotted on at a leisurely pace without the need for much instruction. She seemed to know instinctively what was expected of her, and the route she had to take. Ahead they saw the smoke rising from the chimney of Polgreen Cottage. Polgreen was another neighbouring farm, and its dark green fields stretched out to the boundary walls of the convent, and on into the village of St Mawgan. Their attention was distracted by the heavy clomp of boots advancing smartly towards them. As the sound drew nearer, the girls realised it belonged to the men in the local Home Guard platoon. Marcia reined in the horse a little closer to the hedge, and waited for the men to pass. Ruby's eyes lit up; she had spotted Norman amongst them. He broke file and walked across to peer into the cart. 'Who are the spuds for?' he inquired.

Ruby told him they were delivering them to Reverend Bassett, for the harvest festival. She would have been quite happy to have spent a few more minutes chatting with Norman, but the sergeant in charge had other ideas. He marched over and gave him a right old telling off for breaking the ranks. Poor Norman meekly followed his superior back to the line of grinning men, and Ruby gave the sergeant's rear a look that, if he had seen it, would have chilled him to the bone.

They trundled on through the shaded, dank, leaf-strewn wood, and eventually came out into the clean fresh air opposite the convent. It was just a matter of minutes before Star obediently stopped outside the lych-gate of the church. Through the gateway, on the right hand side, lay the old burial ground with its large, lopsided, granite crosses and grey blotchy angels with chipped wings, that had for centuries guarded and watched over the bodies lying beneath. To the left of the path could be seen carefully mowed grass and gnarled, thick-trunked, lofty trees, which housed a myriad of rasping crows. The top branches had at sometime tried to gain precedence over the taller church tower, but the cruel, withering, Atlantic sea winds had beaten them back. Now their spindly top branches were all slanting and facing inland, and had long ago given up their useless struggle to compete.

As the girls dropped the tailboard of the cart, a rather buxom woman walked past by them and on through the church gate. She was carrying a large basket overflowing with apples which mirrored the appearance of her proud face: round, red and shiny. Following slowly on behind her was a small, cheeky-faced boy. He was struggling with a ripe yellow marrow, almost as big as himself. On a wooden seat just a little further along down the road sat an old man, intently watching every move the two girls made, and no doubt wondering to himself how these two young women were going to be able to carry the heavy sacks all the way up to the church. But this is where Reuben's teachings would come in handy. Marcia pulled a piece of shovel handle, about three.feet long, from the back of the cart. Standing shoulder to shoulder, facing the sack, they held the wooden handle in their outside hands and across the bottom of the sack. Now, with their free inside hands, they grabbed one ear of the sack each, and pulled the bag of potatoes towards them. Then, taking the weight on the piece of wood equally between them, they walked briskly to the church with the first heavy, one-hundredweight sack and dropped it skilfully at the feet of the Reverend Bassett. Panting a little, the girls informed him they were from Reuben of Tolcarne Merock.

The reverend — a tall man in his seventies, with protruding front teeth and thin downy white hair — was in charge of the church while the resident younger man was serving as a padre in the army. His eyes rested on the sack of potatoes. 'Most grateful . . . most grateful. I am sure you will be rewarded in heaven!' he said in his well-practiced ecclesiastical voice.

'Not just yet, I hope, reverend,' Ruby muttered under her breath.

Looking at her shrewdly, his hearing as acute now as ever it was, he said, 'Quite so, quite so, my child.'

The girls informed him that there was another sack of potatoes waiting to be brought in.

'Another one,' echoed the vicar, looking thankfully towards the heavens. 'What a bountiful day this is turning out to be.' As he turned to greet another bearer of gifts, he said, 'I doubt if Reuben will come to the festival; perhaps you may both grace us with your presence tomorrow afternoon.'

After the other bag had been duly delivered in the same way, the girls went round to the back of the cart to replace the tailboard. The old gentleman was still observing them from his seat, and called over to them. 'Did Reuben Gutheridge teach ee to carry a sack like that, me dears?'

'He certainly did,' answered Marcia with a smile. 'You know Reuben then?'

'Should do.' The old man waved his stick in the direction of Tolcarne Merock. 'I worked fer ee fer twenty year er more. There baint many of 'is cunning old tricks that I don't know about.'

The two girls smiled and waved their goodbyes as Ruby took the reins of Star. With a quick click of her tongue and a gentle tug on the reins, the faithful horse turned and began its brief but pleasant journey back to the farm.

After Marcia had explained the procedure of the harvest festival to Ruby, who had never heard of such a thing before, they both decided it would be a nice change to attend the thanksgiving service on the following day.

Next morning Norman came into the kitchen with two pails of milk. Most of it would be put into a large round pan and placed in the dairy until the following day. By that time all the thick cream would have settled to the top of the pan. It would then be placed on the coolest part of the stove for several hours to heat gently. At the end of the day it would produce a substantial bowl of thick clotted cream – some to be eaten on thick slabs of bread and jam, and some to be made into delicious yellow butter. It was no wonder the girls had started to take on a healthy bloom; farm life certainly had its advantages.

'Will you be going to St Mawgan Church this afternoon, Norman?' Ruby was looking at the young farmer in hopeful anticipation. A big smile spread over her face when he eagerly answered:

'Yes, I go every year.'

Ruby then wanted to know who the horrible man was who had told him off yesterday afternoon.

'That's our sergeant, Sid Treloar. Ee's the landlord of the Falcon pub,' Norman explained. 'Ee's not a bad chap really.'

'Ee be a bloody good chap!' – Reuben's broad form filled the doorway – 'The 'ome guard be in good 'ands while there be blokes like Sid in charge.' Reuben looked defiantly at Ruby and Marcia. 'And it's not just cause ee's the landlord of the Falcon either. I was with Sid in the First World War, we fought together at Passchendaele, Delville Wood, and on the Somme . . . a braver man would be 'ard to find!' Turning to Norman, he said, 'Ye listen careful to what ee tells ee, it could save yer life one of these days, me boy!'

Marcia was standing directly behind Reuben and was looking over his shoulder and silently mimicking him as he was delivering his fatherly warning. Poor Norman was trying his hardest to ignore her comical actions. His face took on some weird expressions as he strove to control the laughter that was bubbling up inside him. Reuben, realising what was going on, almost laughed himself, but sternly he said, 'Ye wun't be laughing if them bloody Germans land 'ere, me boy!' A smile did

39

flicker across his face though, when he informed Norman that the pig-sties needed cleaning, and then, without looking at the girl behind him, added, 'Marcia can give ee a 'and!'

Reuben was still wearing a smug grin as he went to go outside, but he halted in his tracks as Norman hastily blustered, 'Boss, it's Sunday, and I'm off to the harvest festival this afternoon. There won't be time 'nuff for that today!'

'Never short of excuses be ye young 'uns. Well it'll 'ave to be done first thing tomorrow morning then!' And with that as his final word, he whistled to William and the pair of them disappeared out of the kitchen door.

The girls had agreed to meet Norman outside the church at a quarter-past-two. Marcia always cooked the Sunday roast, as she was the better cook. Ruby was much happier working outside. One of her favourite jobs was having to fill the mangers with sweet smelling hay. The mangers in the cowsheds would be filled to overflowing before she would leave to start on her next task. The main reason for enjoyment being Norman's company. He worked alongside her, busily cleaning the animal quarters in readiness for the evening.

After enjoying a sumptuous dinner of roast goose, the girls changed into their best uniforms. Ruby wasn't sure whether she ought to wear her hat; but Marcia told her that as they were living almost next door to the aerodrome, it was more than likely some air force officers could attend the service. Even Land Army girls were supposed to wear their complete uniforms . . . so hats it was. Marcia and Ruby looked and felt very smart in their crisp, special best-wear uniform. They had no need of their heavy outside coats as the day was quite warm and humid. The brightly-coloured, leafy carpet gently rustled underfoot as they hurried down the lane. The minutes were ticking by and they did not want to be late.

As they neared the church they saw Norman waiting for them. He failed to notice them until they were almost alongside because, much to Ruby's chagrin, he was too busy talking to three other Land Army girls. But he soon explained to the jealous Ruby that his new acquaintances hailed from Penedra Farm, a little further inland, and that his only interest was the farming news, which the Penedra girls were only too willing to provide.

40

Ruby squeezed Marcia's arm, then looked in the direction of two air force officers who were fast approaching the chattering group. 'Do we salute them?' she nervously muttered.

'I don't think so.' Marcia wasn't really quite sure of the military procedure either. 'Anyway, it's too late now.'

By this time the officers were upon them and the more senior of the two merely smiled and said, 'Good afternoon. Do carry on.' Then he and his many medals followed his colleague through the wide lych-gate.

Norman's group decided they had better make a move as the vibrant strains of the organ warned them that the service was about to start. Just as they were about to enter through the church gate, a red-faced Mr Grenville appeared. 'God bless my soul! . . . if it isn't the charming Marcia and Ruby.' He doffed his hat and carefully patted his remaining tufts of hair. Then his eyes swept appreciatively over the Penedra girls. 'And who might these other delightful young ladies be?' Evidently he hadn't been able to wangle his way into their harvest home supper.

Norman introduced the Penedra Farm girls, and the lawyer shook each of their hands in turn. 'Oscar's the name, me dears. Lawyer of St Columb. If ever you should need my services . . .' The words tailed off as he fumbled into his waistcoat pocket for his gold watch. 'Goodness me, it's time we were all in church; we don't want to be scolded by Reverend Bassett, do we?'

As they all trooped into the old church they were greeted by the lady organist playing '*We plough the fields and scatter the good seed on the land*'. The building's usual fussy ancient smell was replaced by the strong aromatic odour of the fruit and vegetables which were displayed in grandeur around the pulpit and all along the length of the chancel. Apart from a polite cough here and there, silence reigned among the congregation, even though the church was almost full. Norman and Ruby squeezed themselves on to the end of one row, while Marcia, Oscar and the Penedra girls slid into the pews behind them. The old lawyer bent his head in prayer, no doubt thanking God for being squashed between two young women for the next hour or so. As they stood to sing the first hymn, Marcia, who was standing directly behind Norman, noticed that his hand had found Ruby's. It was becoming very clear that they were falling in love.

It was a good service, despite the Reverend Bassett's sermon

41

being a trifle long-winded. Even the younger members of the congregation didn't start to fidget until it was nearing the end. Then the reverend walked sedately down the aisle to the door, where he would meet each member of his flock as they made their way out. His proud gaze swept around the church. It wasn't often these days the pews were filled to overflowing. What with the war, and peoples lives turned upside down, things had changed. But today was almost like old times. Yes, on this Sunday the Reverend Bassett was a satisfied and happy man.

Ruby and Norman decided to take the long way back home, which would take them through a picturesque part of St Mawgan, called Lawreys Mill. It was situated alongside the river, and was adorned with a backcloth of luscious, tall trees. The mill itself was little more than a ruin, but the powerful gigantic water wheel, although rusty from disuse, had beaten the onslaught of time, and seemed to be waiting patiently to team up with the river and start on its noisy and trundling profession once more. There were few courting couples who had never stopped this way. It was the perfect setting, and Norman knew it!

Marcia, now left on her own, made her lonely way back to the farm. She resigned herself to thoughts of preparing Reuben's tea. He would come in with a hearty appetite after doing all the milking on his own. Ruefully she thought, it's a good job for Ruby that I haven't found a boy-friend yet!

When she was part of the way up the valley she noticed Will and Fred coming towards her. They were the ten-year-old twins belonging to Joe and Elsie Trevains from Gluvian Flamank farm. 'You're too late for the harvest festival,' Marcia called cheerily as the two identical faces drew nearer. She could see that they weren't dressed in their Sunday best. Both had short trousers hung at half-mast below their knees, and straw coloured twine belted around their waists to stop the trousers from venturing any lower.

Four skinny legs protruded out of oversized hobnailed boots which looked as if they had already given their hard-working father the best of their days.

Two worried faces looked back at Marcia. 'Father 'ave sent us out to look for two cows that 'ave gone missing.' They both turned and pointed away in the distance to one of their fields. 'Somebody's left the gate open, and father's real mad. He'll 'ave

42

to go into St Columb and buy a padlock; that should do the trick.'

Their faces dropped even more when Marcia had to tell them she had seen neither hide nor hair of the missing cattle. Neither boy relished the thought of spending all afternoon in search of wandering strays. They had much more interesting activities planned.

As Marcia walked on, her thoughts took her back to her own village in Wales. Most of the young ones she had grown up with were no longer there now. Like her, most of them were playing a part in the war. She wondered if one day, when the war was over, things would go back as they were. She frowned to herself, knowing that in reality things would never be the same again.

She was panting slightly after her trudge up the steep hill to Tolcarne Merock. As she crossed the farmyard, she could hear the clanging of galvanised pails. Reuben had already started the milking. Approaching the cowshed door, she smelt the warm strong odour of the animals. They all stood in line, happily munching away at the sweet sun-dried hay which Ruby had placed in the mangers earlier that morning. 'I'm back boss!' she called out to Reuben, then she left him to complete his task while she went indoors to prepare the Sunday tea. Her first job as always was to poke the fire of the range into life, then bring the heavy kettle closer to the heat. She fetched an apple tart which she had baked earlier from the dairy and placed it carefully in the bottom of the large oven so that it would be warm enough to eat when the kettle had boiled. Marcia, like Reuben, loved apple tart. With melt-in-the-mouth pastry and lashings of clotted cream, it was a real Sunday treat. There was never a shortage of apples. If Reuben's gnarled old fruit trees at the bottom of the garden didn't produce much, the farmers around him were more than willing to exchange their apples for a glass or two of his secret supply of port or whiskey.

The kettle was almost boiling and when Marcia glanced out of the window to see if Reuben was on his way, she spotted him in the courtyard, pumping up a large pail of water. She watched as he placed the almost full bucket of water on to the ground, then rolling up his sleeves, plunged his hands and arms into the icy water and splashed it all over his head and neck. She shuddered as her arms were suddenly covered in bristly goose-pimples. Rather him than me, she thought wryly.

43

She was just pouring the boiling water into the teapot when Reuben came in. 'Where's young Ruby got to then? . . . gone off walking with Norman I s'pect?' He sat down at the table with a complacent sigh as Marcia passed him his mug of tea.

'Yes, how did you guess?'

He looked at Marcia, his eyes twinkling under his damp, shaggy eyebrows. 'That's 'ow 'tiz done round 'ere me 'ansome. If you be keen on somebody, ee takes em fer a walk after church. That be always the first step in a romance.' He put a large spoonful of cream on his helping of apple tart, and as it started to melt he dug his spoon eagerly into the fruit and pastry. He raised it to his mouth, and for the moment Ruby and Norman were forgotten.

When the meal was finished, they sat quietly at the table and listened to the news on the wireless. The news always seemed to follow the same pattern. If there was some little ray of hope, it had to be followed by a setback. Tonight's broadcast was no exception. The optimistic voice of the announcer informing the listeners that the Russians were now fighting back, and also that Rommel wasn't having it all his own way in the desert, changed as he gravely spoke of Japanese troops who were pressing southwards along New Guinea's trail. They had succeeded in driving back the Australians to only thirty-two miles from Port Moresby. Reuben sat staring into space and sadly shaking his head; it was a serious business and no mistake.

Marcia cleared the table and washed up, while the old farmer remained seated, catching up with all the paper work concerning the farm. He was still sat there, peering shortsightedly at the forms spread out in front of him, when she finally sat down opposite him to write a letter home. As Marcia's pen scratched out her news, she would hear Reuben, every so often, give a baffled sigh as his brain refused to understand the formal writings. He looked up as the oil lamp flickered. 'I'll 'ave to trim the wick on that ole lamp tomorra. I'm darned if I can see wot these ole forms 'ave to say.' He scooped up all his paperwork and unceremoniously shoved the pile into one of the table drawers. 'Nuff of that rubbish!' he told himself as he moved across to his favourite chair by the warm stove. Leaning forward, he unlatched the fire-door, then settled back to enjoy his pipe of baccy. As Reuben quietly puffed and watched the shimmering hot embers, the silence was suddenly broken by the thunderous roar of the night bomber planes flying over. As the noise faded away into the distance Marcia quietly said, 'I wonder how many of them will come back tomorrow morning?'

Reuben didn't answer. He knew their future was grimly uncertain.

Marcia placed the neatly-written letter to her parents into an envelope and went upstairs to fetch a stamp. She blew out the candle and curled up on the window-seat to look out. Between the dark clouds the moon shone brightly down on to the front garden path. It sloped its weedy way downwards and ended between two large stone pillars from where half a dozen crumbling steps led down to the lane. She thought she saw a movement down by the pillars. Pressing her face closer to the pane she strained to see, but the moon was playing a game with her and quickly hid behind a dark cloud. Marcia waited, keeping her eyes trained to the same spot, ready for the next quick burst of moonlight to reveal what was lurking about out there. At last the moon leapt out from its hiding place and Marcia could now see quite clearly. A small sigh escaped her and her body relaxed as she realised it was just Norman and Ruby outside saying goodnight to each other. She slid back off the window-seat and drew the curtains. She didn't want them to think she was spying on them. When she returned to the kitchen Reuben was dressed to go out and was busily stuffing some twelve bore cartridges into his coat pocket. Marcia gave him a quizzical look, wondering what the old schemer was getting up to now.

Picking up his twelve bore, he told her he was going to take a walk down Gluvian way. 'That dam fox that 'ave bin worrying the sheep might be out on the prowl — just the sort of night to catch Mr Reynard. Moon and cloud, so now be me chance!'

He whistled for William, and the pair sped off before Marcia had the chance to ask him any awkward questions. Marcia smiled to herself, knowing that his fox-trail would inevitably lead him to the Falcon. She was beginning to understand some of Reuben's excuses, although he was a deep one and that was for sure.

The door opened slowly and Ruby's head appeared. Her eyes hastily scanned the clock. 'Sorry, Marcey, I'm a little late.' She walked over and stood in front of the stove. 'Nice to have a warm-up. I got quite chilly outside, saying night-night to

Norman.'

'You've had a nice walk then, Rube?' Marcia noticed her flushed cheeks.

'Ooh yes, it was lovely. Norman is such good company. He explained lots of things about the countryside. It was fascinating – he's so clever, Marcey!'

Marcia smiled and nodded. This girl's smitten, she thought to herself. 'Did you fall for him the first time you saw him?' Her voice was pleasantly soft as she questioned her friend.

'I think perhaps I must have,' Ruby dreamily replied as her thoughts rushed back to their very first meeting.

Marcia listened patiently as her friend talked non-stop throughout the rest of the evening about her wonderful Norman, and she was more than relieved when the clock told them it was time for bed.

Chapter Six

Winter soon engulfed them, and their pattern of working life changed completely. Early every evening the cattle would be brought in from the cold, wet fields to be milked. Afterwards, instead of going back to the wintry pasture, they would spend their nights munching on hay, or just resting in the pleasant warmth of the spacious farm shed. Because of their overnight stay, it would take Reuben and his helpers up until dinner time everyday to clean up after them and replenish food stocks for when they gratefully returned back for their evening meal and shelter.

Some days the girls would stop and listen for a moment to the roar of the waves as they crashed against the rocks. If the wind was blowing in the right direction, the farmyard would be covered with what at first sight appeared to be large snowflakes, but in fact was foamy tufts of white fluffy sea spray. On one dark morning while the three were having breakfast, Reuben informed the girls that the threshing machine would be coming to Tolcarne Merock at the end of the week. He noticed Ruby's baffled expression as he pushed his squeaky clean plate away and wiped his greasy lips with the back of his hand. 'Now then me dears.' He picked up his mug and took a large gulp of tea to help him explain. 'You know the two big corn ricks standing t'other end of yard?'

Both girls nodded and waited expectantly.

'Well,' he went on, 'we feed the sheaves of corn from them there ricks, through this threshing machine, and it separates the grain from the stalks. The grain shoots out into a waiting sack, while another part of the machine sends out the stalks all tied up and 'andy in bundles. This is what we calls straw.' Reuben took another mouthful of tea and noticed that the girls were looking more relieved. It was not as complicated as they had first thought. Cheered by their reaction, Reuben continued with his explanation. 'Them bundles of straw will be made up into two ricks once agin. But first, the thresher be off down Gluvian farm fer a couple of days. Me and Norman will be down there giving Joe Trevains a 'and. Then Joe will come up 'ere and 'elp we lot . . . that be the custom round these 'ere parts.'

Ruby looked at Reuben aghast. Two whole days without Norman! — that part of it was awful.

The Land Army girls found the going tough while the two men were down at Joe's farm. Reuben would return home late in the evening and check the farm and livestock before retiring to his bedroom. A few short hours of sleep, then he would be up and awake again, bright as a button and ready to tackle another hard day's work. For Ruby, it was the longest two days of her life. Every so often she would softly sigh to herself, no doubt missing her Norman. But at night the girls would fall asleep as soon as their heads touched the pillows. They missed the strong help of the two men, and in more ways than one, would be glad when they returned.

Joe's threshing took longer than expected. It was not until. late in the afternoon of the third day that Norman's excited face appeared in the doorway of the cattle shed. 'The machine is on its way!' he told the girls. Donald Johns the driver of the steam engine wants to get it into position before dark falls, so we can 'ave an early start tomorrow morning. The silly old fool is only towing that great threshing machine behind his steam engine, along the valley and up the steep hill. He reckons it's quicker than the usual route he takes along by the beach, but I don't think he's going to make it; it's just too steep for such heavy machinery.' Norman paused to get his wind back.

The girls, excited now, wanted to know where the steam engine would be at that moment.

'It's probably at the bottom of the hill.' Norman turned on his heel. 'Quick! there's a place in the yard where we can look down into the valley and see what's going on!'

The girls didn't need a second telling. They dropped their heavy forks and raced after him.

Norman pointed down the steep slope and, sure enough, there

it was.

'So big!' Ruby said softly, uttering her thoughts aloud. The two machines were lying stationary now, towering high above the hedges, and filling the whole width of the road. Donald had stopped the engine in order to build up plenty of steam for the mammoth task of climbing the hill. Thick black smoke was billowing from the monster's chimney and completely obliterating the fields beyond. Norman and the girls held their breath and watched intently as the smoking giant and its obedient servant started to move slowly up the steep elevation. They watched spellbound as the massive machinery drew nearer and the driver came into view. He was working frantically at the big handles which controlled the engine. Every so often his greasy black face would peer out over the side to check the huge flywheel which was rotating at a terrific speed. A few yards further on, smoke still billowing, wheels still spinning, it started to slow down.

'He's never going to make it!' Marcia's throat felt tight.

'Bet ee 'alf a crown ee will!'

They turned to see that Reuben had joined them.

Marcia took a quick glance down the valley. The machines were now stationary halfway up the hill, not moving an inch either way. She felt sure of the half-crown wager, until she noticed Norman shaking his head in warning to her. Sensibly, she declined Reuben's offer.

For what seemed an eternity the scene below them remained unchanged. Then Donald the driver appeared. He jumped down from the lofty steam engine, closely followed by another black-faced engine-man who they now noticed for the first time. The two men lit up a Woodbine each, then walked slowly around the obstinate machines. Donald lifted up his cap and scratched his head, evidently thinking hard. After taking several long, hard looks uphill and down, they seemed to have arrived at a decision. Donald's assistant, with all the skill of an athlete, leapt up and climbed back into the hissing steam engine. He vanished for a moment, then his face looked over the side, and he started handing down to Donald what appeared to be heavy blocks of wood.

'Chocks, that's wot they be.' Reuben smiled to himself; he had noticed the puzzled expressions on the land-girls' faces.

49

The two men set to work. They placed the heavy wooden chocks behind each of the four wheels of the threshing machine to stop it from moving backwards. Then they unhitched the stout hook and chains which had held it captive to its steaming master. One more slow walk around the thresher, and a hard kick on each of the chocks to ram them home, then the two men, satisfied that the machine wouldn't move, hurriedly took up their positions in the steam engine. Donald took his place behind the huge steering wheel, while his mate busily stoked up the ever hungry fire. Billows of black smoke spurted upwards as the flywheel slowly started to turn. The whole contraption seemed to shake as Donald pushed it into gear. Stones and gravel from the road's surface were whipped up and flung over the bordering hedges as the eight-foot iron wheels spun giddily, fighting for grip under the intense weight and pressure. At last the great machine inched forward and slowly started to climb the great hill up to Tolcarne Merock.

'They're leaving the thresher behind them on the road!' Marcia stared at Reuben in worried disbelief.

Reuben, taking it all in his stride, looked back at the anxious faces and spoke calmly to them: 'Dun't ee go worrying too much 'bout that. Donald knows wot ee's doing!'

They could hear the great engine drawing closer, so Reuben and his workmates hurried across the farm yard to meet it. By the time they reached the entrance gate, Donald had arrived. The beast was brought to an abrupt stop, and the two engine-men, smiles of triumph on their sweaty black faces, jumped down to greet their observers. 'We're nearly there,' Donald assured Reuben as they proceeded to place another set of chocks behind the wheels of the engine. Ruby and Marcia watched intently as Donald's mate took a large hook from the rear of the engine. It was connected to a winch by a sturdy wire rope, and as Donald turned yet another lever the rope was played out for his mate to take it back down the hill and connect it to the stranded threshing machine. Once this was done the man waved to signal that all was ready. Donald hastily wiped the sweat from his brow with an oily rag and concentrated on working in unison with his beloved machine. The wire rope gently left the ground, then with a loud, whistling, twang it straightened out and drew taught. The girls held their breath as the rope started to wind around the winch drum.

'It's going to snap!' Ruby muttered between clenched teeth. But it held fast and the heavy chocks were removed from the thresher. The thresher came up the hill slowly and smoothly as if gliding on ice, and it was only a matter of minutes before the two machines were once more united. It was almost dark but the machines were now in position beside the towering corn ricks. The steam engine was facing the threshing machine with a drive belt connecting them. The scene was set for several long days of hard work.

Donald and his mate — known as Digger to his pals — fetched their dinner bags and coats from inside the warm steam engine, then went around to the back of the thresher to fetch their means of transport to get them back home. It was an old Francis Barnet motor-bike and it travelled everywhere with them, tied unceremoniously on the back with thick, oily rope.

The two men jumped on; the engine was started up, and with a cheery wave and a shouted goodbye, which was almost drowned by the wild spluttering of the motor-cycle engine and a low flying aircraft, they sped away over the bumpy farmyard, leaving behind them a heavy silence as the red tail-light disappeared through the farm gate and down the lane.

Early next morning Ruby and Marcia were in the cowshed, busy with the milking. The animals were still, except for the occasional flick of a tail and the slight movements as they tugged mouthfuls of hay from the mangers. The girls sat with their heads resting against the soft, warm hide. Every so often their eyes would close and they would look to be asleep, but their hands never stopped working until the last drop of creamy rich milk had been drawn and was safely captured in the bucket. They had almost finished their task when they heard the agitated phut-phut of Donald's motor-bike entering the yard. It was barely light but the steam engine would take a good hour to build up steam, so the fire had to be lit as early as possible. The girls finished the milking, then hurried back to the house to prepare the usual fried breakfasts. There would be two extra mouths to feed over the next few days.

Apart from the scraping of the cutlery and a few begging grunts from William, the breakfasts were eaten in silence.

51

Reuben, as usual, was the first to finish. Pushing back his chair, he said, 'Outside in ten minutes. I'll give ee all yer jobs then.' He took his coat off the peg, and disappeared through the door with an excited William hot on his heels.

Reuben soon gave everyone their orders. Donald of course, had a full time job tending to the two engines. Digger would work on the top of the thresher, cutting the cord which bound the sheaves, and then feeding the corn into the hungry jaws of the machine. His job was a precarious one, as the whole contraption would shake and tremble like a bucking bronco, and threaten to toss him off at any moment. Marcia would find herself working at one end of the thresher, replacing the full sacks of corn with empty ones. Working alongside her would be Norman who was Jack of all trades. When everything was working smoothly at Marcia's end, he would dash somewhere else to lend a helping hand, then hurry back to Marcia's side when she would be once again in need of some help. Ruby was put in charge of refreshments. They would be needing gallons of tea, and ample supplies of thick ham sandwiches. Reuben firmly believed his workers couldn't give their best if their bellies weren't completely satisfied.

So the scene was set. Donald threw a lever and the machines burst into action. The noise was deafening. The birds, until then calmly watching the proceedings from the branches above, suddenly shot out of the trees and flew skywards, terrified by the unfamiliar din. Then a shimmering grey form emerged through the swirling clouds of corn chaff – it was Joe Trevains. Reuben and Norman had given their best down at his farm with the threshing, so now it was his turn to help out. He and Reuben collected the bags as soon as they were full. With amazing speed they would carry the heavy sacks up several worn and uneven stone steps, to where the grain would be tipped out on to the bare barn floor, then they would hurry back to Marcia, where another full bag would be waiting for them. In spite of the tedious, dusty work, Marcia couldn't help but smile as Donald kept bobbing up from different angles around the two machines. He was an important man on occasions such as these. Everything depended on the reliability of his contraptions. He would be seen brandishing a rather large spanner in one hand, and an oily rag clutched lovingly in the other. Each time he appeared, he was blacker than the last, and by the end of the day Marcia and Ruby couldn't stop giggling when they looked at him, as by then only the whites of his eyes were in evidence. Nightfall signalled the end of threshing for the day. The workers left their posts feeling tired and dirty, and woefully conscious of the fact that this tiresome work would continue for at least another three days.

Nobody was sorry when those three days were over. Eventually the last bag of corn had been emptied out into the barn, and as Donald and his mate trundled the hard worked machinery through the farmyard gate, Reuben and his crew sighed with relief.

Even Reuben looked exhausted when he sat down for his evening meal. As soon as his plate was empty, he drew his chair closer to the fire, and in seconds he was sound asleep.

The farm quickly settled back to its normal everyday winter routine. Each day's wireless news brought reports of more serious developments in the war, and still there was no likelihood of an end in sight. In this remote corner of England they were reminded each day of the country's terrible plight as the war planes roared overhead. Marcia and Ruby would stop and hold their breaths as sometimes a crippled bomber would fly down low over the farm. Before resuming their duties, they would wait and listen until the ragged sound of the engine slowly faded as it touched down on the runway. Only when they knew it was safely down would they breathe easily again.

Norman and Ruby were now going steady, and by all appearances were very much in love. On one cold damp afternoon Reuben and Marcia were returning from mending a fence in the top field and were walking back through the farmyard, when they caught sight of a movement through the bare window of the cow's house. They both stopped in their tracks, as on a closer inspection they realised it was Norman. He was acting very strangely. All they could see was his head and shoulders slowly moving backwards and forwards along the inside of the window. Deeply puzzled, they crept slowly forward and peered inside.

Norman was holding Ruby in his arms. Being shorter than he, she had previously been hidden from view. The pair were dancing and were serenely oblivious to their curious spectators. Ruby was gazing up at him in adoration as she softly spoke the rhythm. 'One, two, three . . . one, two, three. There, that's much better, Norman.'

Reuben could contain himself no longer. 'One two three,' he bellowed through the opening. 'Out 'ere ye skiving sods . . ! Wot do ye think this is – the blimen bally or summin?'

The dancing partners almost jumped out of their skins, then slowly and shamefacedly they stepped outside. Ruby looked pale as she blustered, 'There's a dance at St Mawgan church hall next week. Norman couldn't dance so I thought I would teach him, boss!' Feeling uncomfortable under Reuben's steely gaze, she lowered her head and studied the ground around her feet. She didn't notice the humorous twinkle that had crept back in his eyes when he said, 'Ye baint learning 'im in working 'ours, missy. Evenin's the time fer that sort of thing. Me work needs to be done . . . dance or no dance!'

The village dance was the main topic of conversation for the next few days . . . that is, when Reuben wasn't around. They all knew their boss's views concerning village dances; he had made his thoughts quite clear. Any man who capered round and around a dance floor, while others stood in groups watching and tittering to themselves, must be a proper sissy. He wouldn't have been seen dead in such places.

It didn't deter Norman though. By the day of the dance he had mastered all the basic steps. Ruby was delighted with his progress, and boosted his confidence by telling him he was a born dancer. Even Marcia had been drawn into the excitement, and was eagerly awaiting the evening's church social.

Chapter Seven

At long last the great day came, and Ruby and Marcia found themselves hurrying down the valley to the village. They both looked fresh and pretty, in spite of the fact that they had only just a very short time to get ready. Reuben had detained them longer than usual with jobs which could have been done at any time. But they realised that he was slightly peeved with them for influencing his Norman. Also they felt that deep down he would have loved to have joined them. And that in fact he was just hiding behind an obstinate, stern exterior.

As they drew nearer, the music from the band came out to meet them, and they almost ran the last few steps in their excitement. The church was in darkness but they carefully made their way along the bordering gravel path until they came to the hall door. The light spilled out for a second while the door opened to let in a group of airmen. The girls stepped in behind them, and excitedly followed them inside. Ruby smiled and gave Marcia a playful nudge. 'I have a feeling you won't be on your own for long tonight!'

Just inside the door sat a very important church committee man who was busy collecting the one shilling entrance fee from each person. On the small table in front of him were placed two large square tins. One was almost half full of shiny shillings, but the other one, reserved for banknotes, was sadly lacking in volume. Alongside the tins of money sat a large roll of green tickets. One of these tickets would be given in exchange for the shilling and had to be kept safe, as some of the patrons might wish to pop over to the Falcon at some time during the evening. If they couldn't produce a ticket when they came back, they would have to buy another one – the wily cashier at the door conveniently had a bad memory for faces.

As the airmen moved over to buy their tickets, the girls spotted Norman waiting for them. Dressed in his finely-creased, grey flannels and sports jacket, he looked very smart and handsome, an entirely different person from the usual dowdily-dressed farm labourer the girls worked with every day. He insisted on paying for both of them, and after carefully stowing the tickets in his jacket pocket, he proudly took their arms and led them through to the dance floor, which was already quite full as they carefully made their way around the side of the room to where there were some empty seats. The band was playing out the last strains of a dreamy waltz as the trio settled themselves down, but the dancers on the floor held their ground, they weren't ready to sit down yet!

Realising there was an exuberant lot on the floor, the musicians struck up a loud and lively quick-step, which was met with noisy cheering and clapping as the dancers leapt into action with gusto. Determined not to miss a single dance, Ruby took Norman's hand and pulled him out on to the floor. He looked terrified. Marcia felt really sorry for him as he tried to move his feet in the right direction. Even his legs looked stiff and wooden. He looked back to where Marcia was sitting and smiled ruefully. Then an exaggerated wink followed the smile as he turned back to Ruby, and they both started to dance. Marcia sat bolt upright in her chair, her mouth open in amazement, Norman's ungainly stiffness had suddenly disappeared as his feet moved to the music with skilled precision. He had been pulling her leg.

Ruby was a picture of pride and elegance as she moved in perfect unison with her handsome partner. Marcia relaxed and smiled to herself as her eyes slowly wandered around the room. She noted that the majority of young men were from the aerodrome. They seemed to be in high spirits, no doubt pleased to have something to take their minds off the perils of war.

'Wanna dance, babe?'

Marcia jumped as the strong American voice broke into her thoughts. The tall airman was looking down at her and looked very smart in his crisp blue uniform. Marcia nodded and smiled as she took his hand and was led out to join the others.

He certainly had a lot of energy. Marcia was enjoying herself hugely, even though her partner only imagined himself to be another 'Fred Astaire'. His lean body writhed to the music, while his feet moved as if he was standing on red-hot coals. Marcia wasn't quite sure what sort of dance he was doing and thought that perhaps it was something he had made up himself. She had certainly never seen a performance quite like it before, but it was good fun. Her eyes swept over the wall-flowers as she obediently followed her 'Fred' around the floor. Then suddenly her eyes rested on one of the men in a blue uniform. She didn't know why, but he seemed to stand out from the rest. For a moment she almost forgot where she was and what she was doing, and it was only when the man turned and looked directly at her that she guiltily averted her gaze and forced her wobbly legs to follow her energetic partner. When the music ended she was glad to get back to her seat. Her lively partner was all right, but only in small doses!

Mustering her courage, she stole a glance across the room and was disappointed to find the handsome stranger was no longer there. Ruby disturbed her thoughts.

'Come on, Marcy it's your turn now. You must dance with Norman.' She looked at him adoringly. 'He's wonderful.'

'You horrible boy,' Marcia said good-naturedly. 'Pretending you didn't know how to dance . . . you certainly had me fooled.'

He smiled broadly and gave her a friendly kiss on her cheek. 'I was a bit rusty at first, but I soon got the hang of it. Besides,' he added with another cheeky grin, 'I rather enjoyed all me lessons with Ruby.'

When the interval came all three were glad to sit down for a rest. Marcia hadn't been short of partners, so the three were really enjoying themselves. Cups of tea and hot appetising little pasties were laid out on long wooden trestle tables, and a hungry crowd soon gathered around the welcoming feast. 'I wish there was a dance here every week,' Ruby remarked, speaking between large mouthfuls of pasty. 'It's ever so quiet down here in the country . . . so different from back home.' She gave a hopeless little sigh. 'There, I could have danced every night if I had wanted to.'

Norman looked at her with a slightly peeved expression in his blue eyes. 'Yer better off down 'ere, me girl, with me to look after ee . . . at least 'tiz safer!'

Ruby cuddled up to him and whispered something into his ear. Marcia couldn't hear what was being said, but by the looks of a now satisfied and smiling Norman, Ruby must have put things right.

The interval was over. All the members of the band had resumed their seats, and the tables of food had been laid bare. A few of the dancers had gone missing. They had probably gone over to the Falcon for something a little stronger than tea, but those remaining were obviously raring to go. An airman with a pretty blonde girl in tow hurried across the dance floor and whispered something to the sax player, who listened carefully, then passed the message round to each member of the band. They looked towards the eager young man and gave him a nod of agreement, whereby, grinning from ear to ear he hauled his girl back to the centre of the floor, and stood waiting. Suddenly the aged members of the band burst into really loud and lively music which quite belied the look of their advancing years. With agile feet tapping and cheeks blown out fit to burst, they happily put their heart and soul into the airman's request. The lone couple on the floor were ready. As soon as the first notes broke the silence, their feet started to move. An excited twitter wafted round the room when it became obvious that the pair were jitterbugging. They had the floor to themselves. Everyone looked on in wonderment as the couple expertly moved together with the stimulating rhythm from the band. They had the floor on their own for several minutes as no one else seemed over-anxious to match their obvious skill. Marcia watched them admiringly, then out of the corner of her eye noticed Ruby and Norman rise from their seats. She held her breath as they walked hand in hand to join the tireless, gyrating couple on the dance floor, hoping that they wouldn't make fools of themselves. But no, it was amazing! She watched spellbound as they started to dance. They were every bit as good as the other couple, if not better even. So this is the result of the secret lessons, marvelled Marcia. She smiled as she watched her elated friend, her thoughts reflecting back to their first days on the farm. Ruby had certainly surprised her; she would willingly have bet a week's hard-earned wages on her not settling down, and now look at her, absolutely loving the country life. A longing sigh escaped Marcia's lips. Norman of course was the reason for the change in her friend. Enviously she thought, it just shows what love can do!

The hall reverberated to the whistles and applause as the music ended, startling her out of her reverie. The dancers stood breathless but jubilant to receive their well-earned plaudits, even the band had dropped their instruments and were now on their feet clapping and cheering as loudly as the rest. The village dance was turning out to be something quite spectacular.

Soon the strains of a dreamy waltz swept smoothly through the air and enticed its listeners to take to the floor again. Marcia sat quietly watching and enjoying the musical activity around her. Some couples were holding each other tightly, their bodies and faces telling of their secrets; others were there just to enjoy the dancing. A few weren't quite sure what steps to take next, and by now were probably wishing they had stuck to harmless tea.

Suddenly Marcia's whole body stiffened. Her eyes had alighted on the handsome airman she had noticed earlier and he was looking her way. Flustered, she swiftly averted her gaze and tried to pretend that she wasn't looking at him, or at anyone in particular. But it was no good, her eyes were inexorably drawn back across the room to see if he was still looking her way. He was!

Before she could again avert her gaze, he smiled and started walking towards her. Instinctively her hands moved to straighten her skirt and she secretly wished that she had checked herself in the mirror beforehand. Too late now; he was standing before her. Her throat felt dry as she looked up into his dark blue eyes. He was even more handsome close up.

'May I have this dance?'

Marcia smiled and took his outstretched hand, self-consciously aware of her hardworking, calloused fingers encased now within his gentle but masterful grip. He led her between the dancers to a suitable bare patch of the floor and put his arm around her waist. His eyes smiled down on her from beneath heavy black eyebrows. 'I have to warn you I'm not a very good dancer,' he said candidly.

Marcia gave a little laugh. That didn't bother her in the least; she was more than happy just to be in his arms. 'You're not an American?'

'No, I'm from Dundee in Scotland. Webster's the name . . . Webster Toddman. I'm a navigator in the air force — stationed at St Mawgan. He drew her closer and rested his head against hers. Marcia could feel the thick softness of his black hair against her cheek, and as they danced, the bristles of his pencil-slim moustache gently brushed her skin. 'And you are?' His voice was low and husky, as if he, too, felt the emotion that she was experiencing.

'My name is Marcia Evans, originally from Wales.' She happily noted his pleased expression when she told him that she now worked as a Land Army girl at Tolcarne Merock farm which was almost next door to the aerodrome.

'That's very handy,' he whispered and snuggled even closer.

Marcia felt sad when the dance ended. She felt as if she could have gone on dancing with him the whole night long, and wished fervently that she had met Webster Toddman earlier. As they vacated the dance floor, another airman tapped Webster on the shoulder and pointed to his watch, 'Sorry, mate, but it's time to go; we're late enough already.'

'Marcia, this is my mate Gerry.' Webster introduced the fresh-faced young airman. 'He's not usually such a rotten spoil-sport!'

A friendly hand was thrust towards her. 'Hello, Marcia, I'm sorry to have to break up the party but someone's got to keep an eye on him.' He looked anxiously towards his friend as if to say, 'Hurry up or we'll both be in deep trouble!'

Webster got the message. He gave an aggrieved smile, squeezed her hand tightly, then hastily followed his friend across the floor to the exit door. Marcia stood and watched their retreating backs, painfully aware of a hollow feeling rising up from the pit of her stomach as she realised that he had gone and hadn't mentioned anything about seeing her again. That's that, she thought despondently as she rejoined Ruby and Norman.

'You seemed to be enjoying yourself Marcy?' Ruby piped up, waiting impatiently for her friend to elaborate on her dancing partner, but Marcia just nodded and smiled wistfully.

Ruby wasn't deterred that easily. 'Come on – what's his name? He looks nice. Are you seeing him again?'

Marcia tried to be flippant. 'His name is Webster; he's Scottish. He's all right, I suppose, but I don't think I will be seeing him again.

Ruby studied her friend carefully. She knew her well enough by now to realise that she was hiding something. But she also realised that it would be wise to let the matter drop for he moment, as apparently things weren't as rosy as they had appeared. Shame, she thought to herself. They seemed to be getting along so well.

Marcia was relieved when the band soon signalled the end of the evening by playing *God Save the King*. She didn't feel like confiding in Ruby, not just yet. Anyway, she was just being silly; there was really nothing to tell. She stood proudly to attention along with the others, but her mind refused to hear the music. Webster filled her thoughts.

She could still feel his warm, manly body close to hers. His strong arm clasped round her waist, and the tingly sensation of his moustache against her cheek. For a moment or two she gave herself up completely to the tender thoughts that filled her mind. Then, with a shrug of her shoulders, she mentally gave herself a strong ticking off. You're a fool, Marcia Evans. Just because he's knocked you for six, doesn't mean that he should feel the same way about you.

A muffled murmur reverberated quietly around the hall as the final notes of the anthem died away and everyone prepared to make a dash for the door. Norman offered her his arm, and with Ruby coveting his other arm, led them both jostling along with the chattering throng to the clear night outside.

They stood and gratefully breathed in the cool, fragrant, country air. Above them the stars twinkled like jewels in the black velvet sky. As Marcia gazed up at the heavens, Webster again dominated her thoughts. Will he be flying up there tonight? she wondered. It suddenly dawned on her that perhaps he had to hurry back for that very reason. She felt a little better then, aware that he could have been feeling anxious if he had to go on a night bombing mission. It was no wonder he didn't feel like hanging about; she should have had more sense. Her breath caught in her throat as she felt something warm and furry moving against her leg. Slowly she looked down, and smiled with relief when she found that it was only William. 'Hello boy!' She bent down and fondly patted his scruffy head. 'Where's your master?' Looking back along the road in the direction of the Falcon, she saw Reuben strolling unsteadily towards her. She walked back to meet him with William bounding joyfully on ahead. 'I'll walk back with you, if that's all right, boss?'

Reuben meekly smiled his agreement and maintained his unsteady gait. Marcia wondered if he was afraid to slow up in case he lost his balance and stumbled over. She fell into step

61

beside him. 'I don't fancy walking on my own, or playing gooseberry to the two lovebirds,' she told him. 'It was just perfect when you came along.'

They walked on in silence except for the sound of Reuben's loud clattering boots. Every so often he would stumble on a loose stone or a rut in the ground and mutter something angrily to himself. As they neared Polgreen farm, the resident dogs became aware of their presence. Marcia cringed as their excited yelping pierced the still air and made her feel that she was intruding in forbidden territory. William happily joined in and ran further along the road to where he could push his snout through the barred gate and greet his friends. After good sniffs all round, the dogs realised there was nothing to fear and stalked nonchalantly back into the murky darkness of the farmyard. The silence now weighed even heavier than before, and Marcia felt the need to talk. Panting a little, as Reuben's feet never paused for a moment, she told him how Norman had turned out to be the star dancer. 'To think that he had all those dancing lessons, and yet he knew how to do it all along. He certainly had me fooled.'

Reuben grunted, 'Yer never knows wot that bloody boy be up to. I s'pose he's further back along the track with Ruby now. I think it's 'bout time I 'ad a talk with ee. We dun't want the maid getting into trouble, do us?'

Marcia didn't answer but felt the colour rise in her cheeks. She was glad of the darkness to hide her embarrassment. After all, Reuben was just an old bachelor, and talk like that seemed out of place coming from him! He was still mumbling and complaining as they made their way up the steep slope to the farmhouse. Marcia could only catch a few of his muttered words but guessed he was still harping on the same old topic when she clearly heard him say, 'Too much bloody work on the farm fer that!'

She followed Reuben into the dark, warm kitchen and waited while he fumbled in his pockets for some matches. She heard the loose wooden clatter as his hand made contact with the box, then a disgruntled curse as he dropped it with a rattling sound on to the hard slate floor. It sounded as if it had fallen quite close to her so she bent down and brushed her hand over the floor. Yes, there it was. She lit one of the matches before straightening up, and in its feeble light she passed the errant box to Reuben. He almost snatched it from her hand, and without saying a word, strutted over to the table and lit the lamp.

Marcia slipped her aching feet out of her best shoes and thankfully wriggled her freed toes. She lit a candle, then, picking up her shoes, bade Reuben 'Goodnight' and hastily retreated up the stairs to her bedroom. Let's hope he's in a better mood tomorrow, she thought wryly to herself. She shivered slightly as the cool sheets touched her warm skin, but a faint smile tickled the corners of her mouth as she drifted into sleep with the memories of the evening still fresh in her mind.

Chapter Eight

One night, about a week later, Marcia was suddenly roused from her sleep by an unfamiliar sound. She sat bolt upright in her bed, her heart racing. She glanced at the clock, its face clearly visible in the moonlight: 1.00 a.m! Had she been dreaming? She glanced down at Ruby sleeping peacefully beside her, whatever it was hadn't disturbed her. Marcia sat quietly and strained her ears . . . no nothing but Ruby's soft, steady breathing. Somewhere out there in the distance an owl hooted. Its lonely, echoing cry carrying clearly through the dark valley. Everything seemed normal. Marcia puffed up her pillow, preparing to settle back to sleep, then her body stiffened. There it was again! She clearly heard muffled voices coming from outside in the front garden. In a flash she was out of bed and nervously peeking through the curtains. Nothing unusual out there. Her eyes combed the moonlit garden, lingering longer on the shadowy patches under the trees. No movement! Nothing! Everything was perfectly normal. Her gaze slowly followed the curving, milk-white path down to the gate. Her breath caught in her throat. Yes, this time there was movement, she was sure! There were shadows where none should have been. She leaned closer to the opened window and strained her ears to listen, hardly daring to breathe in case it blotted out the sound.

Reuben! – there was no mistaking his rough Cornish brogue. What was he up to at this time of night? She was irritated that he had disturbed her much-needed rest. Not nervous now, but curious, she squinted into the darkness. Other low-toned voices joined the old farmer's, and she saw that he was conversing with two other men. Reuben was holding a large box.

Marcia drew back a little so as not to be seen as Reuben carried a heavy box back along the path and into the house. She heard a grunt and a jangle from downstairs as he laid the box on the hard floor. Then he appeared outside again, bustling back down the path to where the men awaited him with another box. There were more hushed murmurings, then the two men moved away to another large dark shape which previously had gone unnoticed to Marcia. She realised it was a van. Perhaps a ghost van! The men disappeared inside and it glided soundlessly away down the hill, without motor or headlights. Reuben stood watching it for a moment before lugging the second box into the house. Marcia heard the front door being closed softly, then everything went quiet. Intrigued, she remained by the window and waited. Before long she heard the squeaky groan of the stairs as Reuben's stockinged feet ascended to his bedroom. This time the faint jangle confirmed what she had already begun to suspect. Spirits! – not of the ghostly kind, but in bottles. The old rascal! – he had been dealing with smugglers. It was clear now why she and Ruby were forbidden to enter his bedroom; it was probably jam-packed full of the stuff.

She shivered. With all the excitement going on she had forgotten how cold it was. She tiptoed back to bed and snuggled under the covers. Ruby hadn't even stirred, so she vowed to keep tonight's events to herself and play the innocent. The less they knew about these fishy dealings, the better, she thought.

The work-filled days hurried by. There were no further unusual events to record, until one day, when all four of them were working on their respective tasks in the yard, the postman came rattling through the main gate on his bicycle.

'Morning, Reuben. 'Ave ee got a Miss Ruby Swabey 'ere stayin?' He parked his bike against a shed and strolled over to Reuben with some letters. One he held apart from the others. 'This one be fer she,' he said, holding the envelope closer to his nose for inspection.

Reuben took his own letters and pointed across the yard to where Ruby was working. 'That there's Ruby, over there – the one with the wheel-barry.'

The postman handed Reuben his letters, then walked slowly across the yard to where Ruby was lifting a bundle of hay expertly out of the wheelbarrow. Marcia happened to glance up as he passed her friend the letter and wished the postman had one for her too. She hadn't heard from home for several days. Still there's always tomorrow, she thought optimistically. She bent forward to finish scrubbing the cattle's drinking trough when something told her to look once again in Ruby's direction. She dropped the brush back into the cold murky water and stood up. Something was wrong. Ruby was staring at the letter in shocked disbelief. Her face was drained of colour.

Marcia dithered for a moment, unsure of what to do next. She saw that Reuben had noticed Ruby's shocked reaction too and now stood anxiously watching her, his own unopened letters clutched tightly in his clenched fist. Even Norman who was several yards away mending one of the field gates, had sensed something was wrong. He, too, had stopped work and was staring over to where Ruby stood. The postman was helplessly looking from one to the other as if to say: Do something! Anything!

Everyone woke up at once and moved towards her as she dropped the letter and sunk to her knees, her hands covering her bowed head.

Norman got there first. He cradled her in his arms, her little shoulders shaking as she sobbed her heart out. His voice cracked with worry, 'What's wrong, Rube? . . . what wuz in the letter?'

Reuben stooped and retrieved the letter from the muddy ground. He wiped it on his trousers and handed it to Marcia. ' 'Ere, you'd better read this . . . can't see without me glasses.'

Marcia read the chilling words with growing alarm. 'Oh no!' she gasped. 'Ruby's home and family have been wiped out by a German bomb!'

No one spoke. Each face registered the deep shock and sorrow they were all feeling. They knew their young friend had come from a very small family, but now she had nothing, all of her past life irretrievably demolished by a senseless act of war. Even the postman looked sadly shaken as he looked down upon Ruby's distraught and pathetic little figure.

Reuben was the first to make a move. 'Bring 'er inside, boy!' His voice sounded oddly gruff as he tried to mask his emotion. Norman's dazed expression spoke louder than any words. Slowly, as if in a dream, he gently lifted the sobbing girl to her feet, picked her up in his arms, and then followed Reuben into the farmhouse. The postman and Marcia followed them. Marcia felt relieved that Reuben had taken charge. Her whole body felt as if it were made of jelly. Thank God for his strength, she thought.

Norman gently lowered Ruby into Reuben's chair by the stove. Her sobbing had abated but she was in a terrible state, her mind numbed by the crushing news. Reuben, having dashed upstairs to his bedroom, now returned with a bottle of whiskey. 'Git the mugs, Marcia, and be quick 'bout it!' He proceeded to open the bottle, his worried eyes flitting back to Ruby as he did so. Marcia, her hands trembling, dropped five mugs on to the table. She knew that the postman needed a drop too, poor old thing, before continuing with his round.

Reuben splashed some of the spirit into a mug and handed it to Norman. ' 'Ere, boy, git it down 'er quick, 'twill do wonders!' He poured a good measure into each of the other mugs, and Marcia handed them round.

Norman held the mug to Ruby's lips and told her to sip some of the fiery liquid. 'Come on, Rube, 'twill make you feel better. You need summin like this down ee fer the shock.'

She took the mug and obediently drank the contents down as if it was as weak as water. 'Thank you,' she said listlessly, glancing at Norman with bloodshot eyes as she handed him the empty mug. 'I'm sorry to be giving you so much trouble.'

Norman knelt beside her and took her hands in his as her face suddenly creased with the onset of a new burst of crying. Marcia felt decidedly uncomfortable as she stood helplessly by. There was nothing she could say or do to help Ruby, she felt utterly useless. She racked her brains for something constructive to do. The only thing that came to mind was tea . . . yes that was it, she would make some good strong tea for them all. She felt a sudden relief to be able to move and do something useful with her hands.

She rinsed out the whiskey-tainted mugs, then crossed the room to get the milk from the dairy. The postman, rooted to the spot since entering the kitchen, now moved to one side, allowing Marcia through to the dairy. She asked him if he would like some tea?

He seemed to come to life then. 'Thankee, no tea, but I wouldn't say no to just a teeny drop more of that whiskey!' Now that he had found his voice he turned to Reuben, 'Nice drop of drink you 'ave there, mister . . . is it the same Irish whiskey that

Carviggy farm do keep? — fer medicinal purposes, they say.' As he looked expectantly at Reuben, waiting for an answer, Marcia noticed her boss looking distinctly uncomfortable. But not for long.

Reuben gave the postman a searing look and said pointedly, 'Dun't ee think it's 'igh time ye wuz on yer way. People ull be wanting all them letters that's left in yer sack!' Without waiting for a reply, he strode over to the back door, opened it wide and ushered the postman on his way. 'Nosy ole sod, good job ee's gone!' he grumbled, shutting the door behind him.

Ruby's sobbing had quietened a little, but she remained understandably distraught. 'My home and family gone — I can't believe it . . . what will I do?' Her voice was pitifully weak. A few stray tears slowly chased one another down her wet cheeks.

Reuben walked over to her and laid his large, rough hand on her shoulder. His eyes looked suspiciously shiny, and his gruff voice held a tremor when he spoke to her. 'There'll always be a 'ome ere fer ee, me dear, dun't forget that.' Then he turned quickly away and whistled for William, the signal that he was going outside to resume his work. He looked back to Marcia as he reached the kitchen door. 'Me and Norman ull manage fer the day. You'd best stay in 'ere.' Then he bustled out, thankful for an excuse to leave the sadness in the room.

Norman looked helplessly at the two woeful faces, shrugged his shoulders as if to say sorry, then followed Reuben out. He knew no matter what, the work on the farm had to be done!

Chapter Nine

December announced its arrival with fierce, biting winds and a sky overflowing with slate-grey snow clouds. The girls were loath to leave their cosy warm bed when the shrill call of the alarm clock pierced the blackness of their bedroom at six a.m. Tentatively, their feet would touch down onto the hard, chilling, linoleum floor, then, hopping from one foot to the other to alleviate the cold, they would dress as hurriedly as possible. With their sleep-befuddled minds making them unusually clumsy, they would descend the stairs like sleepwalkers and step gratefully into the welcoming warmth of the kitchen.

Over the past few weeks Ruby had steadily grown stronger and had come to accept the terrible misfortune of losing her home and family. Norman was without doubt the main reason for her revival, as she spent every moment that was possible in his company. The tragedy had also brought the two girls closer together. They were almost like sisters now, Marcia thought. Yes, Ruby had definitely adopted them all as her new family.

Now Christmas was almost upon them, and the Reverend Bassett was busy preparing for the annual carol service in St Mawgan Church. He was just stepping out of the post office as Ruby and Marcia drew up in the horse and cart. He walked over to them as they tethered Star to a convenient stake, and gave them one of his most gracious smiles.

'Good day, young ladies . . . a little parky though, I must say.' He drew his cloak closer to his thin body as his warm breath took shape in the cold wavering air. 'Will we be seeing you on Sunday next for the carol service?' With his jutting front teeth fastened firmly down on his frozen bottom lip, and trying hard to maintain his warm smile, he said, 'Perhaps you could bring Reuben along

with you . . . we must keep morale up in times such as these.'
With a slight wave he hurried away in the direction of his church,
as if fearful of being frozen to the spot if he stayed there for one
moment longer.

Later that same day Marcia had made some pasties, and now
the three of them Reuben, Ruby and herself — were tucking in to
them at the kitchen table. Glancing at the other two, Marcia was
pleased to note that they were looking as if they were really
enjoying them. Well, they are good, she thought to herself as she
blew away the hot steam and took another bite. Then she smiled
to herself as she remembered the first ones she had made. William
had done well that night. He was the only one who had
appreciated them. But now, thanks to Reuben's help and tips, she
felt she had mastered the art of making a good Cornish pasty.
Glancing across the table to Reuben, she said, 'We bumped into
the Reverend Bassett, down by the post office today, boss. He
asked if you would be going to his carol service on Sunday?'

With a stubby forefinger, Reuben carefully wiped a trickle of
gravy that was speeding down a rut in his chin, then noisily
sucked it clean before saying, 'Dun't 'is 'oliness realise there be
a war on. 'Tiz alright fer 'im, just standin' be'ind 'is pulpit; ee
dun't know wot 'ard work 'tiz, farmin' fer the country.'

The girls looked at each other and smiled knowingly as they
came to the conclusion that there was just no way they could save
their boss.

Marcia had been pleased to hear that another dance was due to
be held in the church hall on the evening before Christmas eve,
and secretly she was hoping that Webster would be there. She
wasn't able to forget him, no matter how hard she tried. And as
the day of the dance drew nearer she was becoming more and
more excited and hardly knew how to hide her restlessness from
the others. It was a help to her that Reuben kept them extra busy
with the feather-plucking of numerous plump birds that would be
eaten on Christmas day. The girls would sit on stools in an
outhouse, and before long they would be surrounded by an ever-
growing mound of soft, weightless plumage. Every so often a
sneeze, caused by the invisible down that filled the air and their
nostrils, would stir the mounds of feathers around them and send
them gently spiralling up to the rafters, where they would hover
as if in slow motion, before gliding back to earth. After the birds

had been laid bare, the girls had the nauseous task of disposing of the birds' grisly innards. At first their fingers worked with utter distaste, but after a while the chore just became another of their allotted jobs. When all the chubby, goose-pimpled packages had been lined up in the dairy, the girls always felt a certain pride as they surveyed their accomplished handiwork and completely forgot that the tempting rows of meat had until just recently been running and pecking around the farmyard. In spite of everything that had happened, even Ruby was getting caught up in the Christmas spirit. Both girls had eagerly discussed decorating the farmhouse for the festive occasion, and had tackled Reuben on the subject. At first he seemed unconcerned, but just when the girls had disappointedly decided he was a grumpy old killjoy, he appeared in the kitchen with a dusty and dilapidated box retrieved from the darkest depths of his bedroom. He placed the box, adorned with thick grey cobwebs and shrivelled dead spiders, on the kitchen tabletop. ' 'Ere you are . . . if you be bent on fancyin' up the place. 'Twas mothers. Dun't know if 'twill be any good now, but yer welcome to it!'

He left as the pair eagerly pounced on the box, both impatient to find out if its secrets would serve their needs. Several pieces had been shattered, and they had to gingerly handle each piece out of the box so as not to cut their fingers on the delicate shards of glass. Others that appeared to be whole, were laid carefully down in the centre of the table.

So engrossed were they in what they were doing, they didn't see Norman who had entered the kitchen and now stood quietly in the doorway watching them. Just like a couple of excited schoolgirls, he thought, as squeals of delight announced another priceless find.

'You two seem very excited?'

Their animated faces turned towards Norman as they heard his voice. Ruby ran over to him and pulled him by the arm over to the table. 'Look, Reuben gave us this old box, and it's full of Christmas decorations! Isn't it wonderful? She reached up and gave him a kiss in her excitement.

Norman put his arms around her and swung her round and round. 'There's more,' he said, lowering her to the ground. 'You and Marcy follow me.'

Looking at each other in happy bewilderment, the girls

71

followed Norman into the yard, where he stopped and pointed to a rich green, red-berried, holly tree which he had cut down from somewhere on the farm.

Ruby's eyes were shining with joy as she looked at her friend. 'A real Christmas tree! Now the house will look really perfect, won't it, Marcy?'

Marcia just nodded. For a second or two her thoughts had transported her back to Christmas's in her own home, and had brought a hard lump to her throat. She kept her thoughts to herself; at least her home was still there. If Ruby had managed to put the past behind her, that was good. She mustn't remind her of it.

On the evening of December 23rd Ruby and Marcia were in the front room admiring the prettily decorated holly tree when Norman arrived to escort them to the village dance.

'Isn't it beautiful?' Ruby said, still absolutely delighted with it.

'It certainly is,' Norman agreed, although his eyes were feasting more on her than on the tree.

Marcia nipped upstairs to bring down their warm coats. Her stomach had been knotted all day. She had been thinking about Webster and wondering whether he would be at the dance. Earlier on she had been optimistic about seeing him, but now the moment was near the gnawing doubts had reared their ugly head, making her almost afraid to attend the dance. After lighting a candle, she took the coats from the wardrobe and draped them over her arm. Raising the candle for a last minute glance in the bedroom mirror, she tutted to herself as she noticed a curl which had strayed out of place. Then, shrugging her shoulders as if to say, 'It will have to do', she hurried back downstairs to rejoin the others.

By the time the three of them arrived, the church hall was almost full. The band was in full swing and several couples were already warming up the dance floor. The hall had been transformed with holly and mistletoe, and chains of brightly-coloured paper which, when added to the sea of happy faces, served to spread a welcoming aura of excitement and anticipation.

Marcia glanced quickly around the room at the numerous blue-uniformed men, scanning their faces with mounting disappointment as she failed to spot Webster amongst them. I knew it, I knew it, she told herself bitterly. Then a wave of utter dejection washed over her as she reflected on the distinct possibility of never seeing him again.

The atmosphere in the hall was so friendly and lively however, that Marcia could not help but start enjoying herself. As the evening progressed, she was never short of dancing partners, and although some of them had been quite dashing and charming, none of them had affected her in the way Webster had.

When the interval came, Marcia sat back and watched the crowds milling around the refreshment table. She decided she couldn't be bothered to join the jostling throng, preferring instead to observe the activities of those around her. Her attention was suddenly drawn in the direction of the toilets by the sound of raised, angry voices. Her interest grew as she spotted Ruby's colourful flowered dress amid the agitated group, then she sat up sharply in her seat as, on closer inspection, somewhere in the centre of the mob, she caught sight of Norman's fair hair. With a sinking feeling that something was wrong, she sprang to her feet and hurried towards them.

When she drew close she saw that Norman was being tormented by one of the airmen who, in turn, was being backed up by several of his uniformed mates who were now urging him on. Just as she reached Ruby's side she heard someone shout above the rumpus, 'Army dodger, outside!' The troublemakers were clearly spoiling for a fight.

Everyone responded to the cue. In an invisible cloud of stale beer fumes they were swept along with the ugly group and, in a matter of seconds, found themselves outside in the bitterly cold air.

The two girls clung together, shaking with fright as the icy wind whipped around their flimsily-clad bodies. The circle of jeering onlookers was now growing larger as more people were enticed out by the dreadful noise. Whacks, slaps, grunts and heavy breathing punctuated the night darkness which was doing its best to obscure the scrappers from view.

'What's happening to him, Marcia? Oh my God, is he all right?' Ruby sounded frantic and was near to tears. Then the noise ceased abruptly as it was realised that only one of the dim figures was left standing. The lone figure extended an outstretched hand

d

and slowly hauled the other man to his feet. Ruby gave a shriek of delight when she realised that Norman was the victor, and neither he nor his opponent appeared to be that much worse for wear. But unfortunately it wasn't yet over. Two of the obstreperous airman's burly mates were closing in on Norman now.

Ruby's squeal of delight died on her lips as she became aware of what was about to happen. She had never felt so scared as she did at that moment. If anything should happen to Norman, she knew she would never be able to cope. *Please God let him be all right*, was her silent prayer.

Suddenly, as if in answer to her fervent prayer, a broad-shouldered figure had pushed his way through the watching crowd and was hoisting one of Norman's cowardly assailants clean off his feet. Then, quick as a flash, he had rounded on the other one and pinned his arms tightly behind his back.

'Save yer bullying fer the Germans,' came the harsh warning in a voice that Ruby promptly recognised as belonging to Reuben.

Boss! — Ruby's mouth silently formed the word as she marvelled at Reuben's timely intervention.

The silence that reigned while Reuben frog-marched his captives through the crowd and across the lane was broken by a loud splash when the unfortunate bullies were dropped unceremoniously into the icy waters of the river. A chorus of laughter greeted the dripping forms that clambered up the bank and scurried away towards the RAF camp.

Rough justice had prevailed.

The shivering group soon lost interest once the excitement was over and hurried back to the warmth of the hall. Ruby saw that Reuben had now been joined by Marcia and Norman. She hastened across to them and clung to Norman for dear life.

He held her tightly as he consoled her. 'Don't worry, Rube, I'm fine . . . they hardly touched me.' Sparing a grateful glance for Reuben, he added, 'But I don't know what would 'ave 'appened if you 'adn't turned up when you did, boss. Ow did you know 'twas me in the scrap?'

' 'Twas easy, boy. Marcy came running into pub an' got me out. In a fair ole state she wuz . . . knew it must be summin pretty drastic. Didn't even 'ave time to finish me pint!'

'Let me buy you another one,' Norman offered gladly.

'Me too,' piped up Ruby, beside herself with relief.

'That I will,' Reuben grinned happily. 'That I will. But another time.' He whistled to William who was busily sniffing around the hedges for the scurrying night creatures that only he could hear. Reluctantly, and with tail drooping, the dog trotted over to his master and looked up at him with big, soulful eyes which mirrored the disappointment he was feeling at having to abandon his playful hunting so soon. Then his tail leapt to life and wagged furiously when Reuben stooped and scratched the top of his head. 'C'mon, Will, 'tiz time to go 'ome.' He grunted at the discomfort of stiff joints as he straightened up, and when he spoke, the reluctance in his voice matched that of his dog: 'I'd best be off now. I be a bit concerned 'bout the cow that's due to calf. Best check 'er, I s'pose.' He waited for a moment in case they decided to walk back with him, but he could see they were itching to get back to the dance, so he turned to go. As he walked off into the darkness he shouted back to Norman, 'Watch yer step, boy — dun't fergit they two maids you be looking after!'

The interval was over and the music and dancing had started again. Norman and Ruby took to the dance floor as soon as they entered the hall, leaving Marcia to squeeze herself through the wall-flowers in search of a seat. Looking at the party now, no one would have guessed there had been trouble here just a short while ago. Noticing that the refreshment lady was still serving a few stragglers at the far end of the room, Marcia realised that a nice cup of tea was just what she needed.

When she reached the table it was bare except for a plate which held a few yeast buns. They looked good and made her feel hungry.

The red-faced, plumpish woman serving behind the table looked overworked and flustered as she waddled closer in her crumpled pinafore. 'Not much left now, dear, 'cept tea and one or two yeasties.' She began pouring milk into a cup as if reading Marcia's mind.

Marcia ordered a bun.

'That'll be fourpence then please, dearie.' The poor woman tutted to herself as more revellers arrived at the table in need of her services. 'Thank you, luv.'

Marcia took a sip of the scalding tea. A bit stewed, she thought, but mustn't complain. Then she raised the bun to her mouth and took a large bite.

'Marcia.'

She knew that voice! She whirled round to find Webster smiling down at her. Her heart leapt, he was even more handsome than she remembered. Her mouth was stuffed full of dry bun crumbs which were the very devil to get rid of in a hurry. She stood looking at him, feeling elated and embarrassed all at the same time.

He said, 'I was hoping you would be here. I couldn't get away from the camp until late . . . almost didn't make it.'

She managed to clear her mouth. 'I'm glad you came.' Her voice, affected by the emotion she was feeling, was little more than a hoarse whisper.

His eyes rested on the partly-eaten bun. 'Is that good. I'm feeling a bit peckish myself.'

Marcia laughed as the tension started to ease. 'Before the war it would have been full of sultanas. Now it's only plain bun. They're okay if you're feeling really hungry.'

As he dug into his pocket for some loose change, the plump woman behind the table shouted, 'All sold out!' and started to pile the dirty crockery on to a large tray.

'That's it then,' Webster said with a rueful smile as he dropped his money back into his pocket. 'Just my luck. I'll make sure I get here earlier next time.'

Marcia offered him what was left of her own bun. 'You can have mine if you like.'

He started to protest but she placed it in his hand, insisting she really didn't want any more of it. She could not have eaten it if she tried. All signs of her hunger had disappeared and a wobbly tingle of excitement had taken its place.

They stood and watched the dancing as Webster polished off the bun and helped himself to some of Marcia's tea. Amid the tangle of swaying bodies, Marcia had spotted Norman and Ruby gently gliding towards them. She stood on tiptoe and waved to attract their attention. Ruby was the first to catch her eye, and she could tell from Marcia's expression that something exciting had occurred. Then she recognised Webster and felt so happy for her friend. Although nothing much had been said, she had guessed that Marcia had been longing to see him. For Marcia, the rest of the evening raced by in a blur of heavenly bliss as she danced with no one else but Webster. All too soon the band had struck up the national anthem and then she found herself standing beside him outside in the bleak wintry night. She shivered as the cold wind chilled away the warmth of the dance hall, and Webster noticed. He put his arm tightly around her. 'Is that better?' he asked.

'Thank you, yes.' She was already feeling the benefit of his electrical warmth pulsating throughout every fibre of her body. Several small groups of people stood around them chatting amongst themselves, all seemingly loath to go home and put an end to their special evening.

Ruby broke away from one of the shadowy clusters and came over to where Marcia and Webster were standing. She smiled to herself as she noticed Webster's arm fastened tightly around her friend's slim waist. 'You can walk home with me and Norm if you like, Marcy. That is, when he's finished gossiping with his friends.' She looked back over her shoulder to where Norman was still happily absorbed amongst his cronies.

Webster swiftly spoke up. 'Thanks, Ruby, but I'm not flying tonight, so I can take Marcia home.'

Although Marcia's face was in shadow, Ruby could feel and picture the delight that was written there. 'See you back at the farm then,' she whispered, squeezing her friend's arm before hurrying back to relay the good news to Norman.

Webster's arm remained comfortingly around Marcia's waist as they walked back through the silent lanes. For a while neither of them spoke. They were both content to be in each other's company.

They had walked almost halfway back to the farm before they found any need for words, then, as if on cue, they both piped up together. Laughing, they stopped in their tracks. Then Webster drew her close and kissed her. He broke away quickly, as if he had been caught stealing. Marcia didn't move. She willed with all her heart for him to kiss her again. He bent forward and this time Marcia was ready for him and their lips met for their first real kiss. They stood for several minutes, locked together, blissfully unaware of the cold night wind that whipped around them and angrily shook the naked boughs of the overhanging trees. Webster took her hand. 'I think we had better move on now. I expect Norman and Ruby will be coming along soon.'

Marcia nodded and stepped out happily beside him, her hand still firmly grasped in his.

'What was it you were going to say just now?' He was suddenly curious.

She had to think back, it was hard, her mind was still reeling. Then she remembered. 'Oh, I was just wondering how you were going to find your way back to the aerodrome. It's pitch black tonight; I don't want you to get lost.'

He smiled and gave her hand a squeeze, 'Don't worry about that; I've got it all figured out. There's a lane which runs from Tolcarne Merock up to the main road, and from there it's just a matter of hopping over the hedge and into the camp. Easy!'

His reply warmed her heart. He must have been thinking of her to have planned all that.

As they were nearing the top of the last steep hill, Marcia noticed the dull glow of a lantern weaving its way across the farmyard and then disappearing into the cowshed. It had to be Reuben. And the cow was probably calving. He wouldn't be in there this late otherwise. She was concerned as she quickened her step. The pitiful moos of the wretched animal echoed eerily around the farmyard as Webster followed closely behind.

She paused to open the shed door and they both stepped inside. Webster closed the door softly behind him. The air inside was hot and stuffy with the strenuous steamy efforts of the poor bloated animal. Reuben was beside her, stroking the damp hide which glistened in the mellow light of the lantern. He glanced fleetingly over his shoulder and saw only Marcia standing there. 'Thank God you be 'ere, we got troubles sure nuff. Calf is wrong way round and can't be born. Poor ole cow is in sum state. Better git Norman to go down and phone the vet quick. If ee dun't come soon we'll lose both of 'em.'

'Norman's not here yet, boss!' Marcia said anxiously as she walked over to where Reuben stood and gently stroked the hide of the exhausted animal.

Reuben's tired and worried face stared back at her. 'We need 'elp soon, Marcy!'

She placed her hand comfortingly on his sinewy arm. 'I'll hurry back and meet them; that will save some time.'

'No need for that, Marcia!'

Reuben started when he heard the strange voice, and turned to see Webster now in the process of removing his overcoat. Marcia had almost forgotten he was there herself in the worry of the moment. 'It's all right, boss,' she explained. 'This is my friend, Webster. He's from the camp up the road.'

Webster had now taken off his tunic jacket and tie and was busy unbuttoning his shirt. 'Can you fetch some soap and hot water, Marcia?' he said, as he laid his uniform carefully down on a bundle of clean straw. Marcia just stood and regarded him in puzzlement, causing him to smile as he noticed her obvious confusion. 'Don't worry, I'm a vet back in civvy street. Now hurry away,' he urged, planting a playful smack on her bottom to send her on her way. 'I presume you would like me to see to her?' he said to Reuben.

Too gobsmacked for words, the old farmer just nodded gratefully.

Moments later Marcia was back with the soap and a pail full of hot water. Her breath caught in her throat as she looked admiringly at her airman. He was now stripped to the waist, and she felt a sudden uncontrollable urge to run her hands over his strong, dark, hairy chest. Directly she had placed the pail on to the floor, he plunged his arms into the hot water and started to lather them with the soap. She watched on lustfully as his hands briskly massaged both arms with the soap, causing the dark hairs on his forearms to appear wetly black against the foaming white bubbles. With his arms wet and slippery he went back to the cow. Murmuring to her softly with the gentle bedside manner of a family doctor, he lifted her tail and his whole arm disappeared easily into her angry rear end.

Marcia was suddenly aware of fresh voices, and then the unmistakable giggle belonging to Ruby. She quietly slipped outside to meet them and to explain what was going on in the cowshed. By the time Marcia had put them in the picture and they had followed her back inside, a steaming little bull calf had been successfully born and now stood teetering on his spindly little legs while his mother eyed him with loving thankfulness.

'There you are, old girl, everything should be all right now.' Webster tenderly patted the beast before going back to wash off the sleeve of pink-tinged mucous which clung wetly to his arm.

Reuben fussed around the cow, giving her a special treat of extra corn for all her troubles, while the other three stood proudly admiring the latest new addition to the farm.

Reuben directed an appreciative glance at the airman. 'Dun't no wot we would 'ave dun without ee, boy. More'n likely lost the both of 'em, I s'pect.'

Webster had fully dressed and was now strapping his watch back on to his wrist. 'Hell, look at the time,' he said. 'It's almost three a.m . . . . it's Christmas eve!' He crossed hurriedly to the shed door. 'Sorry but I must go. I should have reported back at midnight.'

Ruefully, he added, 'I'll probably be on a fizzer for this!' His hand was about to lift the latch when Reuben called out to him, ' 'Ang on a minute, vet. Seeing yer already this late, a few more minutes wun't 'urt. You cum back in the 'ouse with we and 'ave summin to eat an drink. 'Tiz the least we cun do for ee.'

Webster stood undecided for a moment, while Marcia inwardly prayed with all her heart that he would take up Reuben's offer. Then he said, 'I do seem to be feeling a bit peckish; might as well be hung for a sheep as a lamb.' He smiled. 'Or as a calf, as the case might be.'

'Might as well 'ave an early breakfast,' Reuben suggested to no one in particular as he sank wearily into his chair by the stove.

The girls smiled to each other. What he meant was that he wanted them to do the usual fry-up — bacon and eggs — that was the order of the day. They busied themselves with the food while the three men sat and enjoyed an amiable chin-wag. Apart from the room's drawn curtains and artificial light from the oil lamp, no one would have suspected from the look of its occupants that it was the early hours of the morning. Marcia though, worked as if in a dream, every now and then casting a loving glance at her airman and hardly believing it possible he was here. As soon as the plates had been filled, Reuben took his place at the head of the kitchen table. Without taking his eyes off the feast in front of him, he told the still-chatting Norman and Webster to hurry up and join him. ' 'Tiz best eating this while it still be 'ot,' he said, his eyes never leaving the crisp bacon-laden fork as it began its journey to his stomach. ' 'Tiz really 'ansome this,' he added, as it disappeared into his waiting mouth.

Marcia sat next to Webster. He was tucking into his food with gusto, clearly enjoying it. She didn't feel hungry at all, being already full to the brim with excitement. She idly pushed the food around her plate, lumping it together to give the impression that she had eaten some of it. Out of the corner of her eye, Ruby secretly watched as her friend toyed with her bacon and eggs. She smiled to herself, recognising the signs from her own recent experiences. You're love sick, my girl, she thought, delighted now that Marcia had a boyfriend of her own.

Webster placed his knife and fork down on to the plate which was now empty except for a few odd bacon rinds. Lifting his mug, he drained the last drop of his tea, and with a reluctant sigh informed his company that he had to leave them. He rose from his seat and went over to fetch his overcoat which was hanging on the back of the kitchen door.

'Dun't ee go fer a minute,' Reuben said to him, scraping back his chair and hurrying over to the hall door. Before disappearing through it, he called back to Webster, 'Dun't ee move mind, I 'ave to fetch summin fer ee from me bedroom.' The rest of his words were drowned out by the clattering of his boots as they laboured heavily one after the other up the steep stairway.

The four young ones looked at each other, all of them wondering what the wily old farmer had up his sleeve now. Four expectant faces turned towards the hall doorway as the sound of his boots heralded his imminent return.

He appeared round the door clutching a newspaper wrapped package which seemed to have the shape of a bottle inside. Thrusting the package into Webster's hands, he said, 'If you 'ave any trouble, boy, cuz yer late, give this to yer commanding officer. Tell 'im Reuben of Tolcarne Merock sends it fer allowin' ee to see to me cow. That should do the trick!'

The airman thanked him warmly, and while he was saying his goodbyes, Marcia quickly slipped on her warm coat so that she could say her special goodbye outside, on their own.

Webster put his arm around her as they walked together in the darkness towards the main farm gate. 'What do you suppose is inside this parcel, Marcia?'

She giggled as she thought of Reuben's secretive night prowlings. 'Irish whiskey, without a doubt,' she answered without hesitation.

They had reached the gate and Webster placed the package carefully down beside him on the yard floor before taking her in his arms. 'Where on earth does that old blighter get his Irish

81

whiskey from?'

'Believe me, you wouldn't want to know,' Marcia replied softly as she lifted her face towards him for her goodnight kiss.

The rumbling sound of bombers gradually drawing closer above them, brought the two lovers back to anxious reality. Webster gently freed himself from her embrace and picked up his parcel. 'I really must go, Marcia.' He snatched another quick kiss before lifting the heavy latch of the gate and hurrying away. As his footsteps receded into the darkness he called back to her, 'I'll be seeing you soon, I hope!'

'I hope so too!'

Her words were murmured fervently as she walked slowly back to the house.

Chapter Ten

Christmas day brought a change in the weather. The dry, icy winds had given way to blustery outbreaks of rain and a thick, rolling fog that swept in and out at will from the sea. The girls worked happily together preparing the Christmas dinner, although both of them felt a little apprehensive about cooking the large fattened bird, as in the past, it was something that their mothers always did. They had no need to have worried though. As Reuben had declared afterwards, with his lips still shining from the succulent feast, 'That wuz 'ansome, me dears. Can't remember when I last enjoyed me Christmas dinner so much.'

After dinner, Reuben had gone into the parlour to light the fire in the grate, while the girls tackled the large mound of greasy dishes. Norman was calling later in the afternoon to take Ruby back to his home for tea, and she was now beginning to feel nervous at the prospect of meeting his mother. As she struggled to wipe the heavy cooking utensils she voiced her anxieties to Marcia. 'Perhaps she would prefer Norman to have a Cornish girl. She might not like me because I'm a Londoner.'

'Of course she'll like you,' Marcia consoled her. 'Stop worrying. Even boss said she's a good old sort, and if he said so, she must be.'

After Ruby had left with Norman, Marcia joined Reuben in the cosy parlour. He was stretched out on the sofa, and in a deep sleep by the sound of his snoring. Knowing full well that he was bound to be dead beat after the worry of the pregnant animal, and losing a full night's precious sleep into the bargain, she settled quietly into one of the fireside armchairs, careful not to disturb him. Owing to the heavy blanket of fog surrounding the farm, the parlour's small window was offering only a modicum of daylight

83

inside, but Marcia was content to gaze dreamily at the twinkling baubles on the Christmas tree as they gently spun and flashed in the heat of the firelight. She sighed softly to herself, feeling grateful that for a couple of days at least the only work to be done on the farm was the feeding and milking of the animals. That night had drained her as well, but despite her tiredness she was deliriously happy.

Her eyes gradually closed. Even Reuben's snoring and the crackle of the pine logs splitting in the intense heat failed to disturb her. The smile that played around her lips as she slept made it evident that she was happy. More than likely Webster had entered her dreams and she was now close beside him.

'Marcia.'

She stirred, but he was with her in her sleep and tenderly speaking her name, so she was loath to wake up.

'Marcia, it's me!'

This time her senses sharpened and she opened her eyes.

Webster smiled as he saw the incredulity flash across her face as she looked up and saw him standing there.

'I was dreaming about you,' she said. 'I didn't expect to see you so soon.'

'I didn't think so either, but I've managed to get a 48 hour pass . . . so here I am.' He took off his overcoat and placed it beside him when he sat down on the sofa.

'Wonderful!' Marcia said, unable to hide her delight.

As the clock in the kitchen struck five mournful notes, she suddenly became aware that Reuben was no longer asleep on the sofa. He must have gone out to do the milking while she herself had been asleep. She looked guiltily at the grate. The fire had almost burnt itself out while she had been asleep. She knelt down on the hearth and placed a small log and a few pieces of coal on to the remaining red embers. 'There, that should do the trick. I don't think Reuben would be very happy with me if I let his fire go out.' As she rose to her feet, Webster reached out and pulled her down onto his lap. She held her hands away from him, protesting, as he hungrily kissed her, that she must wash them before her coal-blackened fingers soiled his immaculate uniform.

He laughed and let her go. 'Go on then, I'll come with you.'

Four minutes later, when she preceded him in through the kitchen door, Reuben had returned for his tea. 'Boss, look who's here!' she cried, eager for him to share in her excitement.

Reuben walked deliberately over to his seat at the table before answering her. 'Dun't 'ave to look, cuz ee come in to the cows 'ouse when I wuz milking. I telled 'im you wuz in 'ere sleeping, but ee was in no 'urry. Even checked over the cow n'calf afore cummin in 'ere to see ee.' Then he turned and chuckled at the way he had been teasing her.

After they had eaten, Marcia was hardly aware of clearing the table and washing the dishes. With her mind in its wonderful dream-like state, she still couldn't believe how lucky she was to have her airman here with her. It's the best Christmas present ever! she confided to herself as she joined them in the cosy parlour.

She sat down as close as possible to Webster on the sofa. Reuben was sprawled comfortably out in the armchair next to the fire, which thankfully Marcia noted was now blazing away merrily. The old farmer glanced across to Marcia with a twinkle in his eye, before asking Webster if he would consider staying at Tolcarne Merock for the night. 'Marcy'll make up a bed fer ee on the sofa if you like. At least 'twill be nice an warm fer ee in 'ere.'

Marcia could have hugged her boss at that moment, and when Webster told him that he would gladly accept his kind offer she hardly knew how to contain her excitement. Reuben, too, looked pleased to have his company. 'There, that be settled then,' he said as he stiffly levered himself out of the low armchair. 'Marcy, if you git some glasses fer us, we'll 'ave a glass of port, seein' 'tiz Christmas like.'

Between several glasses of port, Reuben had catnapped, and the lovers had not missed the chance of cuddling and kissing at every available respite. At nine o'clock the old farmer left them to go into the kitchen to hear the news.

After a while they heard his chair scrape noisily on the kitchen floor, then the muffled tones of the wireless abruptly stopped. They listened quietly and heard the back door open, then the sound of William's scurrying feet and Reuben's heavy footsteps suddenly disappeared as the door was slammed shut behind them. 'He's gone out to check the livestock,' Marcia whispered.

Webster seized her in his arms. 'Good, now where were we!'

Marcia stiffened and guiltily pulled back. 'Shh, I heard something . . . the door! Perhaps Reuben has forgotten something.'

85

'We're back!' Ruby's beaming face peered round the door. Norman was right behind her. 'It's lovely and warm in here,' Ruby remarked as they came trooping into the room, bringing with them some of the cold from outside. They paused in front of the sofa and looked down at their friends. Marcia could tell by their faces that the afternoon had been a success. Ruby looked absolutely radiant. Then she thrust her left hand towards them. 'Look!' she exclaimed happily. 'We're engaged!' She glanced back at Norman. 'Course, we've agreed it will be ages before we can get married.' She giggled, 'Neither of us have any money.' Norman smiled and nodded, evidently relieved to know that his plans for the future had registered, in spite of her overwhelming excitement.

Marcia took Ruby's cold, work-reddened, little hand in her own and studied the solitary diamond set in its tiny golden nest. 'It's perfect,' she said, as she moved Ruby's hand so that Webster could look too.

'Congratulations,' Webster said, rising to shake Norman's hand.

'It is lovely, isn't it, Marcy?' Ruby's eyes proudly followed the flashing ring as she wielded her hand in front of her. She glanced adoringly at Norman. 'It belonged to Norman's gran, now it's mine and it fits perfectly.'

'Did I 'ear Norman's name mentioned? Wot 'ave the varmint bin up to now?'

Four startled faces turned towards Reuben as he slowly crossed the room and lowered his creaky body into the armchair. No one had heard him come in with all the excitement that was going on. It was Webster who broke the awkward silence. 'Some good news, boss. Ruby and Norman have become engaged to be married. Now isn't that smashing?'

Norman looked sheepishly across at the old farmer, ready for a typically caustic response. To his surprise, Reuben merely grinned and ordered large glasses of port all round to celebrate the happy occasion.

Several glasses of port later, Reuben rose unsteadily from his chair and told Norman it was time he was off home. 'That's nuff celebrating fer one night,' he said. 'I needs me beauty sleep an that's fer sure.' He glanced down at Marcia who was still cuddled up closely to her airman. She'll be the next one with a ring on her finger, he thought. Still, it was good to see her so happy. He realised also that he, too, was much happier in himself since the arrival of the two girls. In fact, he thought fondly, they are almost like daughters to me now. The unbearable thought that they could leave him one day flitted unwillingly across his mind and made his words sound harsh when he told Marcia it was time for bed. 'Better git 'is bed made up, an no 'anging round afterwards mind!' Then he muttered a grumpy goodnight, and without as much as a backward look swayed precariously out through the parlour door.

After Norman had left for home, Ruby tactfully retired to her bedroom, giving her friends privacy for their goodnight kisses and cuddles. They had finally managed, after several loving distractions, to make a bed after a fashion on the sofa. 'It looks good,' Webster said, putting his hands on her arms and looking deep into her eyes. 'How about trying it out?'

Marcia was tempted, but her strict upbringing and Reuben's daunting presence upstairs won the day. Reluctantly she shook her head and slowly drew away from his arms.

'Don't go yet!' Webster said. He slapped his forehead in annoyance. 'I had almost forgotten that I have something for you in my coat pocket.' He hurried out to where his coat was now hanging up on the back of the kitchen door, and returned with a small package wrapped up in Christmas paper. He kissed her as he placed it in her hands. 'I hope you will like it, my darling.'

Her fingers shook with excitement as she unwrapped her Christmas gift. Inside she found a small red box. She carefully lifted the lid to find a dainty gold chain and locket necklace nestling on a plush bed of black suede. 'Oh, Webster, it's beautiful,' she cried. 'Thank you. I will treasure this for ever!' She promptly moved closer and he cuddled her tightly in his arms. They stood for a while, enjoying the warm intimacy, then Marcia slowly drew back. 'I must go,' she said. 'Reuben will be furious . . . I'm sure the rascal will stay awake until he knows I'm safely tucked up in my own bed.'

They snatched one more kiss before Marcia left him and hurried up the stairs to her bedroom, making sure her footfalls could be clearly heard as she passed Reuben's door.

Ruby was sitting up in bed, still wide awake when Marcia gently closed the bedroom door behind her. 'I can't sleep Marcy,

I'm so excited!' she exclaimed. 'Isn't this the most wonderful Christmas for both of us?'

Marcia smiled her agreement as she brought over the candle which had been placed on the chest of drawers. 'Look what Webster's given me,' she enthused.

Ruby gently touched and admired the delicate piece of jewellery. 'He must like you a lot, Marcy, to give you something like this.'

'Yes.'

Ruby detected a wistful note in her friend's voice, which she failed to understand. She had been so happy earlier. 'Is anything wrong, Marcy?' She put her arm around her, sensing her need for some consolation. 'Don't you care for him?'

'Of course I do . . . it's not that. If anything, I think I care for him too much, Ruby.'

'Then what is the matter?'

Marcia carefully placed the lid back on the necklace box before answering. 'He told me tonight that he's a navigator on one of the bomber planes – a Lancaster, he said.'

'So?'

'I feel so worried Rube, he could so easily get shot down on one of his missions . . . he could be killed!' Marcia's voice was little more than a whisper when she added, 'I don't think I could bear it if that happened now.'

Ruby gave her a squeeze. 'Come on, cheer up. Don't even think about it, Marcy, he'll be okay, I'm sure. Anyway it's no good worrying about things that might never happen, is it? I expect the war will soon be over, then you can happily settle down to being a good little vet's wife.'

Marcia had to smile at her friend's cheery confidence. 'I hope so,' she said. 'I really do!'

For the young ones at Tolcarne Merock, Boxing Day sped happily by on giant wings. Dawn had broken to show that the grey mists had cleared, and a weak, watery sun bravely tried its best to ease the chill of the cold wind that rushed headlong straight in from the sea. The girls had been busy all morning, preparing and cooking the dinner. Although it was virtually a repeat of the Christmas Day meal that had been such a great success, they were excitedly aware that Norman and Webster would be dining with them this time, and took great pains to ensure that everything was perfect. And perfect, it was. After the men had tasted their first mouthful and had given praise to the now two beaming cooks, the meal continued in a relaxed and happy atmosphere. Webster kept them laughing with funny stories about some of his animal patients, and a few even funnier ones about their owners. Mindful of Marcia's fears for Webster's safety, Ruby was really glad that they had kept off the subject of war. The less said about that mournful subject the better. After the meal Reuben had slipped quietly away to his armchair in the parlour, leaving the young men to help with the tiresome task of washing the mound of greasy dishes. When the kitchen had finally been tidied, Webster's suggestion of a brisk walk along the beach was readily welcomed by the other three. When they were all ready to go and clad in their warm outside gear Marcia had poked her head round the parlour door to tell boss that they were going out for a walk, but he was dead to the world, stretched out in his chair with his mouth open and snorting like a pig. She didn't have the heart to wake him, so she left him a hastily scribbled note on the kitchen table.

None of them spoke much as they trudged hand-in-hand across wet, deserted sands. The wind was even stronger here, and any words were swiftly whipped away to mingle with the roaring waves and the shrieking call of the frenzied gulls. Webster collected a few sandy sea-shells which he presented to Marcia. She stored them safely away in her coat pocket, already treasuring them simply because it was he who had given them to her.

Breathless and rosy-checked, they arrived back at the farmhouse at around four o'clock. The strenuous walk had given them back their appetites, so the girls then hastily prepared some cold chicken sandwiches for tea. It was all such a quietly pleasant and memorable day, marred only by the fact that Webster had to report back to camp by the early evening.

After he had said his goodbyes and had thanked Reuben for his kind hospitality, Marcia had gone outside with him to say her goodbye in private. They stood cuddled tightly together inside the main farm gate, both of them dreading the moment when it was time for him to go. The wind was still gusting and Marcia was shivering in spite of her warm coat and hastily-donned headscarf. Webster felt her trembling. 'You're cold,' he said with concern. 'You ought to go in now.'

The moon suddenly appeared from behind a cloud and he could see her face clearly as she looked lovingly up at him. 'No, I'm not cold,' she replied untruthfully. Then, sensing he was about to go, she said spontaneously, 'I'll walk back with you!'

'I don't know Marcy.' He frowned and shook his head. 'I would love your company but I don't like to think of you returning alone in the dark.'

But her mind was made up. 'Come on!' she said, pulling on his arm and opening the gate. If we hurry, I won't even be missed.'

Webster sighed; he knew when he was beaten. He put his arm around her waist and they walked leisurely down to the bridge over the river Menahyl.

Halfway across they stopped for a kiss and a cuddle, and listened to the water as it flowed over the stones below them. 'This has been a wonderful Christmas,' Marcia told him between hungry kisses. 'I don't want it to end.'

Webster agreed with her, but the drone of a distant aeroplane reminded him that he had to hurry. 'Reuben's not such a bad old stick, is he?' he remarked as they resumed their walk. 'He certainly has a good stock of port and whisky, hasn't he? I wonder where he gets it?'

Marcia was conscious of their gravelly footsteps and her laboured breathing as she wrestled with the unsavoury thoughts of Reuben's night prowlings. She decided to confide in Webster. After all, she felt she now had a true friend and it would be nice to share her secret with him. As they walked he listened silently to her account of Reuben's night rendezvous with the mysterious smugglers.

'So that's it!' He turned to her and laughed. 'Irish, I expect. I just knew that old rascal was up to something.'

'Please don't tell anyone!' Marcia pleaded. 'It could cause a lot of trouble in the village . . . most of the people are friends and we don't know how many of them are in on this.'

'Don't worry, my darling, his secret's safe with me,' Webster assured her, and she breathed a sigh of relief. She was only too willing to put Reuben's shady dealings firmly behind her.

They had been so engrossed in their conversation that it was with some surprise they found they had reached the top of the lane. Straight ahead of them and just across the main road was the high hedge that formed part of the aerodrome boundary. Webster took her in his arms to kiss her goodbye. 'I want to see where you get in,' Marcia whispered. 'Just let me peek over the hedge, then I promise I'll let you go.'

They crossed the deserted road and quietly walked along the grass verge alongside the hedge, holding hands and stepping carefully so as to keep clear of the trip wires of wayward, thorny brambles that lay in wait underfoot.

'This is it,' Webster said.

They paused at the point where he would climb over. Damp moss and long tough grass covered rough stones to the top, but the brambles had yet to get established. 'It's perfect,' Marcia whispered. 'Can I climb up and look over?'

Webster followed her, supporting her as she picked her way up the steep hedge-bank. After a few heart-stopping slips, she reached the top and was able to look down onto the unlit runway. But the moon was on her side and suddenly bathed the airfield in an eerie brightness. She saw a long row of huge, silent aeroplanes. She shivered as her eyes swept over them, thinking to herself how they resembled giant prehistoric monsters which might burst into life at any moment.

Webster's moustache tickled her cheek as he held her close and looked over her shoulder. 'Those are the Lancasters.'

'Is one of them yours?' Marcia asked.

'Yes, but you can't see it from here.'

A sudden thought struck her, and excitedly she turned her head round to face him wobbling on her slippery foothold as she did so. His arms protectively tightened around her and she had barely time to steady herself before asking him if she could have a closer look. 'I must see your plane now that I am this close,' she begged. 'There's no one around. Can I, Webster? Please!'

Like a fool, he gave in. 'We must be quick,' he said anxiously as he helped her clamber down the inside of the hedge-bank. 'There'll be hell to pay if we're caught.' Keeping in the shadows, moving as quickly and quietly as they could, they advanced towards the row of dark machines. Marcia was shaking with nerves and excitement as they hurried by each of the enormous aircraft. She noted that they all looked identical except for the insignias painted on the fuselage under the cockpit. On glimpsing one such painting of a curvaceous blonde, Marcia jealously wondered what Webster would have on his plane.

They had almost reached the end of the line when he gently pulled her up. 'This is mine.' He spoke softly, almost reverently. 'Not a bad old crate.'

Marcia looked up at it, imagining him inside, then her eyes wandered down to the painted symbol. 'What's that?' she asked.

'That's the Cornish emblem. Fifteen balls within a shield. Look, can you see the words underneath? – *One and All.*' Sensing her curiosity of why such a sign would be on his plane, he swiftly enlightened her: 'Our Captain painted that – he's from Cornwall, you see.'

'It's good, I like it,' she remarked, pleased that no womanly form enhanced this particular aeroplane.

Growing more nervous, Webster glanced around furtively and said, 'We'd better go. Come on, I'll see you safely back over the hedge.'

She took his hand as they made it safely back to the hedgerow. It hadn't really dawned upon her until now, what trouble she could have landed him in if they had been caught. Still, they hadn't, and it had been worth it. She felt even closer to him now, by having this little insight of his perilous working life.

He jumped down beside her and cradled her in his arms. 'It's been lovely this Christmas, hasn't it?' His voice was soft and rich with emotion. Marcia nodded and answered with a lingering passionate kiss. As he drew her tighter to him he almost forced the breath from her body, and she felt the racing beat of his heart, even through the thick layers of their clothing. He kissed her again. 'I don't want to leave you now. If only I – '

She didn't hear any more; his words were obliterated by the sudden roar of a Spitfire engine as a lone fighter plane screamed low overhead. His arms loosened their hold as he looked towards the sound and waited until the noise had receded far away in the distance. Holding her at arms' length, he said, 'I really must go now.' His foot was already searching for the first stepping stone in the hedge. Halfway up he stopped and turned back towards her. 'I can't promise when I will be able to see you again . . . But I will!'

She watched him give a final wave before disappearing over

the top, then stood mesmerised for a moment, her eyes fixed on the spot where she had last seen him and imagining him still to be there.

A vicious gust of icy wind whipped around her as she quickly turned away from the hedge. She felt desperately alone as she hastened across the desolate road and started to run back down the lane, stumbling in her haste on the rough uneven track. She was suddenly conscious that they might have missed her back at the farm. She realised she had been away much longer than she had intended.

Chapter Eleven

The first half of January had flown by for the girls at Tolcarne Merock. The short, wet, dreary days were filled with the endless tasks of feeding all the animals and keeping their winter quarters clean; not to mention their own farmhouse duties of cooking and cleaning. Reuben was quite happy with the arrangement, and left everything to them. They still hadn't ventured into his bedroom though, and sometimes wondered what sort of state it would be in if ever they did. His dirty clothes would be left outside the closed bedroom door on the floor to be washed, and when it was done the girls would put the clean neat pile back in its place.

The pretty festive decorations which had so recently adorned the farmhouse had now been replaced by heavy, wet, outdoor clothes which were hung to dry overnight in the warm kitchen and permeated the house with the steamy smell of the farmyard. Both girls freely admitted to each other that they would be really glad when the rain stopped. Apart from the nasty damp working conditions, it would be heaven to have a fresh smelling home again.

Marcia hadn't seen much of Webster since Christmas, except for a couple of fleeting visits to assure her that he was still safe and well. But today, when she and Ruby were milking in the cowshed, he had walked in and surprised her. She hadn't noticed him at first. Ruby had, but he'd raised a finger to his lips, motioning her to keep quiet. He stood watching Marcia as her hands gently persuaded the warm milk to flow into the bucket below. Her head rested comfortably against the soft hide of the beast and her eyes were almost closed. But some sixth sense told her she was not alone. She drew her head back and her eyes widened with a joyous smile when she saw Webster standing there. Her hands stopped their rhythmic movement as she leapt off her stool and then hurried towards him with arms outstretched. 'Can you stay for a while?' Her voice dropped slightly when she added, 'Or do you have to get back?'

He hugged and kissed her, then looked back over his shoulder with a cheeky wink to Ruby before answering her. Tilting her chin and looking steadfastly into her shining eyes he said, 'Well, my darling, it all depends on whether I'm invited to tea, or not. I'm due back at the camp by nine tonight, so – '

She cut him short with a delighted kiss.

The impatient moo of Marcia's half-milked cow echoed around the shed as the animal looked inquiringly at them with its large, brown, soulful eyes.

'I think she's telling you off,' Webster said, gently pushing Marcia back to her stool. 'You finish your job while I have a wander round to check over the other animals. Might as well make myself useful while I'm here.'

Much later, after tea, Ruby had gone out with Norman, leaving Webster to help Marcia with the washing up. Reuben was comfortably ensconced in his favourite chair beside the stove, enjoying his pipe and quietly contemplating the six o'clock news. 'Did ee 'ear that, boy?' He looked excitedly towards Webster, his pipe forgotten for the moment. 'A German armoured column got to within thirty miles of Stalingrad and their fuel ran out.' He became more animated and almost chuckled as he said, 'They be like sitting ducks to they besieged Russians over there. There's one thing fer sure; they'll fight they uns with anything they can lay their 'ands on . . . do ee see, boy? – it could be the tide turning at last, 'cos 'twas the lack of fuel oil that caused Rommel's withdrawal from the west.' His expression promptly changed to one of annoyance as the newscaster's voice was drowned out by a crescendo of static. 'Damned interference! Bloody planes upsetting everything again,' he muttered. He reached over to turn it off, but not before bestowing a withering look on the poor airman, which clearly showed where he laid the blame.

After smoking his pipe and having his usual noisy forty winks, Reuben had lit the grate fire in the parlour for the young couples comfort. Evidently his earlier annoyance over the crackling wireless had been completely forgotten. He and William had left soon afterwards for their nightly stroll down to the Falcon, leaving Marcia and Webster with a couple of hours to enjoy some warmth and privacy before Webster had to report back. They both had stretched out their legs on the long sofa, and now Marcia sat cuddled in his arms with her back resting against his chest. She blissfully closed her eyes and imagined being with him like this for always.

'Penny for them?' he said softly, as he lifted a stray curl and gently nibbled on her ear.

She opened her eyes and turned her face towards him. 'I'm so happy.'

He started kissing her. Lovingly at first, then hungrily as his passion grew to fever pitch. Marcia felt a growing concern over his obvious ardency. Although she felt the same way, and wanted him with all her heart, her strict upbringing caused her to be wary. She felt she had to do something to quell his rising emotion before things really got out of hand, yet she didn't want to hurt him. Suddenly she knew what to do. She leapt up from the sofa and stood beside him. Before he could speak she bent forward and mercilessly tickled his ribs and waist until he was almost bent double with uncontrollable laughter. She didn't stop until she was sure that the dangerous moment had passed.

'What was that all about?' he asked as he stood and tucked in his loosened shirt. He ran a comb through his tousled hair before rejoining her on the sofa. Marcia sat coyly looking down at her lap as his arm encircled her shoulders. 'Come on, you can tell me . . . is anything the matter?'

Her voice was barely more than a whisper as she answered him. 'I'm sorry. I was afraid something might have happened. I want to as much as you do, but from where I come from, marriage comes first, and that's the way it is.' A solitary tear trickled down her cheek and dripped off to leave a small damp smudge on her floral patterned dress.

'Sweetheart, don't cry.' He smoothed her damp cheek with his hand. 'If that's the way it's done in Pembrokeshire, then so be it. If it wasn't for this blasted war I would ask you to marry me now. As it is, each time I go on a bombing raid I wonder whether it will be my last. It wouldn't be fair on you.'

She turned to him again, damming back the unshed tears. 'I couldn't bear to lose you now.'

He kissed her nose and tried to make light of the matter. 'Do you realise, if it wasn't for the war we wouldn't have met. So it's not all bad, is it? He looked deeply into her eyes and said with total conviction: 'I know the time will come when I will be able to ask you to be my wife — so you mustn't worry about me.'

She smiled then, and he knew in his heart that she would be strong enough to hold her fears in check. They sat contentedly in each other's arms, talking about their families and their different lives, until, all too soon, Webster glanced at his watch and ruefully told her he had to go. Marcia reluctantly got up from the sofa and went to fetch his overcoat from the kitchen. Why did these partings always have to be so painful? she thought, her sadness tinged with anger. When she returned to the parlour with his coat draped over her arm, she was also carrying a little red book in her hand. 'What's this, darling?' she asked, voicing her curiosity. 'It fell out of your pocket. It looks as if it's written in German.'

He understood her confusion as he relieved her of the book and tucked it back into his pocket. 'You see, my darling,' he said, 'if I should ever find myself strolling around in Germany, it might come in handy if I can speak a little of the German language. It's a phrase book.'

'You don't think they will come over here, do you?' Her eyes widened with fear as she looked up to him for an answer.

He smiled reassuringly. 'They'll never do that, my darling; we'll see to that.'

She rested her head against his chest and sighed. 'I hope you will never have to use that horrible phrase book.'

'So do I. But in the meantime it keeps my mind occupied between scrambles. It can be a bit nerve-racking if you haven't anything much to do.' The minutes were ticking by and he realised that he would now have to hurry if he was to make it back to the camp by nine. He gave her one quick last kiss, and after insisting she remain indoors in the warmth, he opened the kitchen door, looked back with a cheery smile and said, 'See you soon.' Then he was gone.

After the rattle of the door latch, the house seemed deathly silent. Marcia remained standing where she was for a few moments, suddenly feeling terribly alone. Even the warm familiar kitchen seemed to be flat and filled with eerie shadows. An involuntary shiver swept through her body, and with a nervous

e

shrug of her shoulders she decided that the best place to be now was in bed. She hurried back into the parlour and poked the dying embers of the fire. Satisfied that it had almost burnt itself out and was safe to be left, she went through to the kitchen and lit her candle. She was about to turn down the paraffin lamp when she heard in the distance the muffled roar of aircraft. Her fingers rested on the spill of the wick as the sound drew nearer, until it seemed to fill and shake the whole house as the bombers flew low over the roof-tops. Marcia looked up and wondered if her Webster was in one of them. She prayed fervently that he would always return safely to her. She remained deep in thought until the house was again still and silent. If only the war was over. She turned down the lamp, picked up her candle, and hurried up the dark stairs.

Chapter Twelve

It was a Monday morning in mid-February. Marcia was on her way to St Columb in the pony and trap to stock up with some provisions. Reuben sat beside her, holding Star's reins. He was in good spirits that morning as two of his finest steers were going to be sold in the cattle market. The day was balmy; the sky was dull and overcast with thick grey clouds. But there was no wind, and as they rode side-by-side in a pleasant companionable silence, Marcia's thoughts turned to Ruby. Normally she would have jumped at the chance of shopping in the town, but today it seemed she preferred to stay at home and work the farm. A slight frown puckered Marcia's forehead as she worried over her friend. Just lately she seemed to have changed, become more withdrawn somehow. And the other night she was sure that she had awakened to the sound of Ruby crying softly into her pillow. There was something amiss she was sure. But when she had tactfully asked her if everything was all right, Ruby had snapped back, 'Of course it is! . . . What could be wrong?' Whatever it was, she apparently wanted to keep it to herself. She decided to mention it to Reuben now that they were on their own.

Reuben listened to her, then pulled on the reins to stop the cart. He sat staring ahead, still clutching the reins and quietly thinking for a few moments. Star turned lazily back to her master as if wondering why he had chosen to stop here. When she realised that no orders were to be given, she impatiently flicked her coarse, tangled mane and slowly sauntered closer to the hedge, where she started to chomp happily on the long grass. 'I bet I knows what 'tiz that be troublin' 'er,' Reuben muttered almost to himself, his eyes still firmly fixed on the road ahead. 'The maid 'ave got 'erself in the family way, sure as me name's Reuben!'

'No!' Marcia gasped, wide-eyed with disbelief. 'No, she can't be . . . can she?'

'I know wot ee be thinking, maid,' Reuben said. You wonder 'ow an ole bachelor like me can know 'bout such things. Well I'll tell ee. 'Tiz like this 'ere, see. I've bin around a little bit longer than you 'ave, me dear. When you gits to my age there ain't much left that can shock or surprise ee.' He tugged on the reins to alert the happily munching mare. 'Trouble is,' he said, as he skilfully guided Star away from the hedge. 'She be keeping it to 'erself . . . and worried sick, I'll be bound. 'Twill be best when 'tiz all out in the open.'

They carried on to St Columb in silence. Marcia hardly noticed the rest of the journey, her mind was too full of concern for Ruby, and how calmly her boss had summed up the situation. But was he right? No, it's probably something entirely different and much more trivial — that at least was what she wanted to believe. After all, everyone has little problems from time to time. Her thoughts were interrupted by a loud call from Reuben, which almost made her jump out of her skin. She looked around and realised they had just entered the main narrow cobbled street of St Columb, and Reuben had frightened her by calling 'Good morning' to Mr Coldvreath, the bank manager. He was standing outside the sturdy door of his domain in his bowler hat, and had been peering short-sightedly at the approaching horse and trap. As the trap drew alongside he smiled as he recognised Reuben.

'Ah, it's Reuben Gutheridge,' he exclaimed. 'I would like a moment of your time, if — '

But Reuben was already steering Star across the road to the Red Lion Inn, where the horse would remain safely tethered in its spacious back yard while Reuben attended to his business. As Reuben guided the horse through the narrow opening on the side of the inn, he shouted back over his shoulder, 'Sorry, Mr Coldvreath, I be late fer market as 'tiz. I'll call an see ee another time.'

Marcia smiled to herself as she glanced back at the bemused face of the bank manager. He stood foolishly at the side of the road with his mouth still gaping open, evidently in shock that anyone should pass up on a chance to speak with such an esteemed dignitary as himself.

Having left Star safely tethered and in company of several

friends of her own kind, Marcia followed behind her boss as he hurried along the street to the other end of the town where the market was situated. The street was already fairly busy, mainly with the wives of the farmers who, while their men were happily employed at the market, had taken the opportunity of leaving the drudgery of housework and cooking behind for a few hours of gossiping and window shopping. Later, when the market closed, they would meet with their husbands for a hand-out of some money. If it had been a good day for selling, a little more than usual would be pressed into an eagerly awaiting palm. A smiling face would then hurry back to the shops that had lured them earlier to spend some of the money that was now clenched safely and warmly in a rough and calloused hand.

Noisy animal sounds mingled with raised, excited voices as Reuben and Marcia neared the market. Reuben hurried along, staring straight ahead. He hated to be late, especially when he had animals to sell. He liked to be standing at the ringside when they were brought out to be led around the ring for the prospective buyers to look over. That way he could keep an eye on things, and make sure he received the best price possible. Even the auctioneer would at times wither under Reuben's stony gaze if the price wasn't rising as fast as he felt it should have done.

They had just reached the market entrance when from somewhere behind them they heard someone call out rather urgently, 'Reuben!' The compelling tone of voice made Reuben stop in his tracks, and turn to see who it was that so desperately needed him.

Marcia suppressed a chuckle to see Reuben's face register with utter annoyance when he realised it was only Oscar Grenville, hurrying to catch them up.

Reuben waited impatiently for the lawyer to reach him. It was obvious by his hurried gait that Oscar's running days had long since gone. His stiff, bony legs were trying their utmost to obey instructions from a livelier brain, and failing dismally. He eventually drew up alongside them, gasping for breath.

'Wot do ee want with me now, Oscar?' Reuben's blunt question held a note of petulance. With one hand the lawyer wiped his damp, flushed face with a large white handkerchief, while the other hand rested in a friendly, yet noticeably restrained, way on Reuben's forearm.

101

'My dear Reuben, it is obvious that you are both bound for the market . . . er hum — ' He stopped for a moment to regain his breath, glancing appreciatively at Marcia as he did so. Then, turning back to Reuben: 'Perhaps I could accompany you both?'

Reuben gave him a suspicious look and pulled his arm away from the lawyer's hot clammy clasp. 'You dun't go to the cattle market as a rule. Wot er ee doing 'ere today?'

Oscar ran his finger along the inside of his stiffly starched collar and stretched his neck for some relief. It seemed so much tighter now that it was damp with perspiration. 'Ah, duty calls, my friend. I am here today to converse with, and hopefully collect certain dues from, a certain farmer who, of course, shall remain nameless. I am well informed that he frequents this market place each and every Monday . . . If Mohammed won't come to the mountain, then the mountain must go to Mohammed, don't you agree?'

Reuben, anxious to be moving on his way, nodded and grumpily muttered, 'I s'pose so. Now if you've finished, Oscar, I'd like to tend to me own business.' He strode off into the market with Marcia and the lawyer grimly tagging on behind.

Reuben resolutely pushed his way through the band of farmers that encircled the ringside. Oscar had given up and tailed off at a tangent, so Marcia stayed close to Reuben and tried to ignore the looks his rude pushing was attracting from his fellow farmers. She listened instead to the unmistakable jargon of the auctioneer rising above the medley of sound from protesting animals and the excited chattering of the human spectators.

'Jus made it!' Reuben breathed a sigh of relief as he rested his elbows on the top of the ring fence. 'See there, maid, they be now bringing our two in.' He glanced quickly at Marcia to ensure she was looking, then turned and pointed to where two men wearing khaki-coloured overall-coats had just entered the ring. Each man held on tightly to a strong rope which was fastened around the neck of a fine and hefty steer.

Reuben's bony fingers gripped the top of the fence in his excitement as his animals started their parade around the inside of the ring. 'Bet yer life, there'll be none better than that 'ere today,' he said proudly.

Marcia agreed with him. They did seem to look much bigger here than when they were amongst the others back at the farm.

The steers turned their massive heads and seemed to look directly at Marcia as they were led past. She was sure they had recognised her, and felt guilty when she identified a look of sad reproach in their big doleful eyes. She was suddenly aware of the auctioneer's furious chanting:

'Sixty . . . sixty-five . . . seventy!' He was already sealing the sad fate of these poor animals.

Marcia had had enough of the market for today. Tugging on Reuben's sleeve, she told him she was off to do her shopping. Reuben tore his attention away from the ring just for a second to tell her that he would meet her in the Red Lion at half-past twelve. She nodded and left.

At twelve-thirty-five, her shopping done, Marcia stood in the doorway and peered through the thick smoke of the noisy crowded bar to see if she could spot her boss. She was a little late herself, but knowing the old farmer, he was sure to be here. She felt silly and self-conscious standing there as her gaze swept through the rough jumble of tough male farmers . . . and looked away quickly whenever an eye would catch hers with a knowing look. Suddenly her gaze was held by a pair of black bird-like eyes glinting knowingly at her from under a shiny dome. Oscar! she thought with annoyance, which immediately changed to relief when she realised that Reuben was sure to be with him. The lawyer beckoned her over with one hand, while the other busily preened the tuft of hair over one ear in her honour. She squeezed her way up to the far corner of the bar to where Reuben stood with his elbows resting on the sticky counter, and his hands clasped lovingly round a half filled tankard.

He remained intent on studying his beer, as if put out that a woman should invade his male sanctuary. 'You didn't stay long at the market?' His eyes never wavered from the tankard in his hands.

'Sorry, boss.' Marcia felt slightly abashed now, as she tried to defend her early departure. 'They looked so sad . . . I couldn't bear to watch!'

Oscar leaned across in front of her. 'Reuben, I don't think it's quite the right place to take a tender young lady.' As he drew back he smiled supportively at Marcia. She graciously smiled back, but inwardly felt nauseous as his hot, ale-soured breath wafted all over her.

It was as if Reuben hadn't heard him. He raised his tankard and took several long swallows before dropping it back on the counter. He wiped the moisture that had collected in the stubble on his chin with the back of his hand, then looked directly at the lawyer. 'You 'aven't a clue 'ave ee, Oscar?' His eyes swept over the smart, dark suit as if that alone proved his ignorance. 'If we dun't sell, we dun't eat — 'tiz as simple as that. Most of the time I loves me work, but — ' He looked at Marcia. 'There be times when 'tiz hard, an a lot of farmers never git used to it. You jus 'ave to go on.' With a despairing shake of his head, he looked down pointedly at his now empty tankard. 'Your round I think, Oscar.'

Marcia studied the sea of boisterous drinkers around her as she slowly sipped a ginger beer. She was quickly becoming bored; her eyes were smarting in the blue, fudgy atmosphere, and the noise was giving her a headache. Each time Reuben's tankard had been emptied, she secretly hoped that they would now be on their way. But somehow, always when she wasn't looking, it was miraculously refilled to overflowing, the soft, caramel cream bubbles sliding gently down the sides of the mug to form yet another dark sticky circle on the counter. The two men talked loudly across her, engrossed in each other's business, ignoring her, except for the exaggerated closeness at times of the repulsive Oscar.

Oscar placed his tankard down with a thud in front of the landlord. 'A refill, my man, to oil my throat, if you please.' He looked drunkenly at Reuben. 'I think a song would be in order, don't you, my friend? — before we depart on our busy ways.' He didn't wait for an answer but discordantly burst into the first verse of *To Be a Farmer's Boy* so loudly that Marcia cringed with embarrassment. It surprised her that such a respected citizen of the town would behave in such a manner. It seemed, though, that everyone around her had expected this, and before long the inn resounded with the lusty, deep voices of the farmers.

As they held their pints aloft and sang with great gusto, the door opened and in sidled a small weasel of a man — who, Marcia learnt later from Reuben, was a Mr Meadows from Padstow way. He was a corn merchant, and on a Monday morning he would attend the market to see if any of his 'owing' customers had made any money. Afterwards he would visit the inn to collect his dues from them before they had the chance to spend it. He now drew up beside one of the farmers who, being so engrossed in his singing, was completely unaware of the little man's presence until he spoke. 'Mr Gates, I believe you've 'ad a good day today?'

Mr Gates glanced down at him, his voice trailing away when he saw who it was. His look of irritation was lost on Mr Meadows who was busily extracting a note-book from his pocket. He opened it to a marked page and held it towards the farmer. 'See there, sir.' His finger jabbed at the paper. 'Thirty-six pounds, nine and four pence ha'penny.' His smile mirrored the smug satisfaction of the victor as he reminded his cornered victim of all the sheep he had sold that day. 'I take it you are in a position, now at last, to pay . . . in full?'

Farmer Gates' hand delved unwillingly into the depths of his trouser-pocket and extracted a rolled-up bundle of banknotes. He looked at it lovingly for a few seconds, then reluctantly handed over a large proportion to a now widely grinning Mr Meadows. As the money and book were being carefully replaced into his overall pocket, the corn merchant's shrewd eyes were already darting from face to face, hoping to find another likely victim.

'Be ee ready to go now, maid?' Reuben's hot breath tickled her ear and made her jump. She had been so absorbed in the corn merchant's tactics that she had completely forgotten her desire to leave. Reuben made for the door on unsteady legs, with Marcia tagging behind. She had one last peep at the corn merchant before the door swung shut behind her. There was no mistaking the look of triumph on the little man's face as he cornered another luckless farmer. The note-book was already in his hand, his pencil poised to strike again.

Chapter Thirteen

The next day, when Reuben and Marcia were working alone together in the yard, she told him that he had guessed right about Ruby. 'She was in such a state last night that I asked her right out.' Marcia stopped and rested her chin on the handle of the shovel she was using. 'She's worried sick, boss.'

Reuben stopped shovelling the pungent manure and wiped his brow. ' 'Ave she told Norman yet?'

Marcia shook her head. 'No, she hasn't; said Norman would be cross with her because they hadn't saved any money yet. Silly girl, I told her that she must.' Clasping her hands round the long handle of the shovel, she forced the spade between yard and manure with a teeth-jarring scrape. Her breathing was laboured as she deftly heaved the loaded shovel away from her body to deposit its contents onto an ever-growing pile. 'I expect he knows by now,' she panted, as the shovel screeched its way with its next load. 'It's a good thing you've got them both crushing corn in the barn this morning, boss. At least she'll have him to herself for an hour or two.'

Later that morning, as Norman crossed the yard to collect more sacks from one of the outhouses, Reuben collared him. ' 'Ere, boy, I wunt a word with ee,' he called. Then, without drawing breath, he blurted out: 'I trust you be going to marry the girl?'

Norman's face registered startled embarrassment, and for an awful moment Reuben wondered if Ruby had yet confided in him. He breathed a lot easier when Norman's reply indicated that she had.

'I haven't had a chance to think about it,' he stuttered. 'It . . . it's been such a shock.'

Reuben, his confident self once more, grunted, 'It be a shock fer all of us. Now you go straight back to the barn an' tell er the time has come fer ee to be married . . . money or no money.' Reuben started to walk away, then stopped and turned back to add sternly, 'There's no time to be lost, mind!'

Reuben was the last to come in for his dinner. Norman and the two girls were already at the table, eating their meals. Silently, the three pairs of eyes looked up and watched him as he crossed the kitchen and picked up his plate. He helped himself to the stew that was bubbling away merrily on the top of the stove taking time to search for another dumpling that was hiding beneath its cover of vegetables. When his plate could hold no more, he carried it over to his place at the table. 'Smells good!' he exclaimed, as he glanced around him. Three heads were bent steadfastly over their dinner plates, to all intents and purposes with nothing else on their minds but the stew in front of them. Reuben smiled to himself as he spooned up a fat dumpling that was threatening to topple off his plate. Best if I eat me dinner first, he decided. I'll be much more ready to talk on a full stomach.

The food was eaten in an uneasy silence. Only Reuben, as he tucked in, seemed unaware of the strained atmosphere that hovered over the hushed diners. When he finally pushed his empty plate aside he noticed that Ruby had eaten very little. 'Come on, maid,' he said, 'this wunt do — you be eating fer two now.' His tone was harsh, but Marcia noted how his eyes twinkled with a kindly glow. I do believe he's enjoying this, she thought. For all his gruff ways, he liked the idea of a family around him — she was sure of it.

Ruby sat with her shoulders hunched in humiliation and her cheeks aflame as she looked towards Norman for moral support.

Reuben was getting impatient. 'Well . . . er ee getting married or not?'

Norman's hand closed over Ruby's. His eyes lingered on her face as he spoke. 'We love each other, boss.' Then he turned to face Reuben. 'We are going to wed — '

That was as far as he got. Before he had a chance to elaborate, Reuben leapt from his chair, his leathery face beaming. 'That's wut I thought you'd say, me boy.' He sat back heavily in his seat and rested his arms on the table. 'You pair better 'ave the afternoon off, I reckon. The both of ee must go 'ome an tell

Norman's mother the good news . . . but if I know anything 'bout Sarah Jane, she will 'ave guessed it already.' He stopped to think for a moment, then: 'Yes,' he said aloud, as if suddenly resolving a problem he had been battling with in his mind. Looking decidedly pleased with himself, he told them that if they wished they could have the wedding reception at Tolcarne Merock. 'I know times er 'ard,' he declared, looking directly at Norman, 'yer poor mother being a widow, an wot with the war and rationing an that – more'n likely she'd be 'appy fer us to see to it.' His gaze slyly shifted to Marcia. 'I'm sure that Marcy 'ere will 'elp to make it the 'appiest day of yer lives.'

'Of course,' Marcia agreed with a smile. 'That would be lovely.' To herself, she thought: I'm not so sure about the 'helping' bit. Knowing crafty old Reuben, his contribution was likely to be limited to words.

Ruby, greatly relieved now that her secret was out in the open, realised how hungry she was feeling after all. She drew her plate closer and greedily began tucking in to the remaining stew, which to the others now looked cold, dull and unappetising.

'When's it to be then, maid?' Reuben's words were laced with a quiver of impatience as he craned forward and studied her face in anticipation.

Ruby cleared her mouth and let the tip of her tongue brush the tasty residue from her lips. 'Sometime in August I think, boss.'

'August!' Reuben looked amazed. 'Then there be no time to be lost, the way I sees it. You'd better call in an see the Reverend Bassett this afternoon, to make yer plans.'

William had been sleeping, or was pretending to be, in his favourite spot on the mat close to the kitchen door. As Reuben's chair scraped back from the table, his eyes pricked up and his head rose to look questioningly at his master. Are we going now – the honest brown eyes almost spoke for him. They followed Reuben with growing disappointment as the old farmer merely crossed to his chair by the stove. His doggy ears dropped forlornly as Reuben switched on the wireless and reached into his pocket for his baccy tin. With one last look of resignation, the collie lowered his head to the mat and shuttered his eyes for a while longer.

At around five in the afternoon Marcia happened to glance across the field to the lane below and spotted a movement. When

108

she took a closer look she saw it was Norman and Ruby skipping up the steep hill together. Marcia hurriedly helped Reuben gather up their scattered tools. She was anxious to learn how they had got on.

Reuben slung the heavy sledge-hammer into the cart along with a couple of spare wooden posts, then stood back to admire the fence he had mended. 'Not bad, even if I says so meself,' he pronounced proudly to Marcia, who by this time was already in the cart with Star's reins in her hands, hoping for a quick getaway. Reuben tutted loudly and clambered aboard.

To Marcia's mind the horse seemed to take for ever in making its way back through the fields. But when they finally approached the farm gate, Norman and Ruby were waiting for them.

Norman hurried over to the cart and held out his hand to help Marcia step down. 'It's all settled,' he said, his blue eyes shining with happy relief. 'The Reverend Bassett has agreed to marry us on the 20th March.' Glancing at Reuben for his reaction, he added, 'It's a Saturday, boss – at two o'clock in the afternoon, if that's alright with you?'

Reuben nodded. ' 'Ave to be, I s'pose,' he said grumpily as he walked away and busied himself with removing Star's harness.

His workers smiled knowingly to one another. The wedding talk would resume later on in the farmhouse. For now, there was still some unfinished work on the farm to be done.

As soon as the work outside had been accomplished, everyone quickly disappeared into the farmhouse, eager to carry on with the plans for the wedding. Reuben was no exception. In spite of his earlier show of indifference, he bustled into the kitchen with his arms laden with logs and went straight to the front room to light a fire in the grate. 'Bit more cumfert down 'ere to discuss yer wedding plans,' he explained, as his back vanished through the hall doorway.

Soon after they were all seated at the table for their meal, Reuben was unable to contain himself any longer. With laden fork poised in mid-air, he glared across at Norman. 'Well, boy, wot did yer mother say 'bout the reception? Er ee 'aving it 'ere or no?'

Norman gulped. The abrupt questioning left him feeling unreasonably guilty. He and Ruby had both felt that Reuben preferred to wait until they were all sat together in the cosy front room before anything about the wedding was mentioned. It wasn't like him to be so impatient. But before he could gather his wits, Ruby intervened, bubbling over with excitement. 'Oh, boss, Norman's mum is lovely! She cried when we first told her, but everything's going to be alright because she said me and Norm were made for each other, and she really likes me — '

'Wot 'bout the reception?' Reuben butted in irritably, as if anything else was of no importance.

'Oh yes,' Ruby answered, too excited to notice Reuben's rudeness. 'She said to thank you for your kind offer, and she would be very grateful . . . if you're sure it's not too much trouble.'

'That's settled then.' Reuben quickly returned his attention to his plate, but not before the others had noticed his stern old features creased by a smile.

There was no stopping Ruby now. She went on to tell them about their visit to the church, and how Reverend Bassett seemed to know they had come there to be married, even before they had opened their mouths. 'I did wonder if he had guessed about the baby,' she added, remembering how guilty she'd felt when the preacher's wise old eyes had looked deep into hers. 'But perhaps I just imagined that.' Her smile returned as she relaxed and looked adoringly at the young man beside her. 'He seemed very pleased to conduct our wedding, didn't he, Norm?'

The heavy roar of aircraft flying overhead was Reuben's cue to turn on the wireless for the evening news.

Ruby sighed. Knowing full well that the boss expected peace and quiet at news time, she knew that her excited chattering had to stop for a while.

That evening the kitchen was tidied in record time, thanks to Ruby's highly-strung impatience. The wireless had at last been switched off, and all four of them were now enjoying the comfort of the warm, restful sitting-room. Reuben picked up the poker and, leaning forward in his chair, gently raised the log that was smouldering in the grate. His action released a myriad of flashing sparks which raced helter-skelter away up the chimney. Bright orange flames brought a pleasant glow to the room as the aromatic pine sap trickled into the red hot embers below. 'Wut wuz ee saying, Rube?'

Ruby suppressed a smile, knowing that he had heard full well the first time. She repeated her question anyway: 'Would you give me away on the day please, boss?'

Reuben dropped the red-tipped poker back onto the hearth and leant back in his chair. 'Dun't know 'bout that,' he replied sternly. 'That ole reverend 'ave bin trying fer ages to git me in 'is church. 'Twill be figs fer ee to git me in 'is clutches.'

Ruby took no notice of his tongue; she could read in his eyes that he would be only too happy to give her away. That settled, she turned to Marcia. 'Will you be my bridesmaid, Marcy? I've always dreamed of having a proper wedding.'

'Of course! I'd love to,' Marcia replied eagerly. 'In fact I have a blue satin dress with a pretty headband to match, back home in Wales. I was a bridesmaid to a cousin of mine — my mum made it especially for the occasion; it still looks like new. I expect it will still fit me.' Her eyes swept down over her body as she ruefully remembered all the butter and cream she had enjoyed since arriving at the farm. Oh well, she thought to herself, she could always let out the seams a little.

'Where er ee going to live, boy, when yer both married?' Having clearly had enough of woman talk for the moment, Reuben now tackled Norman, who was content to lay dreamily back with his eyes half-closed while the two women chatted on and made the necessary plans.

'Don't know, boss,' he stammered, startled back to reality. 'Haven't thought about that yet.'

Ruby glanced up with concern. The old farmer had a point there. What were they going to do?

Marcia in the meantime had been watching Reuben, whose face had taken on a look of smugness at the couple's obvious discomfort. He's up to something, she thought — so she wasn't surprised when, after a few minutes of awkward silence, he said, 'The spare bedroom upstairs is crammed full of junk. If ee clean it out, you'm both welcome to live 'ere.'

'Oh, boss!' Ruby sprang to her feet and went over to him. 'You're like a real dad to us. Thank you,' she said, planting a loud kiss on his leathery cheek.

'You wunt be thanking me when ee sees all the mess in there.' His voice sounded harsh with embarrassment, belying the tender look in his misty old eyes.

It was ten o'clock when Norman hauled himself up out of his chair. After bidding Reuben and Marcia goodnight, and a less than passionate kiss for Ruby, he made his weary way home. With his head still spinning from all the wedding plans, and the inevitable early rise for work in the morning, the thought of his quiet, comfortable bed made him hurry through the darkness back to his mother's house. He knew she would still be up and waiting for him, probably darning while listening to the wireless. He smiled, her fingers were never still. If she had to wait up all night long for him she would still be busy sewing on buttons or darning a worn sock — anything to occupy her bent, arthritic fingers. A wave of love for her washed over him. She had worked so hard to bring him up on her own. He could not even remember now what his dad looked like; he had died when his only son was just five years old. Poor mother had weathered many hardships over the years. But times had been a little easier since working for Reuben. Apart from the regular wage, the kindly old farmer had always kept them well provided with vegetables and dairy produce from the farm. I'll make sure Mum never goes short after I'm married, Norman vowed to himself as he lifted the latch and quietly let himself in.

Chapter Fourteen

'I can't believe I'm getting married tomorrow, Marcy!' Ruby lifted her head from the pillow and let her eyes wander around the familiar candle-lit room. She smiled as she looked down at her friend lying beside her. 'It really will be strange to sleep in another bedroom.'

'At least it's clean and tidy now,' Marcia remarked with a sigh, as she vividly recalled the horrible state it was in earlier. It had taken them hours to lug armfuls of rubbish down the narrow staircase and out into the yard, where Norman had collected it to burn. The bonfire was still smouldering for most of the following day.

Ruby yawned as she rested her head back on the pillow. 'I don't know where the weeks have gone since we first made our plans with the vicar,' she said. 'I hope we haven't forgotten anything.'

'I don't think so,' Marcia assured her, trying to remain awake. Her heavy eyes were stinging for the want of sleep, but Ruby seemed wide awake, bubbling over with nerves and excitement. But in spite of her weariness, Marcia too felt excited, for Webster had managed to get time off for the wedding and would see her dressed up in her finery. Her eyes were instantly drawn to where her blue satin dress hung on its special padded hanger on the outside of the wardrobe door. Ruby's white wedding dress, shimmering in the candle glow, hung alongside, and beneath, placed neatly on the lino floor, were two pairs of dainty satin shoes, identical except for the colour, blue for Marcia and white for the bride.

Ruby's gaze followed her friend's. 'My dress is really beautiful,' she said dreamily. 'Norman's mum is so clever with

113

her needle.' She turned to Marcia with a nervous giggle. 'Poor Norm, he doesn't know yet that I'm hopeless at sewing. Even the smallest job I seem to find difficult and end up with the thread all in knots. I will have to learn how to do it properly now though, won't I, Marcy?'

She sounded anxious, but Marcia just abstractly replied, 'Hmm – yes.' Her mind had already moved on and at that moment was down in the dairy, mentally checking the marble slabs which were laden with cooked meats and other delicacies which had been hastily prepared between the chores of farm-work and the usual running of the farmhouse. I hope there will be enough food for everyone, she thought, with a flutter of anxiety.

Norman and Ruby had spent several evenings visiting friends and neighbours in the village with invitations to their wedding. Most had gladly accepted, and they had estimated that about forty guests would come back to Tolcarne Merock for the reception. Well, it was forty-one really. Oscar Grenville had also been invited. A little smile played at the corners of Marcia's mouth as she thought back to when Reuben had mentioned he had met him in the Red Lion, and how he had somehow ended up by offering him an invitation.

'Crafty ole sod,' Reuben had said. 'Still I 'ad the last laugh on the ole blighter; ended up with ee promising to git Ruby's bouquet – an' a posy fer Marcy too! 'Twas time ee realised Reuben Gutheridge can be as crafty as ee is, in spite of all they fancy words ee's so fond of.' Marcia recalled how, for hours afterwards, Reuben's naturally stern features were frequently transformed by a smug smile and guessed he was reflecting on his triumph over the cunning lawyer.

'I wonder how Norman is feeling?' Ruby's voice interrupted her thoughts. 'I bet he'll look handsome . . . it's not often we see him in his Sunday best, is it, Marcy?' Not waiting for an answer, she rattled on excitedly: 'Wasn't it kind of Joe Trevains to be his best man. I expect the twins are looking forward to the food afterwards. I hope Elsie can keep them under control in the church, I hear they are quite high-spirited.' She paused for breath and her thoughts changed course as she caught sight of her veil which was draped across the top of the chest of drawers, and resembled a flimsy cloud of morning mist. 'I wish I had lovely thick hair like you, Marcy. I hope mine behaves itself tomorrow.'

She brushed her hand over her downy curls, as if willing them to do her bidding.

'Of course it will,' Marcia answered with difficulty as she tried unsuccessfully to stifle a yawn. 'You're going to look beautiful tomorrow. But I do think we should try and get some sleep or else neither of us will look our best. Don't forget we have an early rise in the morning. Wedding or no wedding, the farm work has to be done.'

'Yes, Marcy, you're right.' Ruby blew out the candle and settled herself down under the covers. Squeezing her eyelids tightly shut, she tried to go to sleep, but she knew it was hopeless; her whole body felt fresh and wide awake.

The day of the wedding dawned bright and dry, with the sun soon peeping warmly through lazy puffs of marshmallow cloud. As Ruby worked in the cowshed her eyes kept straying through the open door and across the yard to where her wedding carriage awaited her. A while back, when Reuben had told her that somewhere hidden away in one of the outhouses he had the perfect thing to carry a bride to church, she hadn't taken too much notice of him. But when, a few days later, he had called them over to give him a hand, they had found him busy as could be, removing rubbish from the gloomy interior of a disused outhouse. Dust was flying everywhere as bits of wood, rotten sacks and rusted old farm implements were tossed hurriedly aside. Then he had found what he was looking for. He pushed back his cap and wiped his brow with the back of a grimy hand, leaving a dark smudge over his eyebrows. But he was smiling broadly as he stepped back a pace and pointed proudly at his prize find. There was unmistakable pride in his voice when he spoke: 'There, what do ee think of that then?'

All eyes had followed the pointing hand. They could just make out the shape of two large wheels, but the rest was completely obscured by the dust and dirt of time.

'What is it boss?' Marcia had asked timidly, fearing as they all did, Reuben's scorn of their farm knowledge.

Reuben picked up a piece of sacking and started to wipe away some of the dust and cobwebs. 'Can't ee see?' He looked impatiently at Marcia. ''Tiz plain as a pikestaff . . . 'tiz a jingle to ride in. See 'ere! Look, 'ere's the little door at the back where ee 'it's in . . . and 'ere look . . . ' His hands dusted furiously in his excitement. ' 'Ere's the seats going longways down each side.' He threw down the duster and ran his hand lovingly over the jingle. 'She's a little beauty,' he said. 'We'll give er a good clean up an' she'll be good as new. Ruby remembered her dismay when he had turned to her, eyes shining. 'There you are, Rube — fit fer a princess. What do ee say 'bout that?'

She could only nod and give a strained smile. It looked a total mess but she couldn't hurt his feelings.

Thankfully, he had been too excited to notice her obvious distress, because he had promptly gone on to explain its uses. 'When you rides in a jingle,' he said, 'you sits facing each other, an' the nearest to the pony 'olds the reigns. 'Twill 'ave to be a pony pulling it mind; our shire 'orses won't fit into the shafts of this little cart.' He looked thoughtful for a moment, then added, 'Mebbe Joe's twin boys will let us borrow their pony fer the day — 'twill be just the thing.' Satisfied that another hurdle had been crossed successfully, he had quickly resumed his old manner as boss of the farm and had ushered the two girls away to continue their mundane duties, while he collared Norman to help him get the jingle outside for a wash and brush-up. Ruby had been unable to believe her eyes when, later that same day, they had called her outside to look at their handiwork. The jingle had been transformed. It looked beautiful; almost like new. The seats were red and comfortably padded, and the carriage itself had emerged from its dusty jacket with gleaming stark-black paintwork. With their long spokes coloured bright yellow and a thin black line painted meticulously down the centre, even the large wooden wheels were spectacular.

Reuben had grinned at her astonished expression. ' 'Ow 'bout that then, maid? Is that good nuff fer the bride to be seen in?'

She had merely nodded gratefully, this time too choked to speak because she was overwhelmed with joy.

It was now almost half-past-one. The girls had been far too excited to eat any dinner, and even Reuben hadn't done justice to the cold meat and mashed potatoes that Marcia had hastily prepared for him. But William had been quite happy to make sure that nothing went to waste. He now lay on his favourite spot just inside the kitchen door with his eyes open wide and full of curiosity as he carefully studied his master. Reuben was standing with his back to the coal range and looking uncomfortably smart in his best, slightly outdated, navy blue suit. Every so often his eyes would dart nervously from the clock to the hall door as he waited impatiently for the bride and bridesmaid to appear.

'Wedding'll be all over if they dun't 'urry up,' he muttered to himself. His best shiny black shoes squeaked from lack of wear as he crossed the room to collect his white carnation. While his awkward fingers strove to put it through the tight hole of his lapel, his eyes rested on the flowers which were waiting for the girls. 'Ole Oscar 'ave dun us proud, William,' he said glancing with a smug smile at his canine friend, but the old collie only snorted. He was far more concerned with the strange smell of his master. How was he to know that the old farmer had missed a few of the pungent camphor mothballs that were buried in the folds of his pockets?

The door opened and Reuben gasped as Ruby entered the kitchen. Bright rays of the early spring sunshine that were stealing through the window fell on her, making her appear almost ethereal to the flabbergasted old farmer.

Ruby's face shone radiantly. 'Do I look all right, boss?'

He took a step closer to her, his proud old eyes shining with emotion. 'Rube, yer a vision to be'old.' His voice quivered dangerously. 'I couldn't be more proud of ee if ee wus me own daughter.'

Now Marcia stepped forward to get her boss's approval. This time he couldn't stop the sparkling tears that trickled down his leathery cheeks. She looked beautiful. The thick, dark, curly hair cascading down to her shoulders looked almost black against the dainty circle of artificial flowers that crowned the top of her head. The long, blue satin dress she wore, clung deliciously to the curves of her firm young body, and was set off by the one piece of jewellery fastened around her soft white neck. The dainty gold locket and chain that Webster had given her for Christmas. ' 'Ansome . . . 'ansome,' was all he could manage to say before turning away quickly for fear of letting his emotions take over. He glanced at the grandfather clock, then muttering something to himself, hurried over to the sideboard where several bottles and glasses had been set out in readiness for the reception. Selecting a bottle of port, he poured a small measure into each of three glasses. ' 'Ere you are,' he said to the girls, handing them each a fortifying drink. 'Couple more minutes wun't 'urt – an' anyway 'twill do us all good; 'elp to calm the nerves a bit.'

He picked up his own glass and looked across to Ruby. ' 'Ere's to a long and 'appy marriage, maid,' he said, raising the glass to his lips and downing its contents in a single, satisfying gulp.

A loud rap, followed by the kitchen door opening and three round, smiling faces looking in, reminded them it was time to go. The smiles belonged to three local women from the village who had offered their services as helpers at the reception. Marcia hurried them away from admiring the bride, to quickly show them the dairy where everything that was needed for the large table lay in readiness. Even the wedding cake had been made by the girls themselves, and now had pride of place on the marble slab. Marcia eyed it proudly. It did look nice with its white sugar icing. Her mind raced back to when Reuben had miraculously appeared with a big bag of dried fruit especially for the cake. And how, once they had put the cake in the oven, the coal range had decided to go at full blast so that the outer edge had been charred to a dry black crust. They had hidden it from Reuben, and when it had cooled down had cut off a good inch layer from all over the outside and found to their immense relief that the inside looked and smelled rather good.

'Come on, Marcy, times going on!' Reuben called urgently.

Leaving the women with the food, Marcia snatched up her posy from the kitchen table as she hurried outside to where the old farmer was helping Ruby up into the jingle. The jingle looked every inch a wedding carriage now, with white bows decorating its gleaming coachwork, and two more for the harness of the little pony that the twins had kindly loaned them for the day. The old farmer fussed over Ruby like a mother hen, settling her down on the plush red side-seat, and placing her veil where his clumsy feet would not do any damage. He helped Marcia up and jumped on board himself. Shouts of 'Good luck' and a chorus of cheers from the onlookers echoed around them as Reuben picked up the reins of the pony. The three helpers had torn themselves away from the masses of delicious food just in time to see the carriage leave for the Church. Reuben gave them a dignified wave as he majestically drove the pony across the yard and through the main gate, where he turned, without looking back, into the road which led to the church. The little pony – inappropriately named 'Rascal' by the twins – trotted obediently along the warm, sun-washed lanes, with the three VIP passengers swaying gently to the rhythm of the jingle. They spoke very little as they each dealt in their own way with the attack of nerves that relentlessly squeezed their excited stomachs.

As they drew near the church, they saw that many of the villagers had turned out to greet them. A happy crowd stood milling around the lych-gate, enjoying the pleasant warmth of the sunshine and catching up with the local gossip. Suddenly all ears were made aware of the clip-clop of the pony's hooves, and all eyes turned to the road to watch the approaching jingle.

For the last few yards of the journey, Reuben held the reins standing up, his face registering his moment of glory. It was as much his big day as Ruby's. His gentle tug on the reins brought the jingle to a smooth halt.

The girls gingerly stepped down from the carriage with Reuben's help, then stood to be admired while he tethered 'Rascal' to a post. He was pleased to note that the post was conveniently standing in a bed of tasty long grass that would keep the pony more than happy for the duration of the service.

The villagers stood dutifully aside as Reuben strode importantly back through them, his arm already poised to link with Ruby's for their walk together up the path and into the church. Marcia fell in behind them as they slowly made their way up to the open doorway of the church. The soft organ music that had welcomed them up the path changed to *Here Comes the Bride* as they reached the large arched doorway. Then Ruby suddenly stopped. Reuben felt her grip tighten on his arm as she looked back over her shoulder to Marcia.

'Do you think Norman will be inside waiting for me Marcy?' She sounded truly worried.

'Of course he is.'

'The little bugger 'ad better be,' hissed Reuben from the corner of his mouth. Then, feeling Ruby's grip tighten again, he added, 'Dun't worry, maid, 'e'll be there. Everything will go like clockwork, jus ee mark me words.' He rested his large, tough hand over Ruby's little fingers and with a reassuring smile led her quietly into the church.

To the great joy of the reverend, several pews had been taken, and the bands of sunshine that flooded through the stained glass windows suddenly became alive with dancing dust particles as the congregation rose respectfully to acknowledge the bride's arrival.

Ruby's eyes searched frantically for Norman. Her worried frown gave way to a look of happy relief when she saw the back of his blond head as he stood stiffly beside Joe, in front of a beaming Reverend Bassett.

At that very moment Marcia, too, had experienced the same glorious emotion, for she had spotted Webster standing handsomely out from the rest in his smart blue uniform.

Their eyes met only briefly, but long enough for her to read clearly the loving message that lay deep within them.

Ruby halted beside Norman. They held hands tightly and looked adoringly at each other. She knew in her heart that from this moment on they would always be together. She handed her bouquet to Marcia and the service began.

'Who gives this woman in Holy matrimony?' Reverend Bassett's voice rang out loud and clear for all to hear.

Reuben stepped clear of his pew, clumsily knocking a hymn book off the little shelf in front of him. The thud of its landing on to the wooden floor was magnified, as it echoed embarrassingly around the hushed sanctum. All eyes were upon him as he gave the reverend a withering look and muttered crossly, 'I do.' Then, his work done, he stepped back to his pew, grateful that the eyes of the congregation were no longer upon him.

Marcia stole a sideward glance and saw that Reuben was looking distinctly uncomfortable as the service progressed. The ceremony was really affecting him, she thought. Even her own throat felt tight, which made her realise just how much of a family they had all become. It was lovely.

'You may kiss the bride.'

The minister's words denoted that the pair were now man and wife. A low, respectful titter escaped joyfully from the flock as the new Mr and Mrs Norman Innis fell happily into each other's arms.

The farmhouse took on an air of friendly happiness with its doors wide open to the sunshine, and guests dressed in their Sunday-best filling the kitchen and parlour. The visitors were even spilling over to upstairs where the ladies could avail themselves of the toilet facilities which were placed discreetly under the bed should the outside convenience prove inadequate for the swollen numbers.

Marcia squeezed between the hungry guests to fill two plates from the well-laden table, one apiece for Webster and Gerry. Webster's pal, Gerry, had not been invited to the reception, but he had arrived at the church with his camera and, much to everyone's delight, had stepped in as photographer for the day — a task for which he was now reaping his reward by tucking into a most enjoyable wedding feast.

'I must say you look ravishing, Marcia.' He swallowed with relish a juicy piece of ham, then smacked Webster playfully on the chest. 'Don't forget,' he said, smiling wickedly at Marcia. 'When you get fed up with old Toddy here, I'm always available.'

She gave him a smile before sinking her teeth into a plump chicken drumstick, then threw Webster a look which said, 'Don't worry, there will be no one else for me.'

The musical clink of glasses and the popping of corks made it quite clear that the work of the busy kettle was, for the moment, done. Reuben took charge of filling the glasses, while Oscar stood conveniently by in case he required any assistance, and to ensure that he himself was close to the action. As they were filled, the glasses were placed on trays and distributed to the guests by the voluntary waitresses. Marcia smiled to herself as she noticed the timely appearance of the Trevain twins. They had burst in from outside with just time to exchange a knowing look before trying to get their grubby paws on a passing tray of drinks. But they were thwarted by a withering look from the serving lady, to whom they both grinned sheepishly before shooting off in the direction of the table. At least there was plenty of food — they were on safe ground there!

'Speech! Speech!'

Someone had said it; now everyone had joined in, and all eyes were on Norman.

He smiled nervously and rose self-consciously from his seat. 'I'm no good at speeches,' he mumbled, staring steadfastly at the floor. He stood there, not moving a muscle, for what seemed like forever. Then, when everybody was beginning to think that

f

nothing more was forthcoming, he looked up suddenly and said, 'I'm the happiest man alive.' Picking up his glass, he looked towards his bride and added, 'My own Ruby.' There was no need for anything more. He had said it all. The farmhouse reverberated to the spontaneous applause.

Gerry had taken the final photograph – of the bride and groom cutting the wedding cake – before taking his leave. He was reluctant to go but duty called and he knew that Webster would not want him hanging around.

Marcia and Webster walked with him as far as the main gate, pausing at intervals along the way to chat to guests who had ventured outside to enjoy the warm spring weather. Marcia felt on top of the world, so aware of the handsome young airman at her side, and pleased with her own unusually smart appearance. Such a contrast, she reflected, to her everyday working togs.

She and Webster leaned over the gate and waved until Gerry had disappeared from sight, then Webster turned and drew her tightly to him. 'You are a beautiful woman, Marcia Evans. I love you so much.'

Marcia, not trusting herself to speak, stood on tiptoe to answer with a kiss, when over his shoulder she spotted a flower-adorned hat bobbing with determination as it came inexorably towards them.

As she self-consciously drew back, Webster too had noticed they were about to have company. 'Fancy a little walk?' he said, swiftly taking her hand and leading her through the gate and away up the road. He gave a satisfied grin as he slipped his arm round her waist. Marcia merely nodded as an attack of the giggles threatened to erupt. They walked quickly, determined not to look back until they had rounded the corner and were safely out of sight. Then Webster paused and took her in his arms again. 'Can you walk easily in those shoes?'

'Yes, I think so,' Marcia told him, glancing down at her daintily-clad feet.

'That settles it then. It will be nice to be on our own for a while, won't it, Marcy?'

She smiled her agreement. There was nothing she would like better as she lightly fell into step beside him.

They strolled hand-in-hand along the dusty road, stopping at times to admire and smell the wild primroses that grew in profusion along the hedgerows. As the high walls of the convent came into view, they paused by a gate to watch the antics of some lambs frolicking in the sunshine. Although taking care never to stray too far from their mother's side, they were having the time of their young lives.

'The ewes look in good condition,' Webster remarked, reminding Marcia of his peace-time profession. She tended to forget he was a vet, being so wrapped up with him in the present, and with him looking every inch a very smart airman. Before they moved on, he cuddled her tightly. 'Oh Marcy,' he said, 'If only things could be like this for ever. This damned war – sometimes I . . . ' He didn't finish. It was as if he couldn't trust himself to speak further. Instead, he buried his hot face into her neck and squeezed her body so tightly that for a second or two she found it hard to breathe. 'I need you so much!' His words were muffled, but none the less clear.

Marcia's own emotions were threatening to boil over, but her strict Welsh upbringing strove to push them away. Feverishly, she racked her brain for some sort of diversion, then just ahead she spotted a narrow track, forking off from the road. She knew it would lead them down to the back of the convent, then along and up the other side, to where they would rejoin the road. 'Shall we take that path?'

The urgency of her request broke the spell. Webster loosened his grip and glanced dazedly to where she was pointing. Not speaking, he just nodded and took her outstretched hand, but the message in his blue eyes was clear for her to see. Marcia, you can't fool me.

The path was just wide enough for them to walk side by side. To the right of them some of the convent's trees had bowed their heads to touch the top of the high wall and form an archway. As they strolled along, the bright sunlight seeped through the overhanging branches and danced mischievously across their bodies. It seemed to be much quieter here, more peaceful somehow, than up on the road.

Suddenly Marcia stumbled against Webster. 'Ouch!' The dainty heel of her shoe had slipped on an upraised stone, and had caused her foot to twist painfully.

Webster looked at her anxiously, then propped her against the wall while he bent down to inspect the damage. He carefully removed her shoe and began to gently massage her ankle. His hands worked methodically with gentle pressure, smoothing away the stiffness that had threatened to take over. After a while, when the pain had subsided and she was aware only of his loving touch, he stopped and looked up into her eyes. 'Is that any better?'

'Much better.'

'There's no damage done,' he said as he carefully replaced her shoe. 'A few minutes' rest, and it should be as good as new.' He straightened up and cupped her face in his hands. 'You had me worried there for a minute.' His eyes twinkled as he grinned. 'I didn't relish the idea of having to carry you all the way back to the farm.' Before she could reply he planted his lips firmly on hers, and all she could do was try to suppress the giggles that were doing their best to choke her.

'I guess we should start back now.'

She started at the sound of his voice. Standing cuddled together in the hushed woodland she had drifted into a blissful unawareness of time and place. Her whole being felt a serenity that was completely new to her. She did not want it to end. 'I suppose so,' she conceded reluctantly.

'How does it feel?' Webster watched with concern as she gingerly put her weight on the wounded foot and started to walk. After a few steps she stopped and looked back with a smile. 'It's fine, just a slight stiffness. You won't have to carry me.'

They were about to move on when something caught Webster's eye. 'Funny,' he said. 'I never noticed that before.' He was looking at a small door set unobtrusively into the convent wall.

'Me neither,' Marcia said. 'We probably missed it when I turned my ankle.'

Badly weathered by years of exposure to the elements, the moss-covered door certainly blended in well with the surrounding stone. Webster looped his fingers through the rust-eaten ring of the iron door-handle. 'It's very stiff,' he said, gripping it tightly.

Marcia suddenly felt afraid and laid a restraining hand on his arm. 'Don't open it!'

Deterred by her concern, he lessened his grip and just left his fingers curved around the ring. 'I don't think I could, even if I wanted to. I should think it's been closed for years. Suddenly he gasped, and swiftly drew back his hand from the ring. They both stood transfixed and stared in amazement as the door started to open, creaking painfully as it slowly swung inwards. 'I didn't open it,' he gasped, 'It wasn't me!' He glanced bemusedly at Marcia, but it was as if she hadn't heard him. Her attention was riveted on the scene before her. He put his arm around her and held her close as they looked on in silence. The open doorway had revealed a large well-kept garden bathed in sunshine. They stood silently cuddled together, their eyes following a rough and uneven stone path which led to a large potting shed at the far end of the garden. The garden appeared to be deserted.

Without speaking, Webster led her just a few steps inside, to where they could stand to have a better look. To the left of them, on Marcia's side, was the vegetable garden. Row after row of long, straight, neat lines of tender sprouting leaves could be seen, and not a weed in sight. The vegetable patch ended in what looked like the high boundary wall which had been camouflaged by the trained fork-like branches of soft fruit trees. Situated on Webster's side was a flower garden, which almost took their breath away as their eyes wandered over the blaze of colour from lilies, primroses and tulips, and many other varieties which seemed exotic and were unfamiliar to them. They stood quietly, close together, and let their eyes wander over the natural carpet of delightful blossoms. At the far end of the flower garden, sunlight was glinting on the glass panes of a long greenhouse. It was so perfect here, so tranquil and serene, that Marcia felt strangely relaxed. She was conscious only of Webster's nearness, and of the utter peace which had now entered her body. But suddenly she stiffened. Something wasn't quite right. Her heart leapt painfully in her chest, abruptly reminding her that they were trespassing.

'What's the matter?' Webster asked, sensing that something was amiss. He reached for her hand and realised she was trembling. Her palm was hot and clammy.

She made no attempt to answer him. Her gaze was riveted to the door of the potting shed. His eyes followed hers, and he too now froze as his gaze fell upon the silent, watchful figure of a nun. He suddenly felt decidedly uncomfortable, plagued by strange emotions. Guilt for invading the order's privacy. Remorse, for landing Marcia in this situation. His throat felt dry as the nun walked slowly but determinedly towards them. He glanced at Marcia, his eyes desperately apologetic, then he turned to face the advancing nun. He had to speak to her, to tell her how sorry he was.

She stopped just a few paces away from them, enabling them now to look beyond the habit and to see her face. Webster was surprised to note that she was young; about Marcia's age. He didn't know why, but he had expected her to be much older. And the stern, disapproving look which he expected, was not there. She was smiling, and even the large, dark eyes that shone out from her pale oval face, seemed happy to see them. He swallowed hard as he spared a glance for Marcia, but she was unaware of him as her eyes were still firmly fixed on the nun.

'I have been waiting for you.'

This time Marcia did meet Webster's eyes as they looked at each other in stunned amazement.

'But how could you know we were coming?' Incredibility sharpened his words as he looked once again at the angelic face before him, but his question went unanswered.

She said, 'You are both very much in love?'

They nodded slowly, both wondering where all this was leading to, and not understanding why they were not yet hearing the words of reproof that they had fully expected. Then the sister's expression suddenly grew serious as she turned to Webster, her eyes sweeping over the blue uniform as if seeing it for the first time. 'Will you be married?' The words were softly spoken as her inquiring eyes bored into his.

He met her gaze and paused, startled by the utter despair he saw in her eyes. Then she smiled and the look was gone, leaving him to believe that he had only imagined it. 'Yes, oh yes,' he said. 'As soon as this terrible war is over.'

Smiling, he looked down to the girl cuddled in his arm as if asking for some kind of reassurance.

The nun merely nodded, but he was relieved to see she bore them no malice. Nevertheless, he still felt oddly strange and would feel much happier in himself once they had left the garden. He glanced pointedly at the watch on his wrist, and then at Marcia. 'Gosh! – is that the time? I'm afraid we really must go.' They both looked back towards the nun to take their leave, and were surprised to see only the back of her black, flowing habit gliding over the path and away from them. It seemed so strange that she had left so abruptly without a parting word. When they next looked, she had gone. The garden was once again deserted.

'Come on!' Taking Marcia's hand, Webster hurried her back along the path and out through the garden door. With a gasp of relief he closed it firmly behind them. 'Wow!' he said, leaning back against the wall and rubbing his hands over his face. 'I'm glad to be out of that garden, aren't you?' He drew her closer. 'I'm sorry I led you inside but it looked so peaceful. He looked deeply into her eyes, willing her to understand as he tried to explain. 'It was as if I had no control . . . I had to go inside.'

'It's all right,' Marcia said. 'It really was beautiful in there, and I suppose the nun's reaction to us can easily be explained by the solitary life they lead.

Webster nodded and kissed her, feeling much calmer now that everything seemed back to normal. With his arm fastened lovingly around her waist, they headed back to the farm and to the remainder of the wedding festivities.

Chapter Fifteen

Marcia tried to suppress a nervous giggle as she tiptoed barefoot up the stairs to her bedroom. The candle in her trembling hand flickered crazily, sending her shadow to mingle and dance with Webster's, who was close behind her. He, too, was in his stockinged feet. His shoes were tightly clutched in one hand, whilst the other helped him to feel his way up the unfamiliar narrow staircase.

They had made it back to the farmhouse in good time, in spite of Marcia's sore ankle. They had not spoken much about their strange encounter in the convent garden. Marcia could tell that Webster was still feeling guilty, and tried to think of other things to say to try and forget the incident. It was funny though, it had unnerved her in a way. She felt different; changed in some weird way. She hadn't told Webster – it was hard to describe feelings she couldn't explain to herself – but it had happened when the nun had looked directly at her. Her whole body had suddenly ached with love and longing for the airman beside her. It was as if the bond between them had in that moment become much stronger. So much so that for several seconds she had found it difficult to breathe. She had timidly followed Webster into the still crowded kitchen, afraid that someone would read in her face what her feelings were, but she soon relaxed when she realised that they had not even been missed. Everyone was having too good a time. Occasions like this were few and far between in these terrible times and they were all making the most of it. Even as her eyes met Ruby's, she could only see happiness shining there. It was obvious that Norman held pride of place in her thoughts today, as was to be expected, of course.

As the evening wore on, Norman and Ruby left them to spend

their wedding night in a cottage by the sea. The cottage belonged to Norman's cousin and was about four miles away in the town of Newquay. The cousin's old Austin Seven car had disappeared through the main gate with the happy couple waving furiously from the small back window, but the clatter of the tin cans tied to the rear bumper could still be heard when they were almost a mile away.

When the metallic clatter at last faded into the distance, the laughing, chattering guests hurried back to the warmth of the house. The evening, they had discovered, had turned quite chilly. The merriment had continued for the rest of the evening. Even those who were normally shy and retiring had been singing and doing their own special party pieces, no doubt helped along by one or two glasses of Reuben's potent liquor. Although Marcia had thoroughly enjoyed herself, she was relieved when the last guest had reluctantly decided it was time to go home. She left Webster standing in front of the stove warming his back while she went through to the front room to check on Reuben. She heard his loud, regular breathing as soon as she put her head around the door, and smiled to herself when she saw he had company. Oscar was stretched out on one chair, and the old farmer on another, both fast asleep and wearing the satisfied expression of enjoying the comfort of numerous powerful nightcaps. She gently closed the door on them, and tiptoed back to the kitchen.

Webster caught her in his arms. 'I suppose I should be getting back,' he sighed, not relishing the thought of leaving her.

She reached up and kissed him, then rested her head against his chest. Her mind was in turmoil. She couldn't bear to let him go, not just yet. She wanted him. She wanted to feel his body lying close beside her in bed! But she was a good girl — would it cheapen her in his eyes? Could she live with the knowledge that she had gone against her upbringing? Her thoughts raced back to the nun, and the doubts suddenly vanished, leaving her mind as clear as crystal. She had to be with him; nothing else mattered!

'Will you stay?' Her voice was just a whisper as she looked up at him, her eyes almost pleading.

'You know how much I want to, but are you sure?' He studied her face, wondering if he had understood the full implication of her question. Yes, it was there in her eyes, the answer he so desperately wanted. She really wanted him. 'Oh Marcy, of course

I'll stay.' He spoke softly as he lifted one of her long, dark curls and kissed the silky smoothness of her neck. Impishly she looked up to him, then gently touched his lips with her fingers for him to keep silent while she fetched the candlestick. She turned the lamp on the table to low, struck a match to light the candle in her hand, then looked back for him to follow her.

Marcia crossed to the bedside table and laid down the candlestick as Webster silently closed the bedroom door behind him. She turned nervously to face him, wondering for a moment what had possessed her to act in this way, yet at the same time she was thrilled and excited.

Loosening his tie, he moved towards her. 'I expect you will need some help to get out of that dress?' She just nodded, and turned her back to him so that he could unfasten it for her. His fingers that normally were so sure when dealing with the animals in his profession, now trembled so badly that he had to will himself to calm down. At last the dress loosened from her body and he gently slid it down over her shoulders. Catching it at the waist, she turned once more to face him. He could feel her nervousness, even though the weak candlelight betrayed no emotion in her large dark eyes. To ease the tension he looked down and concentrated on removing his own clothing. He laid his clothes neatly on the linoleum floor at the bottom of the bed, then standing naked he turned to look at her. He had imagined that she had a beautiful body, but his thoughts had not done her justice. His breath caught in his throat at the sight of her. She was more than beautiful . . . she was perfect! He moved slowly towards her.

Taking her hand, he guided her to the bed. They slipped between the cool sheets, then he moistened his fingers on his tongue to extinguish the candle flame. The darkness was complete. He turned and drew her soft body close to his own, and in that most wonderful of moments nothing else existed. Their surroundings, the war, other people, even time itself – all were forgotten as they embarked together on their first sensual voyage.

Marcia stirred, and snuggled deeper down under the covers. Was it morning yet? She felt blissfully relaxed and content. She didn't want to get up, not yet . . . she just couldn't.

'Marcy.'

Webster calling her name? Her sleep fuddled mind told her she was dreaming. The soft urgency of her name being called yet again alerted her senses. She opened her eyes to see Webster standing beside the bed. He was fully dressed and bending over her, his face almost touching hers. He kissed her.

'Is it time to get up?' She drew her arms from under the covers and clasped them round his neck, this time kissing him.

'No, my darling, it's just after four. But I must get back before I'm missed . . . my pass was only 'til midnight.'

'Because of me, you could get into serious trouble,' she said ruefully.

'I won't, I promise.' He cupped his hands around her face, sensing rather than seeing her anxious look in the darkness of the room. 'Even if I do, it was worth it, wasn't it?' He stifled her intended 'yes' by putting his lips to hers in a lingering kiss. 'I'll see you soon, my darling.'

Webster straightened up and pulled the bedclothes snugly up around her neck. Marcia suddenly felt very alone as the gentle click of the bedroom door signalled that he had gone.

Chapter Sixteen

The busy planting season had arrived at the farm, and although the marriage was only one week old, Reuben, to outward appearances at least, had dismissed it from his mind. Even the fact of Norman moving in with them had made no difference, it was as if he had always been part of the family.

At breakfast that morning, the two men had been discussing the busy week ahead. Potatoes were their first priority, and it went without saying that as the hours of daylight grew longer, so their workload increased. Reuben waited for the girls to take away the empty breakfast dishes before opening the table drawer in front of him and taking out a large brown envelope. He extracted a booklet from the envelope, then, passing it across the table to Norman, said, ' 'Ow would ee fancy driving summin like that, boy?'

Norman's face beamed as he placed the booklet on the table in front of him and studied it for a moment. 'It's a tractor, boss! You're not thinking of having one, are you?'

The dirty breakfast dishes were forgotten for the moment. Marcia hastily rung out the dishcloth in the bowl, and wiping her wet hands on her breeches, hurried over to join Ruby. Ruby, still clutching a tea-towel, was staring intently over Norman's shoulder. A glossy picture of a dark green 'Fordson' tractor stared back at them.

Marcia looked towards Reuben with concern. 'It looks smashing, boss, but what about the horses?'

'You dun't 'ave to worry 'bout they, maid,' he said. 'They'm like meself – gittin' on a bit now. They'll still 'ave their uses, but life will be a bit easier for 'em from now on. Anyways,' he added. 'Seeing as 'ow we need to produce more fer the war effort, I can

132

see no other way out.'

When a few days later the 'Fordson' arrived, riding sedately on the back of a lorry, the four members of the farm were excitedly waiting in the yard to greet it. The driver jumped down from his cab, touched his cap, and said, 'Mornin'.' Then, with an agility that belied his years, he swung his thin, overalled frame up into the back beside the tractor. The four watched on expectantly as he picked up two flat metal girders and placed them under each of the front wheels, then lowered the opposite ends of the girders down to rest on the yard. He jumped down and without saying a word stood back from the lorry to size up the situation. After making a slight adjustment, he leapt back up to the tractor and turned a tap under the fuel tank before going round to the front of the machine where he started to swing a large starting handle. He did this three or four times. When nothing happened, he straightened up and pushed his cap further back on his head. With a look of utter bewilderment, he gave his scalp a thorough scratching. As if this action in itself had given him his answer, he pulled his cap into its former position, then swung the handle again. This time, a gentle chug and a puff of smoke from the tractor's chimney signalled that the machine was ready to go. The watchful eyes still trained on him noticed the smug smile that flickered across his face before he again hurried round to the rear of the machine, where he jumped up and leaned across the large driving seat to grip the steering wheel. Still standing, he kicked the brake with his foot to release it, then slowly but surely steered the huge tractor wheels down the girders and safely on to the farmyard.

'Who will be driving it?' he asked.

Reuben pointed to Norman. ' 'Ee'll be driving it,' he said. 'All this newfangled stuff is beyond me, I dun't know wot the world is coming to,' he added grumpily.

Norman jumped happily up onto the tractor and made himself familiar with the controls, while the delivery man placed the two girders back into the lorry. By the time the lorry had gone, Norman was confidently cruising round the yard amid squeals of delight from the two girls and the doubting watchful presence of Reuben. But whatever thoughts were going through his mind, he realised that the 'Fordson' would now play a major part in their everyday lives. Life on the farm would never be the same again.

Over the next few weeks the farm implements that had been previously horse-drawn, had been taken one by one to the village blacksmith in St Mawgan. By adding a drawbar, each item had been converted for use with the new tractor. Its first job was to have the chiseller connected to its rear in order to soften the earth of the fields that had been ploughed by the horses over the winter months. When that was done, the tractor then changed over to the bankers which formed long straight lines of grooves, enabling the farmers to walk up and down with their buckets of seed potatoes and drop them uniformly into the prepared furrow. This was done by placing down one booted foot, with one potato planted at the heel and another at the toe. When the tractor had finished one field and had moved to the next, Reuben was happy to revert back to his old way of farming. With the help of Star pulling a single banker on behind, they worked as one, drawing back from the sides of the furrows the rich crumbly soil which the tractor had dug out earlier, and gently covering the potatoes with their tender shoots. By the time they had finished, the field once again looked flat and dull, but Reuben smiled as he left by the gate. Looking back he could already envisage the fruits of their labours. Soon there would be row upon row of healthy green leaves, and underneath – his mouth watered – potatoes, new perfect potatoes.

In just five days, six acres of potatoes had been planted. Without the help of the tractor it would have taken them twice as long. Reuben was beginning to wonder why he hadn't invested in a tractor long before.

Chapter Seventeen

The girls were eager to 'have a go' on the new tractor, and with Norman's help soon mastered the chugging beast. They both loved driving it, but Reuben always seemed to find something else for Ruby to do when it was her turn. She felt slightly peeved about this, until the others pointed out to her that, although Reuben hadn't said anything, they guessed it was because she was pregnant. In fact, Ruby had never felt better and thought that Reuben was being silly. But on the other hand, it was nice to know that he cared.

Marcia was thankful to keep busy. She hadn't seen much of Webster since the wedding, apart from an odd hour or two snatched here and there, and she was missing him terribly. Apart from that, just lately she had been having nightmares about him, and they were beginning to play on her mind. Last night was the worst yet; she had awakened herself with her own screaming. All of her dreams had been almost identical. She would find herself standing outside in the darkness. She couldn't see anything around her, just total blackness, but she knew she was standing alone on a large, open, grassy plane. The wind was cold and whipped and whirled around her thinly-clad body. Above the howling of the wind she would hear someone calling her name:

'Marcy! . . . Marcy!'

She knew it was Webster and he needed her. She tried to walk in the direction of the sound of his voice, but the wind shrieked even louder and blew with a force that held her fast, as if her legs were paralysed. The extreme desperation she suffered forced her mind to awake from the horrors of the dream. But it would leave her restless and melancholy until the alarm signalled the start of a new day.

She tried very hard to be her usual self at breakfast time, but Reuben somehow sensed that something was amiss and had asked her if anything was troubling her. For a moment she did not answer him, reliving the nightmare again in her mind. All of it was there in vivid detail. Once again she found herself on the dark wind-swept plane, but this time she was not alone. The nun whom they had met in the garden now stood watchful before her. Neither of them spoke, but Marcia saw that the nun's eyes were filled with an intense sorrow. Then the spectre suddenly vanished and Marcia was alone. The wind still shrieked and tore at her body, but this time no one called her name. Instead, in the black distance, she saw a great light in the sky. As she watched, the light slowly descended to the ground. She saw that the light was in fact flames. It was an aeroplane! It was Webster's plane! She screamed.

'Marcy, what is it? Whatever is the matter?' Ruby leapt from her chair and hurried round the table to comfort her. 'What's troubling you? You're as white as a sheet.'

Marcia took in the worried faces around her and felt ashamed that she had caused such anxiety. After all, it was only a dream. 'I'm sorry.' She forced a strained smile. 'It's nothing really, just a dream. Well more of a nightmare really – it just got to me, that's all.'

'Tell us 'bout it then, maid. 'Twill do ee good to git it off yer chest.' Reuben spoke light-heartedly, but failed to hide his look of concern.

It was on the tip of Marcia's tongue to blurt out the whole frightening episode, when suddenly she remembered they had decided to keep secret their strange encounter with the nun. She limited her account to the dream.

'I dreamt that Webster's plane crashed. I keep seeing it, in vivid detail!'

'Blimey!' Reuben said. 'No wonder you've bin upset. But 'twas only a silly dream, maid; dun't ee go fretting 'bout it. I'll tell ee what – you can 'ave a day driving the tractor if you like.' He looked to see her reaction, and when she gave him a grateful smile he added gruffly, as if embarrassed: 'Ground needs to be turned over in the higher field anyways.' Then, picking up his mug as if the problem had been resolved, he said, 'Any more tea in the pot, Ruby?'

Chapter Eighteen

Marcia's hand left the steering wheel to acknowledge Norman's wave as his cheerful face disappeared through the field gate. On Reuben's instructions, he had rode up in the tractor with her and explained the best way to work this stony and particularly large acre'd field. Even with the help of this new machine, Marcia guessed it would take most of the day to plough it and have it in a workable condition for planting, which would follow early the next morning.

Marcia drove the tractor slowly, continually glancing behind to check that the furrows were straight. She would be the butt of everyone's jokes if the earth was patterned in wavy lines when she had finished. Scores of shrieking seagulls were keeping her company, picking on choice fat worms which were rudely evicted by the machine's powerful blades, and chasing along behind her like a bride's white veil fluttering in the wind.

Some way ahead was the hedgerow which divided the field from the road, and on the other side of the road was the boundary hedge of the aerodrome. Marcia sighed as she thought of Webster. So near, yet so far. If only she could talk to him, even for a moment. A shiver rippled through her body as she recalled the vividness of her recurring dream. 'Come on, girl!' She spoke the words aloud, angry at her own profound misery. 'Pull yourself together!' Gritting her teeth, she forced her mind to concentrate on the job in hand, and her grip tightened on the steering wheel as if in defiance of any unwelcome thoughts that might stand in her way.

It was almost dusk when she finally halted the tractor close to the field's open gate. She switched off the engine and rubbed her hands over her dusty eyes and face. It had been a long day. She grimaced as she shifted her position on the hard seat in order to look around to survey her tractor skills. 'Not bad,' she told herself, confident that Reuben would be pleased. 'Not bad at all.' Her foot nudged her dinner bag, reminding her that she was feeling hungry. She remembered that she had eaten only a couple of sandwiches at dinner time, being anxious to carry on with her work, afraid that she wouldn't complete it in time. She bent down and retrieved the bag from the floor of the tractor. She brushed her tongue over her dry lips as she also remembered the hot tea which was remaining in the thermos flask. Placing the dinner bag on her lap, she was about to open it when she heard the unmistakable drone of an aeroplane. She stopped to listen. Probably on a test flight, she thought. Webster had once told her that after a damaged 'kite' had been repaired, it would be sent up for a spin to check it out. She remembered how he had joked with her saying, 'You won't find me up there in the daytime. I'll probably be enjoying a rest somewhere and be thinking of you slaving away on the farm. As her hand felt around inside the bag for the sandwiches, her fingers came in contact with the battered tobacco tin which contained an old pocket watch. She took it out, curious now to know the exact time. She gasped as she lifted the lid. The watch told her it was a quarter to six. She couldn't believe it. The time had simply flown. She had no idea that it was so late. Too late now for a snack, she realised, putting the watch away; her tea would be waiting for her back at the farm.

She could still hear the deep drone of aircraft engines in the distance. Her heart almost stopped as it suddenly dawned upon her that this was no test flight; this was for real. They were about to set out on a bombing mission. Take-off time was supposed to be a secret, but everyone at St Mawgan knew exactly when the bombers took off.

'I must warn him!' Marcia spoke aloud to herself as the nightmare returned to haunt her with ghastly realism. There was no time to be lost. She had to see Webster! To warn him! Then another thought struck her: he would probably think she was crazy. What could she do? She felt strongly that she should at least voice her fears to him, and yet she knew in her heart that nothing would stop him from doing his duty. The only sensible thing to do was go back to the farm and try and forget last night. She had almost convinced herself that was the right thing to do, when once again the image of the nun appeared in her mind. Marcia was mesmerised by those eyes. It was as if nothing else existed. The eyes of the holy woman stared unblinking into her own, probing deeply, urging her to hurry, to warn him! Suddenly she knew what she had to do. Grabbing her coat, still clutching her dinner bag, she jumped down from the tractor and raced out through the gate. She prayed that she would be in time as she ran across the road to the airfield's boundary hedge. She clambered up the steep bank, heedless of the brambles which tried to hold her back.

She reached the top, gasping for air as her lungs felt fit to burst. The noise of the engines was louder here. She glanced across and saw the line of waiting aircraft. She couldn't tell if Webster's plane was among them; she was too far away to see. She only knew that they would soon be airborne . . . she had to hurry!

She leapt from the bank to land heavily on all fours. No one had seen her. Remaining close to the hedge, she ran with all her might until she reached the tail-end of the first parked aircraft. The engine noise was deafening. A swift glance along the side of the fuselage told her this one wasn't Webster's. She ran on awkwardly, her bag bouncing uncomfortably on her hip, her hands covering her ears, along to the next giant tail. She paused to look for the Cornish emblem. Yes, it was there! Her heart missed a beat as she found herself staring up at Webster's Lancaster bomber.

Marcia glanced around anxiously, not sure what her next move would be. She thought she could hear voices above the din but she could see no one. As she drew closer to the rear fins, she spotted a short ladder leading to an opening in the fuselage. Perhaps Webster was already inside. She only wanted to speak briefly with him. She crept up to the foot of the ladder. With her foot on the bottom rung she gazed up at the dark aperture. From the corner of her eye she detected a movement. Hardly daring to breath, she slowly turned her head and saw two airmen standing and talking together. They were near the front of the plane, partly obscured by one of the huge wheels. Her mind worked furiously, Webster had told her that engineers always checked over the aircraft prior to take-off. If they turned and spotted her she would have a lot of explaining to do. Hide! – it was the only way. She scrambled up the metal rungs and ducked into the fuselage.

For a moment she couldn't see anything; it was so dark in there. She closed her eyes for a second to accustom herself to the gloom and felt her stomach churn as she breathed in the hot piquant smell of oil and engines. She ventured a little further, until she found herself beneath a large perspex canopy. She felt claustrophobic as her eyes swept over the dim, poky area, and she was about to retreat when she heard voices. She strained to listen above the din; was it her imagination? No. There it was again. They could be inside at any minute. Frantically she looked for somewhere to hide. Everything looked alien. Sour bile rose in her throat; she thought she was going to be sick. Extending a hand to steady herself, she almost lost her balance as the solid obstruction she encountered moved inwards with the gentle pressure of her fingers. She choked back a nervous giggle as she collided with an object which was familiar to her. She had stumbled upon the lavatory. It was an Elsan. She stepped inside and closed the door.

Sitting on the Elsan in the pressing darkness, she strove to collect her thoughts. Never before had she felt so frightened. Then she heard more voices — closer this time. Transfixed with fear, she strained to listen over the noise of the engines. Her worst fears were confirmed as she clearly heard talking; not one voice but several, drawing nearer. Then a brief moment of relief. Whoever it was had passed by.

She thought and hoped that the voices belonged to the ground crew who were checking over the plane before take-off. Webster had often spoken to her about its huge Merlin engines, and how they were the finest in the world. And how everything was checked and double-checked before each flight. She reasoned that if she waited for just a few more minutes, she could gently open the door and leave without being seen. She realised now how stupid this idea of hers had been. Webster would think she was mad. Suddenly the noisy vibration was much louder. The engine-note rose to a thunderous roar. She covered her ears with her hands as the noise threatened to burst her eardrums. She almost lost her balance. Terrified, she realised the plane was moving. As she sprang to her feet in sheer panic, her head struck metal with a sickening thud. She was pitched forward into an abyss of blackness.

Chapter Nineteen

'Marcia! Marcia!'

The words slowly filtered through to her fogged mind. She blinked and opened her eyes. It was another dream, another nightmare – it had to be! She was lying on a hard floor; her head was hurting. There was so much noise. And there were faces – three blurred faces – all staring down at her. She struggled to bring them into focus. 'Webster!' Her voice was a feeble croak. It had to be a dream! 'Webster, is that you?'

'Take it easy now,' Webster said, looking more worried than she'd ever seen him, 'you've had a nasty crack on the head.'

Marcia tried to sit up. 'Where am I? What happened?'

'Stay there. Don't move.' It was Webster's pal, Gerry. 'We don't know how you came to be here with us, but you're in our Lancaster high over Germany. We just found you on the floor. I'm sorry, but it's too late to abort this mission now; you're coming with us all the way.'

This time Marcia did manage to struggle into a sitting position. 'Over Germany?' she echoed, aghast.

'I'm afraid so,' Webster replied grimly. 'Whatever possessed you to – '

'Not now,' the third man cut in, placing a hand on Webster's arm. 'Give me a hand to help her into a seat.'

A nightmare maybe, but it was certainly no dream. Marcia found herself being half-carried to the rear of the cockpit where she was eased into the Wireless Operator's seat. 'What now, skip?' Gerry enquired of the pilot.

'Maintain radio silence. Carry on as normal,' came the sharp reply, barely audible above the roar of the four Merlin engines.

Marcia stole a look out of the cockpit window and saw the

unmistakable black shapes of several other Lancasters flying in loose formation. Her heart missed a beat as she imagined their bombs being released and wondered if she would be able to cope with the reality of war.

'Find her some warm clothes,' the captain ordered Gerry.

'Right, skip. Do you feel well enough to stand?' Gerry asked her gently.

'I think so.'

He took her arm, helped her to her feet. 'This way then. Steady now.'

'I'm really sorry, sir,' she called to the captain as Gerry led her from the cockpit.

The captain did not answer.

Gerry left her in the bowels of the plane for a few moments, then returned with a very creased and soiled boiler suit. She wrinkled her nose at the strong smell of oil as the garment was passed to her.

Gerry laughed. 'It's a bit big, but it will go over the rest of your clothes — coat and all. It gets pretty cold up here.'

As she struggled into the heavy suit, she realised she was shivering. 'Where's Webster?'

'Up front with his charts again. We need him to show us the way to our target.'

'What happens then, Gerry?'

'Could get a little scary, Marcia,' he replied, no longer laughing. 'They'll try to capture us in their searchlights and there's bound to be a lot of flack. Then we drop our load and head for home.'

'If we're lucky,' Marcia said, reading the look in his eyes.

'We always have been so far,' he told her, with a confidence that was not entirely felt. 'Now put this on.' He thrust a leather helmet into her hands. 'Found it spare. It will keep your sore head warm and you'll be able to hear what's going on through the earphones. Must dash, see you later.' He flung her a wry grin before disappearing in the direction of the cockpit.

She didn't take kindly to the hat. It felt tight and uncomfortable. Her head felt squashed and hot, and she wished now that she had less hair. But her annoyance with the helmet paled into insignificance as the hollow voice of the skipper suddenly erupted from the headphones:

142

'Message from leader. Six to ten bandits off starboard bow!'

'Get down on the floor, Marcia!' Webster's voice. 'Hang on for dear life!'

She grabbed hold of a metal handle and crouched low as the rear gunner's voice screamed, *'Dive, skipper! Bandits on our tail. Dive! Dive! Dive!'* The staccato sound of machine-gun fire reverberated throughout the plane. The Lancaster banked to one side, almost tearing her arms from their sockets. Then there was a terrifying sensation of falling, accompanied by a sound of screaming – she wasn't sure if it was herself or the engines. She clung relentlessly to the support as the gunfire continued.

The plane shuddered! Had they been hit? The engines roared as the skipper climbed steeply on full power. She thought the ordeal would never end as she registered the gunners shouting their urgent and demanding instructions to the skipper.

But finally it did end, and Webster came back to check that she was okay. 'Are you still in one piece, old girl?' He was visibly relieved as he helped her to her feet.

Fighting back the welling tears, Marcia merely nodded.

Conjuring up a thermos flask, Webster unscrewed the top and filled it with hot tea. 'Here, drink this.'

Marcia wrapped her hands around the metal cup as she gratefully sipped its contents. She was still cold in spite of the boiler suit and helmet, but the plane had levelled-out and the gunfire had abated. 'Are we going home now?'

'Not yet, darling. We're halfway between Bremen and Hannover, passing over a town called Diepholz. Just a few more minutes before we're over our target zone, then we can drop our load and head back.' He squeezed her arm. 'Don't worry, you're in safe hands. I'll be back soon.'

She closed her eyes and tried to shut out the terrible world around her. Her arms locked around the sturdy support as the plane bucked violently again, threatening to hurl her off balance. She just wanted to get away – away from the sheer hell of screeching whines and frantic voices. Even with her eyes tightly shut she could see flashes of glaring white light. She was frozen with fear.

Was that Gerry's voice? She tried hard to concentrate, listening intently as the plane lurched upward. *'Bombs away . . . bombs away!'* The excitement was evident in his voice as he shouted,

'Go, Go, Go, skip! Get the hell out of here!'

She ventured to open her eyes. Was it all over? She wanted to believe that the worst was behind them, but the frantic dialogue between the gunners and the skipper confirmed that they were not yet out of danger. The plane was shaking like a rag in the wind. Another brilliant flash erupted around her, followed by a moment of deathly silence. Then the calm voice of the skipper again: *'Flying at 19000 feet. A direct hit on port outer engine. We've lost a wing tip. Difficulty in holding her. Hang on, chaps.'*

Webster gave him their position: *'Hohenhausen directly beneath us. River Weser ahead to the north.'* Now the wounded plane was diving.

Then the captain's voice again. This time more urgent. *'Losing altitude; can't hold her. Order to crew: Bale out. I repeat, BALE OUT!'*

Webster was already out of his seat and stuffing items from his desk into the pockets of his flying suit as the pilot's final words came through the headphones: *'Good luck, chaps!'*

'Get off the deck, Marcy!' Webster grabbed her arm. Her body felt like lead; she wasn't sure if she could stand. He hauled her to her feet and shouted to Gerry. 'Here, give us a hand, mate.'

Gerry rushed over to them, relieved Webster of the length of webbing he was carrying, and hurriedly began tying the two of them together.

Marcia tried to break free as it dawned on her what was about to happen. 'I can't! I can't!' She was sobbing now, but she was already strapped securely to Webster. She was shouting hysterically as Gerry double-checked his knots before aiding their clumsy progress to the open fuselage aperture.

Noise, wind, blackness, fear! – it all happened with mind-boggling speed.

She screamed as they were flung out into the black nothingness. The cold, rushing wind tore at her face and numbed her fingers as she clung to Webster's shoulders with every last ounce of her strength. Unable to breathe, she was convinced they were both hurtling to their death. Then came a sharp crack of exploding silk and their terrifying dive to earth was slowed with a vicious yank. The parachute had opened; she found she could breathe!

'We'll make it now!' Webster shouted triumphantly.

Thank God, she thought, but the makeshift harness-strap felt as if it was cutting her in half. Some of the Lancasters were still visible as the parachute continued its descent. She was at the point where she felt she could stick it no longer when her feet touched down. Her body was jarred painfully as she and Webster landed on the hard soil of war-torn Germany.

g

Chapter Twenty

Marcia was still gasping for breath when Webster levered her to her feet. 'You okay, Marcy? How's the head?'

'All all right, I think.'

He produced a jack-knife from his pocket and proceeded to sever the straps which bound them both to the parachute. He lost no time in pulling in the collapsed canopy, then stood with it still bundled in his arms while he listened intently for any sounds of impending danger. 'We must get away from here as quickly as possible,' he whispered.

'Can you hear something?'

'No, but our chute might have been spotted. Come on, quickly.'

Marcia felt stiff all over, and her legs ached with every step she took as she trailed along behind Webster while he looked for somewhere to conceal the parachute. Suddenly he stopped and bent down to examine what looked like a large rabbit hole in the grassy bank beside them. 'This will do,' he said softly.

Taking one end of the chute, he began stuffing it into the hole. It was hard work, but with Marcia feeding the silk tidily through her hands to him it eventually disappeared. 'Now for our helmets,' he said.

Marcia had almost forgotten she was still wearing hers. She took it off and shook out her hair. It felt so good to be free from its constriction. Webster pushed both helmets well down into the hole, then with his hands and knife he rammed some earth on top of them and overlaid the hole with clumps of grass. 'There, that should do the trick,' he declared, satisfied that it would take some finding, even come daylight. He straightened up and stood once again quietly listening.

'Do you think Gerry or any of the crew could have landed near us,' Marcia whispered.

'No he whispered back.' He listened again. 'It's very quiet. We were first out of the plane; the old kite could have flown on for at least thirty miles before it crashed. It's possible the nearest bloke could be ten miles away from us.' He put his arms around her. 'I'm afraid we're on our own, my darling — just you and me.' He held her tightly for a few moments, then felt in his pocket for the compass and map reading torch he had grabbed from his desk. A quick glance at the compass showed him the route he had decided to take. He took her hand. 'I think the best plan for us is to try and head for the ports of northern Germany. As far as I can see, it could be our only means of escape. Let's go.'

Marcia was soon lagging behind. She felt as if they had been walking for miles, and had lost count of the many times she had stumbled over the rough and unfamiliar terrain.

Webster glanced over his shoulder. 'Getting tired old thing?' He waited for her to catch him up. 'We'll stop and rest for a few minutes,' he whispered. 'It should be okay; we're well away from where we landed.' On looking around, he noticed, just a few yards away, the dark silhouettes of several old trees. 'Over here,' he murmured.

Marcia sighed with relief as she lay back against the hard trunk. It was sheer bliss to sit for a while and rest her aching feet and legs. A reassuring silence enveloped them. She closed her heavy eyes as Webster took her hand in his own. They didn't speak, neither of them felt like talking. Then she started as Webster let go of her hand and stood up. Her heart started to pound. 'What is it?'

He quickly knelt down beside her, 'Nothing to worry about,' he assured her. 'But I think I can hear running water.'

'Is that good or bad?' There was a note of concern in her voice.

'It's good for us, my darling. It may be a stream, which could mean our salvation. Come on.' He helped her up, then stood quietly listening. She remained silent as he tried to pinpoint the location of the sound. She heard it for herself now, but it seemed to be coming from all around them.

At last he spoke. 'I think it's somewhere ahead of us, perhaps a little to our right.' He grasped her shoulders and turned her towards him, seeming excited. 'Marcy, are you able to go on? I can't judge how far away it is, but the sooner we find it the happier I'll be.'

Marcia couldn't imagine why the stream was so important to them, but she agreed to go on. She trusted him implicitly and his new-found enthusiasm had lifted her spirits; even her aching body felt much lighter now.

They couldn't believe how far they had to travel before they found it. The watery sound had seemed much closer when they had first heard it, but evidently the stillness of the night had magnified the sound greatly. Luckily it was still dark, although not for much longer. Already, shapes were beginning to take on their own identity. Webster picked up a stick and held it in the water to judge its depth. 'Good,' he said. 'Not too deep. Take your boots off, Marcy.' He sat down and began to remove his own flying boots. 'I'm sorry about this, old thing. I know it's going to be freezing but if they have dogs out searching for us, we have to lose our scent.'

'Is that why you were so pleased about the stream?' she whispered, as with some difficulty she prized off her boots and stuffed her socks into one of the many pockets of her boiler-suit.

'Partly,' he answered. He stood barefoot, his boots clenched securely under his arm. 'But the main reason, my darling, is that from this part of Germany the rivers run towards the North Sea. I think this little stream could meet with the River Weser. It could lead us to the port of Bremerhaven. If we can make it to there, we might have a chance.'

They waded downstream for almost an hour, although it seemed like eternity to Marcia. If she didn't step out of that icy water very soon, she was sure her feet would never recover their warmth. Daylight had arrived as they waded onwards, which at least made it easier for them to pick their way over the stream's stony bed.

Webster paused and pointed a finger at a road bridge spanning the river some sixty yards ahead. She followed him as he hurried to reach the cover of its moss-encrusted stone arch.

Once there, he again stopped to listen. Nothing. Satisfied that all was quiet, he whispered to her that he was going to venture up onto the bridge. 'No, you stay here,' he said, as she moved to follow. 'I'll only be a few minutes.' Then, recognising the flash of panic in her eyes, he explained, 'You see, they will only be looking for one. They won't know a Land Army girl has dropped in uninvited, will they? I'll walk just a few yards along the bridge, then retrace my steps back to you. If they do have sniffer dogs out searching, they'll think that someone has stopped and given me a lift. It will give us a little more time, hopefully.' He slipped away before she could protest.

She shivered from head to toe and her teeth chattered uncontrollably with the cold water swirling round her feet, and the fear of Webster being seen. What would she do if he was caught? She waited, straining her ears to listen. Where was he? Fear gripped her. She dithered for several long moments, wondering whether to go looking for him. But he had told her to wait there. Then an almost overwhelming surge of relief flooded over her as she saw him scramble down the bank towards her. He smiled, indicating that all was well, then beckoned her to follow him.

Bending low, they passed under the bridge. He pointed again, this time to where some overhanging branches dipped into the flowing water. 'We'll get out by those branches.'

She lip-read the words he mouthed, relieved to know that this freezing ordeal was almost over.

Webster clambered out first, then lent her a hand as she pulled against the tree. The bark bit into her hands as with grim determination she struggled to scale the vertical bank. She bit down on her bottom lip to stop herself from crying out, determined not to be a burden to Webster. She had landed him in more than enough trouble already. One final heave and she was on dry ground. The cool grass was sheer heaven.

A tree-lined path led them away from the stream, until Webster's vigilant gaze homed in on a particularly thick patch of vegetation. 'Perfect,' he breathed. 'Come on, old thing – time we were holed up for a while. We're sitting ducks out here in the daylight.' He found what he was looking for and drew her down to sit beside him. 'Now, my darling,' he said. 'I'm afraid we're in for a long wait.'

Chapter Twenty-one

William growled and lifted sleepy lids to warn his master that someone was coming.

'Marcy?' Reuben pushed back his chair and crossed to the door, breakfast forgotten in his excitement. ' 'Bout time too,' he snapped to the others, not wanting to appear too happy in front of them.

Norman winked across at Ruby. They were both only too well aware of his true feelings. Late last night they had received word from the camp of Marcia's extraordinary escapade, after an early message had been relayed from Webster's plane. Reuben was dumbstruck. He had remained seated in his chair with his eyes closed. Not asleep, but just to warn them he wanted to be left alone with his thoughts. Later, he and William went out. The Falcon was the only place to drown his sorrows. But now, perhaps, the agony was nearly over.

Ruby swiftly stacked the dirty dishes to one side of the table before dashing over to the stove to heat the kettle. She couldn't wait to sit down with a nice hot cuppa and listen to Marcia's account of her adventure. None of them could figure out what had possessed her to go and do such a thing. 'Boss is taking his time,' she remarked as she took down another mug for her returning friend.

They both looked up expectantly as the kitchen door was slowly opened, only to see Reuben entering alone. His face was ashen. He looked twenty years older – a pitiful, shrunken old man.

'What's up, boss? Where's Marcy?' Norman and Ruby were both talking at the same time. 'What's the matter?'

'She's bin shot down!'

It was as if Tolcarne Merock had suddenly been draped in a deathly shroud. 'Oh no!' Ruby gasped. 'How? Where is she? Is she all right?'

Reuben struggled to speak. He uttered the words with obvious difficulty. 'Two of 'em from the camp this time. Knew as soon as I clamped eyes on 'em 'twas bad news.' He pulled a soiled rag from his pocket and wiped his eyes. 'They said the One and All was shot down somewhere over Germany.'

The kettle had started to boil, splattering and frizzing beside him. He seemed not to notice.

Norman took it off the heat and asked Ruby to make some tea. 'Sweet and strong,' he said to her, with a meaningful nod in Reuben's direction. He brought over a chair and sat beside his boss. 'What else do we know?'

'Six others were lost as well. They 'ad a bad night of it . . . there is one thing though . . . ' Reuben sat up straight and stared at Norman, his sad eyes suddenly looking more hopeful. 'They officials said that one of the kites that made it back reported seeing some of the crew baling out. Only trouble is . . . ' The old farmer's eyes misted over again. 'They might take 'er prisoner . . . '

Ruby gently placed the mug of hot tea into his trembling hands. Controlling her own painful emotions, she gave him a confident smile. 'I'm sure they'll make it back, boss. Webster will look after her.'

Reuben nodded slowly, grateful for her reassuring words. 'Aye,' he said, 'if the lad 'imself be alright.'

He tried to smile, but his heart was too heavy.

Chapter Twenty-two

Webster peeked out from their hiding place, careful not to awake Marcia who was sleeping fitfully. They had agreed to have two hours' rest each, then two hours' watch throughout the hours of daylight. Then, when it became dark, they would be able to move onward, reasonably refreshed. He had insisted on taking the first watch himself. He yawned. His eyes felt heavy; all he wanted to do was join her in oblivion, but he was on guard and their safety depended on him. He glanced at his watch, remembering that Germany was an hour ahead of English time, he advanced the hands to local time. He prided himself on his good vantage point. He was also grateful for the fact that, unlike England, here there were no hedges to impede his view. A sudden movement away in the distance caught his eye. He squinted, straining to see, then chuckled softly to himself. Some six hundred yards away, three cyclists were peddling furiously along what had to be a road. 'Thank you,' he said under his breath. 'Now I know where it is.' It was easy to see how he had missed it before. It was masked by the trees and greenery on either side. He rubbed his tired eyes, willing them to remain open as he forced his mind to focus on planning a viable escape route.

Marcia stirred; something had roused her. She smiled sleepily, thinking she was back at the farm and listening to Norman working with the tractor in one of the fields. Then her eyes snapped open as realisation dawned. She knew that it could not be. She saw that Webster had moved some five or six yards away from her, and was seemingly intent on watching something not too far from their temporary hideout. Exercising extreme caution, she moved to join him. 'What is it, darling?'

He pointed towards the sun.

As her eyes gradually focused she saw a tractor chugging along with a trailer-load of women, all of them wearing brightly coloured headscarves. She thought they looked strange; they seemed to be riding high. Then she noticed several galvanised buckets. She smiled to herself, as she whispered in Webster's ear. 'They're going to plant potatoes.'

They watched as the tractor chugged and spluttered along the road before turning into a field which, by the look of its tender green hue, would soon yield a mass of golden corn. The women alighted nimbly from the trailer as the tractor slowed to a halt, already pulling out the sacks of seed potatoes that had served them as seats. 'Perhaps we can pinch some out of the earth when it's dark,' Marcia ventured. She was beginning to feel hungry.

'I suppose a raw spud is better than nothing,' Webster replied ruefully. 'But won't they be green, unfit for eating?'

'That's not always the case,' she told him. 'They won't be green if they have been kept in the dark, in which case it should be okay to eat them.'

'I see. It's lucky for me that I have a knowledgeable army girl by my side, isn't it?' Webster said smilingly. 'How do you feel now?'

'Much better. Why don't you grab a little sleep for yourself now.'

It wasn't a question; it was an honest suggestion, and he did not need twice telling. As soon as she had assured him that she was able to manage for an hour or so, he had crawled over to the spot where she had lain, and was asleep in an instant.

Marcia settled down to watch the toiling women going about their business. She couldn't see exactly what they were doing; the distance was too great. But she nevertheless knew every move they would make. She thought back to gruff old Reuben and how well he had taught her. A lump built in her throat as she clearly heard his instructions: 'See, maid, 'tiz like this. The spacing must be right. One spud at the heel and t'other at the toe of yer boot. Carry on like that, an we be sure to 'ave a good crop.' She certainly knew now just how much she missed him and the others back home at the farm.

The sun was stronger now, causing Webster to squint as he finally opened his eyes. 'Any activity old thing?' His voice sounded gruff with sleep.

'Nothing except for the potato planters still hard at it,' she answered, pleased to see him awake. The time had dragged and she felt lonely. She also felt uncomfortable. She was bursting to use the toilet and didn't know what to do. Embarrassed, she reluctantly told Webster of her plight.

He took the jack-knife from his pocket and opened the blade, trying hard to suppress a smile. He knew how difficult this was going to be for her, but he couldn't help but see a funny side to it; she looked so serious. 'I'm afraid we will have to rough it out here, old thing. We daren't leave any trace of our being here so we have three things to remember. One, find a suitable spot. Two . . . ' he held up the knife, 'dig a little hole. And three, cover it in afterwards.' He grinned. 'Oh, and by the way. A few large leaves will come in handy for your own use.'

Her cheeks scarlet, she held out her hand for the knife. But he told her to hold on for just a minute or two more while he ventured out first to check whether the coast was clear. 'Won't be long,' he told her, before he vanished silently behind a thick screen of bushes.

Each minute he was gone seemed to her like five. She was just thinking to herself that she wouldn't be able to hold on any longer, when he returned. 'Phew, that's better,' he said. 'It's all clear. There's an ideal spot if you go a little way to your left.'

She grabbed the knife and was gone in a second.

Webster felt for her. It wasn't really funny. He thought about the boiler suit she was wearing. It wasn't the easiest of garments to remove, especially if you were in a hurry.

After what seemed an age, Marcia came back smiling, so he felt sure that everything had gone according to plan as she handed him back the knife.

They were both greatly relieved when darkness finally fell. Each hour had slowly dragged by and neither of them had felt like sleeping any more. Luckily for them the weather had remained dry. So apart from the discomfort of the early evening dampness, they were thankful that things were no worse. They were both very hungry. They had shared a solitary bar of chocolate earlier, but that was all they had. There was nothing else. But thirst was the more pressing problem.

The road had remained relatively quiet, with little activity to interest them, apart from the tractor with its trailer-load of women returning homewards after their hard toil of the day. Satisfied that the coast was clear, they emerged at last from their hiding place and hurried back to the stream, where Marcia drank greedily, scooping the cold, clear water up with her hands. Afterwards, her thirst quenched, she rinsed her face and wiped it dry on the sleeves of her boiler suit.

'Are you ready?' Webster voiced the question softly as he reached for her cold hand.

'Ready?'

'For the spud field,' he elaborated.

'Yes please,' she whispered eagerly.

From their hideout, Webster had earlier plotted the exact position of the potato field. Now he led her by the hand as they moved stealthily through the damp undergrowth. Every now and then he would stop to listen for any unusual sounds, making sure they were in the shadows. The night wasn't as dark as he would have wished, but the area was apparently deserted, and he had plotted well. It wasn't long before Marcia detected the sweet smell of freshly turned earth. Almost running now, she hurried till her boots sank into the spongy earth carpet of the potato field. She bent down and plunged her fingers into the soil.

'I've found one!' Gleefully, she passed the small potato back to Webster before resuming her frenzied digging along the row. They soon filled their pockets. Then, feeling guilty, they scurried back in the direction of the stream.

Marcia said, 'When they don't come up, the poor old farmer will think that the rabbits have taken them.' They emptied the potatoes out on the bank then washed them one by one in the flowing water. She asked Webster for his knife, then cut one in half. She sniffed it and breathed a sigh of relief. Yes, they could eat them. If they had been green and inedible her nose would have told her so.

They ate a couple of them each, then put the rest back into their pockets to nibble on later. Marcia hadn't enjoyed them at all, but she forced them down. At least they served to fill her stomach and give her strength to carry on. Her nobbly filled pockets bounced heavily on her thighs as she followed Webster northwards along the banks of the stream.

They made good progress. The moon kindly showed them that it was on their side by appearing every so often, just long enough to reveal the countryside around them. Webster stopped and used his torch to check the time. They couldn't believe they had been tramping for four hours. The moon once again lit up the area around them, and pointed out a large farmhouse situated a little way ahead of them. 'I'm glad we noticed that,' Webster hissed. 'We were heading straight for it.' He drew her close, facing her so she would hear his low whispering. He needed to explain. He told her that most German farmhouses held family and livestock under the same roof. People one end and animals the other. 'We have to be careful,' he said, 'or the animals could pick up our scent and cause a rumpus. There's only a slight breeze but we'll play it safe and skirt round the leeward side of the building.' He looked up to test the wind direction. 'Yes,' he said, 'just as I thought. I'm afraid it's the long way round for us, old girl.' He kissed her cold face. 'Come on, the quicker we can get back to the stream the happier I'll be. And remember, we have to move with the utmost caution.'

Webster cursed his heavy flying boots. They were not at all suitable for cross-country hiking. But despite his aching feet, they made it safely back to the stream and for that he was grateful. Daylight was fast approaching and their immediate concern was to find another suitable hiding place. Luckily, it wasn't too difficult. The thickly-covered banks around them looked promising and soon Webster beckoned for Marcia to join him. It looked perfect and not too far away from the water if they should get really thirsty.

The first thing he did was to sit down and take off his boots. Marcia knelt down and removed his damp socks, then started to gently massage his feet. He closed his eyes; the sensation felt wonderful.

'Shall we have breakfast now?'

Marcia was putting his socks back on when he opened his eyes. He must have dozed off while she was rubbing his feet. He wriggled his toes; they certainly felt better now. She handed him one of her potatoes. It didn't look so appetising in the daylight, but there was nothing else. She had not complained but he knew she must be terribly hungry. His own stomach had started to rattle like the plumbing on a faulty boiler.

Webster again chose to do the first watch. Marcia had found a fairly comfortable spot to lie down and was already curled up on one side and sleeping like a baby. The responsibility of her safety rested heavily on his shoulders. Heaven only knew what dangers they had yet to face. He wondered if perhaps it might be better after all if they gave themselves up to the Germans. Then the dreadful realisation of what might happen to her if they did, decided him. No matter what, they had to go on! He scrutinised the crumpled map which he had stuffed into his pocket along with the other items from the plane. He wasn't exactly sure of their present position, but working from his last report to the pilot he reckoned they were fairly close to the River Weser. That, he decided, would be their immediate destination. From there they would have to play it by ear.

During Marcia's first watch she happened to notice a beech tree close by. It was a young tree bearing fresh and tender leaves. Her mouth started to water. She recalled eating them as a child. The memory made her feel hungrier than ever and she instinctively edged towards this possible source of food. She looked over to Webster . . . fast asleep. But he wouldn't want her to take any chances. She paused, trying to resist the temptation, then her eyes swept back to the tree. It was no good; her hunger was too strong. Crossing to the tree, she plucked frantically at the tender leaves, glancing around furtively as she did so. With her hands and mouth stuffed full, and her heart pounding fit to burst she raced back to the hideaway. Later, when he awoke, she presented Webster with her special dish of the day. She received a gentle ticking off for leaving her post, but he had to admit they were nice for a change, and he could see by the green hue of her lips that she had enjoyed them as well.

That night as they walked on Webster was pleased to see the stream had become much wider. It was a good sign that his calculations could be right. He was worried though. Both of them were tiring much quicker now through lack of food. He knew he had to find something for them soon. Marcia bumped into him. Walking with her head down, she hadn't realised he had stopped. He raised a finger to his lips and stood stock still, staring into the gloom ahead. 'I think it's okay,' he whispered eventually. 'As far as I can make out, it's just a sluice gate . . . at first I thought there was someone standing there.'

The gate was directly opposite, on the other side of the river. They could see that it controlled a broad water channel which flowed away from the river and somewhere to the right of them. Webster was curious. He told Marcia to wait while he went to check it out.

After wading across the fast-flowing water he was able to see that the man-made channel led to a rather large building. He decided to move on and get a better look. The first thing he noticed was the huge water-wheel, now lying still on the nearside wall. His spirits lifted with the possibility of food in the shape of crushed corn waiting inside. He smiled to himself, feeling that his hunch had proved right. He advanced stealthily, looking for a way inside. There was no sign of a farmhouse so he reasoned that thankfully it was situated some fair distance away from the mill. He moved nearer and found the door. He turned towards it then froze as the low growl of a dog broke the silence. It was directly in front of him, barring his way.

Careful not to alarm the snarling mongrel, he slowly dropped to one knee and spoke gently to it, hoping fervently that his training with bad-tempered beasts as a vet would stand him in good stead here. He spoke soothingly to the animal until gradually the deep throaty growl faded and he noticed the first flick of the mongrel's tail. He was winning. He continued talking softly as his hand moved slowly forward to touch the dog's head. The tail moved faster now, and the vet knew that the bond between them was almost complete. He straightened up slowly and held out his hand for the dog to lick. When he obliged he knew he was safe from him and that their friendship had been sealed. He hurried to the door of the mill, regretting the time spent in gaining the mongrel's confidence. He was worried about Marcia, thinking how she would go crazy if he didn't get back there soon. Now to see if the door was locked. It wasn't; it was slightly ajar. He grinned at the thought that these German farmers were just like their English counterparts as he noticed a missing hinge. He prized the door open, just enough to enable him to squeeze inside. A quick movement down by his feet told him that his newfound friend had joined him. He closed his eyes for a moment as the blackness hit him. It wasn't much better when he opened them. But he now detected the unmistakable aroma of freshly crushed cereal. There had to be some in here somewhere. He moved slowly, feeling his way between unfamiliar objects which threatened to trip him up. His outstretched hand encountered several wooden items, then his fingers touched sacking cloth. Excited now, he was soon able to distinguish the silhouettes of several full sacks. He would need his jack-knife to cut the string which tied the top. He opened out the blade, then a terrific crash coming from somewhere close by made him jump with fright making him drop the knife. Something raced by his feet.

'That bloody dog,' he muttered crossly, guessing that it was after a rat. He crouched down and gingerly felt around the floor for the knife. He was sweating now, knowing that he was wasting precious minutes; the damned knife could have landed anywhere. His fingers touched hessian — an empty sack. He decided to take it to carry the cereal — if only he could find the bloody knife! Then something clattered to the hard floor as he picked up the sack and relief coursed through his whole body as he located the object and his fingers closed around the handle of his knife. He lost no time in cutting the sack's thick cord. His fingers sifted through the soft floury grain, then he tasted some. 'Perfect.' he breathed. He ran his hands quickly down over the spare sack, then, satisfied it was sound, opened the top and began filling it as fast as he could. After scooping up countless handfuls, he tested its weight. 'That should do us,' he muttered to himself, realising that if he filled it any more he would have difficulty in carrying it.

As he neared the door, his boot slipped awkwardly on something lying beneath it. Cursing, he bent down and picked up the offending article. It was a large enamel mug. His fingers encountered several rough patches, signifying that it had seen better days and probably had been discarded long ago. He shoved it into his pocket, thinking how handy it could be if it was still serviceable to hold liquid. He squeezed his body back through the gap and stood for a moment, listening to the night. Everything seemed quietly normal.

Even the mongrel had left him for something more challenging. Gripping the sack firmly, he hurried back to Marcia.

He found her in a terrible state. She had been worried sick. When he hadn't returned after a few minutes, she had started to imagine him being in trouble. Her mind went berserk with one horrible thought after another until she firmly believed that she would be left out here on her own to fend for herself. When he had finally come back she was in a pitiful state. Crying and

159

trembling so much, that for a little while she couldn't even swallow the food he had brought her. He had cuddled her tightly, quietly explaining what had happened, until her fears had eventually subsided. Then, with her pocket filled with grain, enabling her to nibble on the way, they set off once more to follow the stream. Webster was anxious to make good use of the remaining hours of darkness. By his makeshift reckoning, they had covered four or five miles that night.

They sat now in their hideout for the day. It had been harder to find a suitable spot this time. It seemed that the countryside was changing and the thick areas of undergrowth which had served them well would soon be a thing of the past. They had noticed before diving under cover the glint of a large amount of water, far away in the distance. As soon as they had settled down, Webster told her that he believed it to be the River Weser. He studied the map now resting on his thigh, and Marcia smiled to herself as she watched the frown of concentration pucker up his forehead. He looked so different now. The neat moustache had changed into an unruly tuft, and already his beard had grown long enough to catch a few of the grains which had escaped his lips.

He looked up, sensing her watching him. He rubbed his chin as if reading her thoughts, then reached down between them for the enamel mug. He took a long sip and felt glad he had brought it back. A good wash in the stream had revealed a battered and worn monstrosity, but it did hold water, and for that they were really grateful. Returning his attention to the map, he said, 'With any luck we should reach the Weser before daybreak tomorrow.'

Chapter Twenty-three

Several days had now passed since they had reached the River Weser as Webster had predicted. Arriving at dawn after a gruelling non-stop trek, they had stood together staring at the vast river before them, hardly daring to believe that they had actually made it. Webster had grasped her to him, forgetting in their excitement that they stood out like sitting ducks in the new light of morning. Suddenly, a dull throbbing sound had alerted them of their precarious position and with safety now uppermost in their minds they ran for cover to a patch of tall reeds.

They threw themselves down on to the spongy damp surface of the reed bed. Trembling from head to toe, and hardly daring to breathe they listened as the sound grew louder until it appeared to be not more than a few feet away from them. Marcia had been so frightened. Her heart was in her boots as she waited for the inevitable discovery. Then, to her amazement, she realised that the sound was diminishing. Whatever it was seemed to be moving away from them. When they had raised their heads to look they had seen the tail-end of a laden barge receding from view. They had waited until the gentle thrumming of its engine had faded into the distance before stealthily crawling out of the reeds, and had then continued on their way until they reached a small pine forest which would serve as their cover for the day. The thick, dark, feathery branches hung down around them like heavy curtains which made them feel safe from the very real dangers of the outside world. They lay in each other's arms, happy to be together, yet dreading the thought of another long day of endless waiting.

The following night Webster had acquired a new pair of boots. They had holed up for the day quite close to the Weser in a

161

ramshackle hut. The roof had long gone and some of the walls were crumbling away. By the looks of the sturdy vegetation growing up and around it, no human had ventured inside for a very long time. There was a door of sorts, faded, peeling and shrunken from its frame by the weather and the passage of time and never to be opened by the looks of the long green grass which had fastened itself along the bottom. It hugged the door tightly like a long lost friend, holding it in a vicelike grip. They clambered inside through an opening which once could have held a window overlooking the river.

Picking their way through rubble and crude tufts of grass, they came across some rusty corrugated sheeting which had dropped down from the roof. Webster prized them from the tangled undergrowth and carried them over to the door. Using the door as a backrest, he placed the rusty sheets around them. If prying eyes did look inside, he felt confident now that they wouldn't be seen.

Several times throughout the day they had heard the now familiar thrumming sound of the barges as they glided past on the water. It made them realise that the river was a very busy and industrious place. That same evening, just before dusk, they had heard voices. With hearts beating uncomfortably fast they had peered through a crack in the door to see a group of young men and women outside. They looked to be part of some organisation or youth movement, as without exception all were attired in a special sort of uniform. Laughing and chattering excitedly together, they had all sat down and removed their boots. Then, with even more boisterous shrieking, they all stood up and started to take off their uniforms. 'They're going in for a dip.' Webster hissed.

Marcia had been almost too afraid to look, but she had no need to worry, they were all wearing swimsuits underneath. One by one, with war-cry shrieks, they dived into the cold, fast-flowing water, leaving their clothes scattered in unruly heaps at the river's edge. After some minutes it became apparent that they were playing a game with the river. After diving in, the current would swiftly carry them downstream where, at some point, they would leave the water and race back along the bank, whereupon the whole procedure would be noisily repeated. Webster was waiting for them to return for the second time when he noticed the boots. Although the light was fading fast, they were close enough for him to see that they were roughly his own size. Flying boots weren't made for cross-country tramping and his poor feet had become extremely painful. He made up his mind. If and when they next jumped in, he would dash out and help himself.

He was lucky, they were clearly in no hurry to abandon their shared fun. Once the coast was clear it had only been a matter of a few seconds before Webster stood proudly clutching the stolen boots. Then he and Marcia stealthily retreated around the back of the shack to make their silent getaway.

They had travelled a fair distance before Webster had dared to stop and try them on. His calculating eye had served him well. Much to Marcia's surprise, they had fitted him like a glove. A little later, the old flying boots had been filled with stones then dropped without conscience into the dark depths of the mighty River Weser.

At one point in their journey they had left the main river to skirt along the boundaries of the town of Minden. Webster knew it contained several military barracks and they needed to be extra vigilant. The night had not been without its perils. At one stage while walking close to a road, they had to dive on their bellies to avoid discovery. Night flyers and the distant booming of heavy artillery had disguised the sound of heavy transport approaching until it was almost upon them. They had lain rigid, hardly daring to breathe when the ground beneath them trembled as a convoy of military trucks drove by. The last truck had been well out of sight before either of them had dared to move.

On wobbly legs they had forced their bodies onwards. Still with the feeling of disbelief that somehow nobody had spotted them. They had eventually rejoined the river and managed to hide up for the day in an old disused boat-house. Since then, one day had blended into the next as they had continued their hazardous nocturnal journey along the banks of the River Weser.

Chapter Twenty-four

Webster gave his jaw a good old scratching. His beard had grown considerably over the last few days and at times the itching got on his nerves. He glanced down to see that Marcia was still fast asleep. It really worried him to see her looking so pale and thin, and he hoped that his latest plan would work. It had to, he thought grimly, if he wanted to get her safely home.

His plan involved the barges which he had been tirelessly observing throughout the day. Last night, by a strange quirk of fate, something had happened to them which had sown the seeds of his latest plan. It must have been in the early hours of the morning because it was still extremely dark when he had heard something. He had stopped and touched Marcia's arm, warning her to stay put while he slithered forward a little way to check it out. At first he couldn't quite make out what was going on. He had recognised the long dark shape of a barge in the water, but for the moment the reason for the clamour and the sound of voices had eluded him. Suddenly, however, a movement at the waters edge gave him the answer. He had stumbled on to a bunker stop. The barge in the water had tied up to refuel.

His plan had already started to form in his mind as he crept back to her. They had retraced their steps for a few yards, then branched away from the river to seek some sort of cover for the long hours of daylight. They had indeed chosen the right path. A distressed burnt-out ruin of what appeared once to have been a large thatched house now welcomed them. They moved with hurried caution to a safe position inside.

The first light of day had shown Webster had made a good choice. They were roughly a quarter of a mile away from the river, but because of the flatness of the land between, he could see the river and the bunker most clearly. He had spent most of the day watching and planning, afraid to sleep in case he missed something of importance. His eyes were stinging but he refused to give in. As soon as Marcia was awake he would tell her what he had planned.

Marcia could hear the waves gently lapping on the shore. She stretched out her limbs, savouring the moment. It was so peaceful here . . . and yet something told her that it was too peaceful. Something was wrong. She could hear no seagulls' cries, no roar of breakers as they pummelled the cliffs further out to sea. She opened her eyes and her heart sank; it was just another dream. She wasn't back home, there was no familiar beach. Somewhere nearby, the soothing ripples of the Weser seemed to be mocking her.

'You awake, Marcy?'

She propped herself up on one elbow to look at him. 'I dreamt I was back home.' She couldn't go on, knowing that the tears weren't far away.

Webster could see that she was at a low ebb and was thankful he now had something positive to tell her. He knelt down beside her and with his hand under her chin raised her face so that she could look into his eyes. 'We've done okay so far, haven't we?'

She slowly blinked her eyes in agreement, still afraid she would make a fool of herself by speaking. He sat down beside her and drew her closer as he outlined his latest plan. Throughout his daylight watch, he told her, he had vigilantly observed the comings and goings of the barges on the river. Several of them had stopped to refuel at the bunker, and he had learnt that they received their fuel by means of a hand-pump. He had timed them and the barges had been there for twenty or thirty minutes before resuming their journey down-river. He had also noticed some of the barges had been towing one or two others. His guess was that the towed barges were carrying cargo of some sort because they were low in the water and securely covered with heavy tarpaulin. It was these that had taken his interest. He explained to her how the overall length of three barges together would be considerable, and how the last one being towed would be quite a distance away from the activities of the fuelling bunker. 'We could easily slip into that one without being seen,' he told her excitedly.

Marcia still said nothing as her mouth exhibited a nervous

165

twitch.

Taking out his well-worn map, Webster laid it before them and traced his finger along the river. He said, 'I have a gut feeling these cargo boats are heading for Bremerhaven. And if that's so, my darling, we stand a very good chance of reaching the North Sea . . . and we will be doing it in style!'

Marcia was visibly more cheerful as they shared the last of the cereal — a meagre handful each while they waited for nightfall. It seemed to take a long time in coming and they were both painfully aware that with summer fast approaching the days would soon be even longer. Webster was grateful the moon had been trapped above a thick blanket of cloud. They had been forced into their position of dubious cover by his meticulous study of where the third barge would lie in the water. This precise spot would enable them to quickly jump aboard if and when the chance arose.

Marcia was feeling stiff and cold, missing the old boiler-suit which had been disposed of somewhere along the way. It had been an encumbrance to her then, but now its warmth would have been a great comfort.

Their excitement started to build as they detected the faint engine-note of an oncoming barge. The sound steadily grew, until with a soft vibration of the ground beneath them the barge sailed on by. It didn't stop!

'Never mind, Marcy.' Webster spoke softly. 'It wouldn't have helped us if it did stop; it wasn't towing anything.' He knew her disappointment matched his own, so he tried to force a note of cheerfulness into his voice when he told her not to worry. He was sure that one which suited their needs would come along soon.

Now it seemed a lifetime ago since they had seen the last barge. Never before had she felt such cold and discomfort. Several times her hopes had been dashed. What she had thought was the sound of river traffic had turned out to be nothing more than the muffled rumblings of distant bombing. She felt that perhaps she could take no more.

She was on the brink of giving in and telling Webster she'd had enough when once again a pulsating drone reached her ears. Webster had heard it too. He gripped her hand tightly. 'Keep your fingers crossed, Marcy, we could be in luck this time!'

With hearts beating overtime they watched until the purring

166

shadow of a barge drew alongside them. And it was towing another!

Marcia held her breath, hoping and praying that a third one would be following along behind.

Suddenly, Webster's body stiffened, 'Get down quick! Stay quiet,' he whispered urgently. His trained eye had warned him that the second barge was carrying human cargo. Their shadowy outlines had revealed them to be German troops. He felt sick with fear as he realised the barges were slowing down. If the soldiers did get off to stretch their legs, they would be discovered in no time at all. He had to think of something and fast. He swiftly realised that there was nothing else for it but to retreat to the hideout they had been so pleased to abandon just a few hours ago. Warily, he lifted his head to look for any moving shadows. Nothing had changed; he felt safe for the moment. Rising to a crouching position, he quickly explained to Marcia why they had to go back.

He took hold of her hand to pull her up, then gripping it firmly almost dragged her unwilling body behind him until they reached the comparative safety of the ruin. All they could do now, was wait throughout another long day and try their luck again.

The moon decided to shine brightly that night. Webster would have been in two minds whether to chance their riverside wait if it wasn't for Marcia. Eating nothing whatsoever that day had seriously sapped her strength. He knew something had to be done quickly or she could become ill. On their way back to the river he had collected an assortment of leafy twigs and ferns which he had used to camouflage their bodies. It wasn't perfect by any means, but there was nothing else – it had to do.

As yet only one single barge had used the fuelling facility and he was getting really worried in case they ended up having to spend another long day in the old ruin. Beside him the branches rustled as Marcia shifted her position. Something was happening. Webster opened his eyes and cursed, he must have dozed off. Noises along the river led him to peer cautiously through his leafy camouflage. He rubbed his eyes, not quite believing what he was seeing. He called quietly to Marcia, telling her to have a look.

There, before them, gently swaying in the current, rested a cargo-laden barge. He knew by his earlier reckoning that this one must be the second one being towed by the mother barge.

'Can we sneak aboard that one?' Marcia whispered with renewed excitement, feeling her body slowly regaining its strength with the gratifying knowledge of fresh hope.

'I think so,' Webster murmured, knowing it wouldn't be easy with the adjacent countryside lit up like day. He decided they would wait and watch for a little while, then, if they saw nobody, they would crawl all the way to the barge. He explained to her that the cargo was covered by a stout tarpaulin which was securely fastened by hemp rope to large cleats situated around the lip of the craft. His plan was to untie the rope at the point nearest to them and then to slip quickly under the tarpaulin. Hopefully, he would be able to re-tie the rope afterwards so as not to arouse suspicion. The nagging worry of the moon's brilliance took the edge off his excitement, but he knew if there was a chance then he had to take it whatever the consequences; they couldn't go on like this for much longer. He lifted the branch a little to give Marcia a reassuring kiss, then hating the thought of dampening her spirits told her what to do if they were to get caught. 'Just tell the truth,' he told her softly. 'You are still wearing your Land Army uniform so that will bear you out. But we're going to make it, aren't we, Marcy? I reckon we will soon be in Bremerhaven.'

'And what then?'

'Then, my love, the North Sea will be the only thing between us and England.'

They had waited long enough. No one had been near the barge and Webster was assuming that if there was any activity it was happening up by the fuelling bunker. He gestured for Marcia to follow him.

Feeling naked in the moonlight, they slithered forward towards the river. Even the rustling sigh of the springy undergrowth as their bodies moved to flatten it, sounded terrifyingly loud in their ears.

By the time they had reached the river, Webster's eyes were stinging madly with the sweat from his brow. The fuelling bunker was a good distance away, and as he had suspected earlier the mother barge was indeed towing two more fully-laden barges. He listened carefully as the faint murmur of disjointed voices reached his ears. Wiping the sweat from his eyes, he tried to focus on the scene up ahead of them. He noticed movement, but it was too far away to be easily distinguished. He was grateful for that, knowing that it would work both ways. If they were careful they wouldn't be seen. Frantic now to get aboard, he swiftly moved forward holding his jack-knife at the ready in case there were any problems with the rope. He stretched out his hand to grab the barge but his fingertips merely brushed along the side; it was just out of reach. Cursing under his breath, he glanced fearfully towards the mother barge, knowing that if they stayed there much longer someone would be sure to see them. With a heavy heart he was about to tell Marcia they would have to return to their hideout, when a thud made him look towards the river. He couldn't believe his eyes; the barge had swayed in the current and now stood closer to them. Without wasting a second, he hauled himself up onto the deck and untied the rope nearest to him. He extended a hand to Marcia and hauled her roughly aboard. They ducked under the loosened tarpaulin and pulled it to behind them. Within seconds the rope had been tied back securely round the cleat. They had made it!

h

Chapter Twenty-five

Now safely concealed by the tarpaulin, Webster and Marcia were able to crawl along a narrow gap between the cargo and the port side of the dark hold. On reaching the stern of the vessel, their outstretched arms told them there was much more room there. They sat down gladly and snuggled together in the claustrophobic darkness to wait for the barge to resume its journey. They didn't have long to wait. Some twenty-five minutes later the gentle lapping of the water changed to a more regular whooshing sound as their barge was towed smoothly along in the frothy wake of its leaders.

As soon as he was sure they were safely on their way, Webster took out the map-reading torch from his pocket and told Marcia he wanted a better look at the cargo. 'I'm just going to scout around those crates nearest to us,' he told her. 'It will be interesting to know what's keeping us company.'

Moments later she could see nothing but the faint circle of light from his torch as it flitted over what appeared to be large wooden containers. It wasn't long before the small disc of light vanished and Webster came shuffling back to her.

'Good news, Marcy!' he exclaimed, giving her a delighted squeeze. 'Are you still hungry?'

'Of course I am.'

'Well my darling it looks as if we're surrounded by crates of food. The couple I checked are full of canned bully beef.'

'That's wonderful!'

'Not only that,' he went on excitedly. 'I saw from the markings on the crates that they're bound for Bremerhaven, possibly to be loaded onto German warships. That confirms our port of destination. So all we have to do now is sit back and relax, and

170

hopefully catch up on our sleep before the next stage of our journey. Sound good to you, my darling?'

'Yes,' she whispered, nestling closer to him. 'Do you think we could try and get some of that bully beef now!'

'So you *are* peckish,' he laughed. 'Come on then, lend me a hand.'

She guided the torch light over the crate while Webster studied its surface for a means of easy entry with his jackknife. 'Hold it right there, Marcy,' he said, spotting a promising gap near the top of the crate. The blade of the knife slipped inside and he worked the handle to try and loosen the stout wooden lid. He began to sweat as the knife seemed to be making little headway, then it gave with a crack of splitting wood. The knife was quickly returned to his pocket, then with his hands he tried to force the gap even wider.

Marcia watched and waited with baited breath as she heard him gasping with exertion as he struggled feverishly with the stubborn crate. Suddenly the wood splintered and screeched as if knowing its battle was lost when Webster, with one almighty heave, prized the top from its bottom to reveal its contents. He reached inside and withdrew a tin which he handed to Marcia. 'Right then, my girl,' he said, replacing the lid carefully, 'let's go back and sit down to a decent meal. That's if I can get it out of the tin,' he added ruefully.

The point of his knife-blade pierced the thin tin with ease, and soon a jagged line appeared around the can, releasing the delicious aroma of the tender meat hiding inside. After carefully pulling back the razor-edged lid, he cut out a generous chunk of bully beef and dropped it into her waiting palm. 'Go easy, Marcy,' he said, fearing they would be sick if they ate their first good meal too heartily.

She bit into the succulent meat, it tasted heavenly. She rested her back against the hard surface of the hold and for the first time in ages began to feel more optimistic about their future. She leaned over and planted a kiss on Webster's hairy cheek. 'I love you,' she said.

Chapter Twenty-six

Webster put the mug to his lips and took a large mouthful of water. 'Ugh!' he gasped, spitting it out again and rubbing his mouth as if it had been scalded with boiling liquid. 'That's disgusting!'

'What is it? What's the matter?' Marcia cried, wondering what on earth could be wrong. After all, it was only cold water, and they had been drinking it for several days now.

'It's salty!' he complained, rubbing his mouth furiously with his handkerchief. 'It was fine yesterday, wasn't it? – unless . . . ' He stopped for a moment as the realisation dawned upon him – he must have drawn up sea water in the mug. 'Marcy!' he said, really excited now. 'I think I've just tasted some of the North Sea . . . we must be almost there!'

She felt a mixture of excitement and terror at the prospect of leaving the safety of the barge. For a few days now, they had travelled with ease along the Weser. No one had bothered them, and their stomachs had been well satisfied with the cans of bully beef. So much so that they had both vowed never to eat it again if they were fortunate enough to reach home.

It was almost noon when Webster peeked from under the tarpaulin to check their surroundings. Raising the covering just enough to enable him to see, he was instantly aware of how much the river had widened now. And he was conscious of the fact that the barge seemed to be travelling much slower than before. Then it hit him. The mother barge up ahead was planning to stop. He quickly dropped back the tarpaulin and hurried across to look out from the other side of the barge. It was difficult to see clearly up ahead from his vantage point on this side, as the vessel's raised prow was impeding his view. He realised he would be able to see more from the stern, but instinct made him wary and told him to stay where he was. By straining his neck he could just make out the side of a rather large building which he assumed, by the faint sounds of hammering he heard, to be some sort of workshop. He guessed that the mother barge could be stopping for some repairs. They would have to sit tight for the moment, as any idea of leaving the barge would be impossible during the day. Going back to Marcia, he thought grimly of the hours ahead of them without any water to drink. And he knew without doubt that whatever happened during the day, they would have to leave the safety of the barge that night.

At about six-thirty that same evening the barge started moving again. Webster was apprehensive at the thought of what might be waiting for them once they reached Bremerhaven and told Marcia to come and sit by his side while he kept watch through the gap in the tarpaulin. During the afternoon he had opened another can of beef in readiness to take with them when they left the barge. Marcia had turned up her nose when she saw him wrapping it in his very soiled handkerchief. But he told her that once they were ashore the Lord only knew when they would find food again. 'Better to eat a bit of dirt than starve, my darling,' he told her.

She knew he was right.

'Marcy, come here and take a look!'

Webster's urgent whisper startled her; she must have nodded off. She sidled up beside him and peered out through the tiny opening. She was surprised to see that dusk had crept in while she had been asleep, and it was a moment or two before she was able to distinguish anything in the deepening gloom. 'What is it?' she asked as she rubbed her sleep-bleary eyes, coaxing them to focus more clearly.

'I think we've reached the North Sea, Marcy.' He spoke calmly to her, even though his stomach churned and was knotted with the fear and worry of what now awaited them.

'Yes, I think you're right,' she answered nervously, awaking suddenly to the chorus of different sounds now filling the air around them. She watched, mesmerised, as they coasted alongside a busy quay lined with warehouses, and with men toiling away under the dimmed wartime lighting.

A sudden swaying of the barge, and the quayside seemingly still, warned them that the leader barge must have stopped. Webster inhaled deeply. He knew they were in great danger now and he had no idea what their next move was going to be. He tried to see what was happening with the mother barge, but it was useless from so far away. Quickly, he brought down the tarpaulin and tied it to its cleat. Telling Marcia to follow him, he felt his way along the inside of the hull until they reached the prow.

He was glad he had moved. He now saw that the first barge was tied to another one already moored alongside the wharf. There was quite a bit of activity on the wharf itself, with several people dashing around, each of them seemingly intent on contributing their own special skills for the smooth running of a busy dockyard.

A motor-bike and sidecar clattered slowly by. He stiffened and automatically drew back as he saw that the rider and passenger were German soldiers with rifles slung across their backs. Positive that they were patrolling guards, he made a mental note to study their movements, knowing they must at all costs stay clear of them. Instinct made him turn and he caught sight of two shadowy figures nimbly stepping off the leader barge and onto the one alongside them which they had been fastened to. He watched as they walked across its deck and from there climbed up a vertical ladder to the quay. They paused for a moment to look back at the moored barges. Then, as if satisfied that all was well, they moved quickly away from the water, eventually disappearing into the shadows of the huge sheds which lined the waterfront.

It looked as if they were on their own at last, and Webster realised they would have to move quickly if they wanted to get off the barge. There was no telling how long the crew would be away, and if they missed this chance there might not be another one.

Dropping to where Marcia sat waiting in a frightened huddle at his feet, he quickly related what he had seen. 'Come on, old thing,' he said, sounding much braver than he felt as he took hold of her hand. 'It's now or never.'

After checking once more through the tiny gap in the tarpaulin that they had no unwanted observers, he opened it wider and squeezed his body through. Marcia followed him out and they

174

crawled along the side deck to the prow. Not daring to breathe or move an inch, they waited and listened, expecting at any minute to be spotted. But rolling in from the sea was a cloying, thick sea-mist. With his confidence gradually returning as he began to realise that nobody could have spotted them, Webster ventured a glance towards the wharf. But he couldn't see a thing. He was aware, however, that the mist could lift as quickly as it arrived, so in great haste he helped Marcia across the watery gap and down into the second barge. They scrambled along its deck and onto the mother barge. In a matter of seconds they had crossed the barge lying alongside of them and Webster had his foot on the bottom rung of the ladder. Warning Marcia to be careful as the ladder felt slippery underfoot, he started to climb.

His foot was on the third rung up when he stopped suddenly. He was sure the armed guards were on their way back as he distinctly heard the faint sound of a motor-cycle engine approaching somewhere up above them on the wharf. Marcia had heard it too and was waiting, petrified, with her feet seemingly frozen to the bottom rung.

The sound grew until it seemed to be directly above them. Instinctively, they both flattened themselves against the ladder, sure now that it was going to stop right by them, and that the guards would look down over the side and see them. The sound of its engine hovered above them for several long seconds, then to their overwhelming relief they heard it moving away.

After taking just enough time to steady their breathing, they moved on quickly up the ladder until Webster was in a position to peek over the top and scan the waterfront. The mist swirled across the quay, severely restricting his range of vision. Realising there was no going back, he hoisted himself up on the wharf, then took Marcia's hand and pulled her up alongside him. Even in the gloom he could see she was terrified. She seemed unable to move or speak. He whispered soft encouragement, even though his own heart was racing madly. 'Come on, Marcy, you can do it.' He gripped her clammy fingers and started to run, pulling her along behind him.

He raced on blindly across the waterfront, painfully aware that every next step could land them in deep trouble. Just in time he noticed the slippery damp lines of a rail track lying across his path. He slowed down just enough to point out the slithery obstacle to Marcia, then raced on wildly, pulling her leaden body along behind him with an energy laced with fear.

Painfully aware of ghostly shadows moving close by he charged on regardless, and when all of a sudden he realised that the obstruction in front of him was the huge shuttered doorway of a shed, he couldn't believe his eyes. Swiftly glancing along to the end of the building, he noticed a gap between this shed and the next. Pulling her roughly in his anxiety to be hidden from view, he hastened towards the darkened alleyway.

He told her to stay in the shadows while he cautiously stuck his head round the corner of the building. It was still misty, but he could make out a few things which were close to him. He could smell food and guessed that the square of muted light from across the way belonged to some sort of café. The odour of smoking fat and stale vegetables would normally have turned his stomach, but tonight he longed to go inside in the cheerful warmth and eat and drink whatever was put before him. With difficulty he forced the thoughts of such luxury from his mind and concentrated on sizing-up the layout of the immediate area around them. He spotted more railway lines and assumed they were the continuation of the ones they had crossed earlier along the front. He was positive now that this area was yet another working yard, which sharpened his desperation to find somewhere safe for them to hide. With dawn fast approaching he knew that this whole area would soon come alive and their chances of being caught would be a certainty. They were virtually trapped. He glanced worriedly towards his left and was just able to distinguish the dark silhouette of the neighbouring shed. He was sure the mist was hiding several others and decided there was only one thing for it; they would have to chance a closer look. Beckoning Marcia to follow him, he emerged stealthily from the alley and, keeping to what little cover there was, they both skirted the adjacent shed. They were both praying with all their hearts that they would soon find something which would suit their purposes, but it didn't look very promising. They passed four more huge warehouses, and not one of them seemed to be accessible from the rear. Webster was just making up his mind whether or not to change direction when he heard the motor-cycle returning. He grabbed Marcia and hurried with her into the nearest passageway. In the darkness they waited with bated breath until the guards had gone by and the sound of the engine had dwindled into the distance.

'We'll stay here for a few minutes, Marcy,' Webster said quietly. 'Then we must try again.'

She rested her head against his shoulder and closed her eyes and wondered what was to become of them. Suddenly her mind transported her back to the farm. She could smell the fresh pine logs as they spluttered crazily in the grate in Reuben's front room. She could even smell the yellow sawdust that fell softly round the chopping block as Norman wielded the heavy axe to chop off neat little sticks to use as kindling when they lit the fires. She opened her eyes to dispel the images; the memories were too painful. She found it odd, however, that the scent of the pine still lingered in her nostrils. Sniffing the air, she realised this was the real thing. Somewhere nearby there had to be a woodshed. She excitedly explained to Webster that when she was a girl she and her friends sometimes played around the Welsh dockland area. Although the waterfront itself was forbidden territory to them, sometimes they would go there and sneak into a huge open-sided timber shed to hide. Because of the various sizes of planks stored inside it meant that where one stack had ended and the other stack had started there was usually a sizeable gap. As children they had used these gaps between the planks as a stairway to climb to where they could sit and watch the comings and goings of the big ships. 'If there's a woodshed here,' she said, 'I'll show you how.'

Marcia's sense of smell hadn't let her down. They only had to pass by one other building and there it was. She hurried towards it, already searching for a way in.

Webster wasn't so sure. It looked tightly packed to him. He placed his hand on her arm. 'Are you sure about this, Marcy? There must be boat-loads of timber stacked in there – it looks impossible!'

She paid him no heed; she knew she was right.

He waited, expecting her to give up soon. He was almost out of his mind now with worry. It would be daylight soon and they had nowhere to hide. His roving glance suddenly fell on something on the warehouse wall. A standpipe! His hand went immediately for the mug in his pocket. Glancing around and seeing that nothing stirred, he held the mug underneath and carefully turned on the tap.

Marcia came up beside him just as he was taking his first

mouthful. She ran her dry tongue over her lips and looked longingly at the tap. 'You've found water.' The relief in her voice was evident. In a flash he had drained the mug, refilled it, and placed it into her waiting hands. She drank greedily.

'Where do we go from here, Marcy?' He was at his wits end, not knowing which way to turn.

She passed him the empty mug and gave him a cheeky smile. 'Into the timber shed,' she said smugly. 'I've found us a way in.'

The door Marcia had located was unlocked. Once inside, Webster was surprised at how easy it was to manoeuvre their way through the stacks of timber. From outside it had looked like a solid mass of wood. In fact there was plenty of room. To him it felt maze-like, but Marcia seemed to know what she was doing so he followed on behind her, trying not to spill any of the precious water from the mug he had refilled. It might well have to last them throughout the long day.

With a sigh of relief Marcia sat down. Her legs ached terribly with the climb through the timber; so different to how easy it had been when she was a girl, she remembered ruefully. Webster sat down beside her on the stacked planks. He placed the mug at a safe distance away from them, then took her in his arms and gave her a lingering kiss. 'Well done Marcy,' he whispered.

As the early morning light sifted through the wooden planks they were amazed to discover how far they had travelled. Without realising it, they must have clambered along the whole length of the shed, gradually climbing upwards as they went, because now they found themselves on the far side of the shed and if they moved their position only slightly it gave them a bird's eye view of the wharf below. It was already busy down there. A large ship was moored alongside the wharf while a tall crane effortlessly removed its cargo of iron-ore and loaded it into a line of waiting railway wagons. They watched fascinated as busy crew members and stevedores scuttled hither and thither, shouting their orders to be heard above the din. Two more ships were berthed nearby, waiting to have there respective cargoes off-loaded. All three ships flew the flag of the enemy.

Webster felt decidedly uneasy. It looked as if they could be stuck in the timber shed for a very long time.

Chapter Twenty-seven

For two long days and nights they had remained concealed in the timber shed, only daring to move during the quietest part of the night. Apart from their nightly trek for water, and napping fitfully in their hard and draughty wood-hole, they had both kept a faithful watch on the wharf below. They now knew when to expect the patrol guards. Every half-hour, with Teutonic punctuality, they would hear the now familiar sound of the motor-bike's engine. It never once failed them. They had also learned by the late night antics of some of the ships crews, that there must be a drinking house somewhere along the wharf. But the arrival of more cargo ships did nothing to lift their spirits, as each one of them had been flying the flag of a hostile country. They waited now for the sounds of morning.

Webster broke the last piece of canned beef in two and gave a piece to Marcia. She accepted her share just to please him. Although he hadn't said much, she knew by the expression on his face that he was really worried. She felt the same way, but kept silent so as not to add to his troubles. Her fingers closed over the beef to hide it. The thought of eating it made her feel sick. Already her stomach was churning violently with the fear of being captured. She knew that time was running out for them; their luck couldn't hold for ever.

Webster looked down wearily from his elevated vantage point. The noisy activity had started quite a time ago, and Marcia had wondered if he had decided not to bother to keep watch anymore. It sometimes appeared to her that he had now resigned himself to the inevitability of capture. While his gaze was averted, she stuffed the sticky warm meat into her pocket with disgust, then reached for the mug, hoping that a few sips of water would take away the nasty taste in her mouth. The mug was halfway to her lips when Webster startled her by suddenly calling out her name. Her hand shook and some of the precious liquid spilled down over her front. It was the last straw. Even with the mug full, it had barely been sufficient to last out the day. She was close to tears when he spoke to her again. Unaware of her predicament, and with his own eyes still glued to the wharf below, he urged her to come and look.

Wiping away a tear, she drew herself up beside him and looked down at the waterfront. Webster gave her a hug and pointed to one of the berthed ships. 'See?' he said.

She gave it a cursory glance, still baffled by his obvious excitement. It had been there last night. It was Italian – she remembered the flag with its green, white, and red vertical band.

Webster knew what she was thinking and told her to look at the flag again.

'Why?'

'Look more carefully,' he said, his voice now edged with a hint of exasperation.

She looked back at the flag, frowning – then she realised her mistake! It wasn't green, white and red bands – it was green, white and *orange!* The night lighting had deceived them into thinking it was red. 'It's not Italian,' she breathed.

'No my, darling,' he answered her joyfully. 'Look at her name!'

Marcia directed her gaze at the words proudly emblazoned on the ship's stern:

THE LADY OF KILLARNEY

'It's Irish!' she cried.

'Now all we have to do is to get on her,' Webster muttered ruefully, realising that this was much easier said than done. His words brought her back to earth. She found her hopes quickly dispersing as she realised what lay before them. 'Don't worry,' he said, sensing her anxiety. 'As soon as it's dark we'll go down there and see what we can do. We're going to get on that ship, Marcy, I promise you.' He prayed fervently that he wouldn't let her down.

'Time to move, Marcy.'

She opened her eyes to find that the warehouse was in

180

darkness. She hadn't been asleep, her mind was too active for that. But the exhausting watch on the Irish ship throughout the day, coupled with the lack of any food, had made her weary and lethargic. Webster's eyes were heavy too. All day long he had watched as the great crane swung with precise monotony from ship to wagon, precariously gripping several large weighty sacks which he guessed could contain sugar. He had watched it for seven hours. Now, rubbing his hot, gritty eyes, he decided it was time for them to go. He took a deep breath, then spoke to Marcia. 'Are you ready?'

'Yes.'

'Let's go.'

Some sunshine had seeped through the timber during the day and had kept them pleasantly warm, but tonight a cold wind swept between the sheds and Marcia shivered as she waited for Webster to fill the mug with water from the tap. When they had had their fill, he took her hand and they moved stealthily to the other end of the alleyway. Telling her to stay back in the shadows, he edged forward to where he could scrutinise the waterfront. He heard someone coughing, then coming towards him out of the darkness he saw a group of four men. They were coming from the direction of the Irish ship. Webster stepped back into the shadows beside Marcia and gestured her to remain silent. Standing stock still, they waited and listened as the voices drew nearer. Marcia almost cried out with fright as a hearty laugh reverberated through the alleyway. It was as if it was right next to them. But the men carried on past, unaware of their presence, and despite his still pounding heart, Webster was greatly cheered by the sound of their Irish accents. The rich brogue was unmistakable. Another lone figure materialised from the gloom. Webster watched with bated breath as the man sauntered towards the alleyway with his hands in his pockets. Acting on impulse, Webster called out softly: 'Irishman!'

The man stopped and looked down the dark passage. Webster froze, and cursed himself for being such an idiot. He couldn't understand what had possessed him to do such a stupid thing. It just happened.

'Is someone wanting me?' The voice was hesitant, but again there was no mistaking the soft Irish lilt.

With soaring confidence Webster stepped forward so that the

181

man could see him. 'I need your help!' he said desperately.

The Irishman glanced at Webster in disbelief and looked as if he was about to hurry away when Marcia stepped out from the shadows. 'Please help us, sir,' she pleaded.

The desperation in her voice caused him to hesitate. He glanced furtively over his shoulder, then stepped into the alleyway to join them.

Allowing the seaman no time to gather his thoughts, Webster explained that he and Marcia were English, desperately trying to find a way home. 'We'll give anything to get aboard your ship!' he said.

The Irishman shook his head. 'It won't be easy, boyo,' he said, but it was clear from his tone that he was sympathetic of their plight. 'The cap'n has no love for the Nazi's, even though he does carry for them from time to time. But he's a strange old bugger, to be sure. Oi'd be telling the pair of you the truth now if I said I haven't a clue as to what his reaction would be if he found a couple of stowaways aboard. Even if you are English.'

Webster thought quickly. They had to get on that ship, with or without the sailor's help. 'When do you sail, mate?' he asked.

'Tomorrow at midnight,' came the prompt reply. 'We'll be going out with the tide.' There was a strained silence as the Irishman battled with his conscience. He was well aware of the dire consequences if he was caught helping them by the German authorities, but his own daughter was roughly the same age as this English lass . . . and if it was her needing help! His mind was made up. 'If you can manage to get aboard her she'll take you right back to your own waters. At first light we start loading her with industrial coal for southern Ireland.' He grinned as he sensed their growing excitement. 'There isn't much I can do, you understand, other than give you a few details which might help. The rest will be up to you.'

'We're deeply indebted to you, sir,' Webster said with conviction.

The Irishman said, '*The Lady* will be at her quietest at around ten. By then the cargo will have been loaded, and most of the crew will be resting while she's waiting for the tide.' He went on to suggest that if they did find themselves on board their best bet in his opinion would be to hide away in the oil store. 'The smell will probably make you feel sick, mind, but the forty-gallon

182

drums should give you some good cover.'

Webster nodded gratefully. 'How do we find this oil store?'

The sound of the guards' motor-cycle combination froze them into silence. They waited for it to pass. It clearly made the Irishman more aware of the imminent dangers and he lost no time in giving them the vital instructions. They hardly had time enough to thank him before he turned on his heel and was gone, perhaps wishing to himself that he had stayed quietly on board this evening.

To help fill their empty stomachs they drank a full mug of water each before returning to the sanctuary of the timber warehouse. In spite of their gnawing hunger pains they felt a joyous relief to know that tomorrow night could bring them the chance of going home to dear old blighty.

Chapter Twenty-eight

The following evening found the nervous couple again sheltering in the dark alleyway. It had been raining off and on all day. What with the cold, damp air caressing Marcia's bones and the dangerous mission they were about to undertake, she couldn't stop her body from shaking. Webster felt the same way but tried his best to cover it up for her sake, but he found it very difficult. He stood back in the shadows just far enough to enable him to see the wharf and *The Lady of Killarney* lying sedately in the water alongside. Every few minutes he would step back beside Marcia as various persons suddenly appeared and came much too close for comfort. 'We're never going to leave here!' Webster muttered to himself, despairing of ever finding the coast clear for their covert dash to the ship. 'If we go on at this rate,' he said miserably, 'the damn ship will sail without us.' He put his arms around her and rested his head on her shoulder to find solace, thinking to himself how excited they had been throughout the long day, with their confidence growing with each hour. By the time they were ready to leave the timber shed they really believed they would soon be on their way home. Their nerves were stretched to breaking point as they again heard the familiar chilling rumble of the guards' motor-cycle combination. Still huddled together, they waited until it had passed and the sound of its noisy exhaust had again faded into the distance. Webster whispered that he was going to take another look. This time he was unable to believe his eyes: the waterfront looked deserted. This was it! With his heart thumping madly he called softly back to Marcia.

'Here! Quickly!'

He felt for her hand and gripped it tightly, preparing himself to run like hell.

'No!' she gasped, desperately tugging at his hand to draw him back into the dark alleyway. 'Guards!' Her voice was hoarse with fear as she pointed feverishly in the direction of the wharf. 'They're still out there!' She was clinging to him like a limpet.

He held her for a few moments, then went back to look for himself. He felt sure she was mistaken, he hadn't seen anyone. Not then – but now he did! Two men, barely thirty yards away, and coming towards him. But no – deep in conversation, they were sauntering on past. By the looks of their garb they appeared to have come off one of the ships. Scanning the waterfront again, he saw nothing untoward and was about to go back for Marcia when the slight shifting of a shadow directly in front of the Irish ship caught his eye. He looked harder, and could see now the guards were indeed there. The motor-cycle engine had been switched off and the two men now sat with their backs to him, seemingly intent on watching the big ship which lay serenely before them. His fragile morale teetered precariously close to breaking-point as he wondered if the Irishman had double-crossed them. He felt Marcia close beside him. In a tone of utter despondency he murmured, 'I think we've had it, Marcy!'

Motionless, they stayed where they were. The disappointment of not being able to reach the ship had rendered them both speechless. In his mind Webster knew it was time to give themselves up to the authorities. They'd been without food for far too long now, and they couldn't expect their presence in the timber store to remain undetected for very much longer. That they would soon be captured was a real certainty. So far they had been extremely lucky with the absence of timber ships, but he knew that one was bound to come along sooner or later. His main worry was Marcia. He would have to tell her, but he felt he had failed her. These depleting thoughts were instantly driven from his mind by the sudden, unexpected roar of the motor-cycle engine. 'Thank God!' he whispered.

Within a few minutes the wharf had settled quietly back into its muffled chorus of gentle night-time sounds. As far as he could see the coast was clear. Webster took a firmer grip of her hand and gave her a hasty peck on her cheek. 'Ready?' he said.

She just nodded, feeling too numb to speak. Her arm felt as if it was being pulled from its socket as he told her to 'Run like

185

Hell!' and bounded forward across the quayside.

Gasping for breath, they reached the top of the gangway and silently thanked their lucky stars that no one was there to challenge them. They had seen nobody on their reckless dash across the quay, and Webster felt fairly confident that if someone had noticed them they would know all about it by now. They stepped down onto the deck, and with the Irish sailor's directions clearly etched in his mind, Webster hurried Marcia along the side of the steel superstructure that supported the ship's bridge. It was here they would find the entrance to the oil store. He had warned them to be extremely careful at this point, as situated above the store was the Captain's quarters, and above that was the wheelhouse. The captain was sure to be around there somewhere. Flattening themselves to the cold steel side of the building, they slowly edged their way along until they found a doorway. The door had been left slightly ajar and the thick sickly odour of oil came out to meet them. Afraid even to whisper, Webster guided Marcia inside and thankfully closed the door behind them.

Inside, it was pitch dark and the smell was overpowering. But it was just as they had hoped and expected. The store was full of 40 gallon oil drums. With the meagre help of Webster's small torch they managed to find a way round to the rear of the store. Here they felt a mite safer. They managed to find a spot where there was room enough to sit down and stretch their legs.

'Well, Marcy, we've made it this far.' Webster said softly.

'How long will it be before we reach Ireland?' she asked wistfully.

'A couple of days or so,' he replied confidently. Then, as if afraid of tempting fate, he added, 'That is, if everything goes well for us, my darling.'

They sensed rather than heard the presence of someone close to the storeroom door. They strained to listen. Dull-sounding footfalls and the chatter of excited voices permeated the steel bulkhead, and Marcia covered her face with her hands, terrified that any minute now the door would be flung open and they would be discovered.

After endless minutes of mind-torturing worry they realised the commotion outside could have nothing to do with them. They would have been found and apprehended by now if the Irishman had betrayed them. The cacophony of unfamiliar sounds was merely the normal hustle bustle as the ship's crew prepared the ship for sea. Their excitement mounted as the floor thrummed and vibrated beneath them, and the sounds of rattling cables and quick urgent shouts told them they would soon be on their way. The humming vibration grew until it reached its peak, then remained steady.

'We're on our way, Marcy . . . we're going home!' Webster felt her body shaking and knew she was crying. The ordeal of the last ten days had taken its toll. Holding her close and rocking her gently in his arms, he let her be.

They had been sailing for almost an hour and although they had heard movements outside, nobody had yet entered the oil-store. Webster was beginning to wonder if the sailor had forgotten all about them. Marcia seemed to be much calmer now and he gratefully shifted his aching arm from behind her back.

'Feeling a little better now, old thing?' he asked.

'Yes . . . I'm sorry f– ' The sentence died on her lips as the store door was flung open.

Two shadowy figures stepped inside. A switch was flicked and the whole store was flooded with light. Then they heard the scrape of oil drums being shifted and the indistinct mutterings of busy men at work. It sounded as if the drums were being moved closer to the door, and after a few minutes of hectic activity the noise suddenly ceased. They waited for the men to leave, but they didn't. Panic started squeezing their insides as they wondered why everything remained so still.

'Airman?'

Just one clearly spoken word, but it brought them instant relief.

'Thank God . . . it's our sailor friend,' Webster breathed. He rose slowly to his feet, pulling Marcia up beside him. 'We're over here,' he called.

The sailors were dressed alike in dark coloured boiler suits and flat greasy caps, and by their lined and weather-beaten faces appeared to have been seafarers for a very long time.

The shorter of the two men held out a thick-fingered hand in greeting. 'It was so quiet in here oi was beginning to think you hadn't made it,' he said with a smile.

Webster took his hand and wrung it gratefully. 'It's thanks to you that we have, my friend. I hope we haven't caused you any trouble.'

After a quick exchange of names, Joe — the sailor who had befriended them — and his taller work buddy, Danny, lost no time in explaining what they were to do next. Joe and Danny were the ship's engineers and worked together in the bowels of the ship. Joe had sailed with the captain many times over the years and a certain bond of trust had developed between them, in spite of the captain being a man unto himself and preferring his own company. Joe had thought it best to tell him of his meeting with the unfortunate young couple, but decided to wait until they were well out to sea before doing so. If by some miracle they had managed to sneak on board, by then it would be too late for the captain to refuse.

As Joe had half-expected, it hadn't gone too well. The captain had remained silent and poker-faced for several long moments after he had been informed of the situation. Then, accepting that the damage was done, he told Joe that the responsibility was his. It was on his own head. Scowling, he told him he was a fool to get mixed up in other people's business, and hadn't they enough trouble already without going out to look for it. After telling Joe in no uncertain terms to get rid of them as soon as they anchored in Ireland, the captain had dismissed him with an angry wave of his hand.

'The cap'n has given us the job of looking after you,' Joe said with a good-natured grin. 'We'll look after you down below; you'll find it nice and warm down there.'

Danny nodded his agreement and told them it was time they went. He gave Marcia a roguish wink. 'Skip will give us hell if he thinks we're shirking our duties,' he said dryly.

As they followed the two seamen down into the bowels of the ship, their presence attracted some puzzled stares from several of the other crew members. Marcia stared straight ahead, not wanting to meet their eyes because she felt ashamed of her unkempt and filthy appearance. As soon as they reached the engine room, Danny disappeared to attend to his duties, leaving Joe to take care of them. The engineers shared a cabin near to the engine-room and Joe ushered them inside. The cabin was very small, with just two bunk-beds, a tall cupboard, small sink and table, and several manly possessions scattered untidily around. To Marcia and Webster it felt like a palace. After telling them to sit down on the lower bunk and make themselves comfortable, Joe hurried off to the galley to rustle up some food and drink for them.

'I can't believe we're on our way home,' Marcia said, with tears of relief glistening in her blue eyes.

Webster cuddled her close. 'I reckon there's someone watching over us,' he told her in a voice heavy with emotion.

Joe was soon back with a laden tray of steaming hot tea and an assortment of sandwiches. After offering them the use of his own toilet facilities, he left to resume his duties in the engine room. 'Lock the door behind me if you like,' came his meaningful parting remark. 'We won't be back for a good couple of hours.'

They felt their strength returning as soon as they sampled the stimulating hot sweet tea and bit delicately into the thick wedge of a cheese sandwich. Neither of them did justice to the food. One sandwich each and they were full; their stomachs could take no more. But it was deliciously satisfying nonetheless.

After they had eaten, they stood naked to cleanse their bodies. Neither felt any qualms about their nudity; they had been through too much together for that. Slowly but surely the smooth hot water and the silken suds of soap washed away the grime and distress of the last few weeks. Their ordeal was nearly over. Afterwards they rested their bodies on the lower bunk. Cuddled tightly together, exhausted but content, they soon drifted into a blissful sleep.

Chapter Twenty-nine

In spite of sharing the cramped cabin with the engineers, the last two days had been wonderful. Webster had gladly removed the abundance of hair from his face, and with the sea air and their appetites slowly being regained, they were both beginning to look more like their old selves.

They had just finished their evening meal when Joe's smiling face appeared round the cabin door. 'Next stop, Rosslare,' he told them cheerily. 'We'll be dropping anchor soon, me shipmates. Me and Danny boy will come down for you when it's time to go ashore. He gave Marcia a cheeky wink. 'Unless that is you would rather stay here on board with me.'

Marcia's chuckle followed him out of the door.

It seemed a silent age since they had felt the tired judderings of the dying engines upon arriving off the Irish port. Even the atmosphere in the cabin felt different without the reassuring throb of the engines. It was as though they no longer belonged there.

Joe appeared at long last and told them to get their coats on quickly, as it was time to go. As they hurried along to the upper deck he told them they were to join some of his fellow crewmen. He explained that if they were surrounded by sailors when they stepped ashore, they would be less likely to be targeted by any prying eyes. If they walked out on their own and were spotted by some zealous official, they could be involved in a lot of red-tape, and the captain would be furious if the ship was held up.

The little band of sailors were waiting for them at the head of the gangway. They were clearly impatient to get ashore and afforded Joe's party only a cursory nod before falling in around them and sweeping them along with them down onto the jetty. If someone had shouted 'FIRE!' they couldn't have hurried more.

Their feet hardly touched the ground.

'Fitzwilliam's Bar,' panted Joe, pointing directly ahead.

The thick, strong smell of stout washed over them as they entered the bar. Marcia felt conspicuously naked as the group around her swiftly melted away and several knowing eyes looked up from frothing beer mugs to appraise her. She wedged herself between Joe and Webster, hoping their supportive presence would give her the courage to remain in what was obviously a rough-tough seafarer's bar. The black-haired, red-lipped barmaid, who looked young only from a distance, rested her bouncing cleavage on the counter and looked seductively towards the two men for their order.

'Three of your best, love,' Joe said, carefully counting out the right small change before slamming it down on the sticky counter.

The brassy barmaid looked peeved as she gingerly picked up the coins between her manicured claws and saw that his attention was drawn to something more interesting in one of the room's dimly-lit corners. Joe's eyes shone with satisfaction as his glance alighted on one particular fisherman. 'Oi think we might be in luck, me boyo's,' he breathed. 'O'Riley's in tonight.'

Having deposited three glasses of stout on the counter, the barmaid was already engaged in fluttering her eyelashes at a new conquest.

Joe handed Webster and Marcia their drinks and picked up his own. After taking a prolonged swig, he wiped the creamy moustache from his upper lip and invited the pair of them to accompany him to the fisherman's table.

O'Riley, who looked too old to still be active as a seaman, was deep in conversation with another old salt, but they both looked up as Joe's long shadow invaded their untidy table. For a split-second, O'Riley's crafty eyes narrowed with annoyance at the intrusion, then, as recognition swiftly dawned, his expression changed to one of pleasant surprise. 'I didn't know *The Lady* had docked, Joe!' he exclaimed, giving them all the benefit of a nicotine-stained grin.

Joe pulled up some more chairs and they settled themselves around O'Riley's table. Joe answered the old fisherman's puzzled look by introducing his friends and outlining briefly the circumstances that had befallen them. When he had done,

O'Riley merely nodded and waited, knowing there was more to come. Joe didn't disappoint him. 'So, moi old friend,' he said. 'How soon before you take the *Megan* back down to Cornish waters for the fishing? Me boyo here and his lovely wee colleen are after a ride.'

On hearing this request, a look of what can only be described as sheer panic washed over the faces of O'Riley and his drinking partner. But in an instant, O'Riley had composed himself, and with a smile that was evidently forced told them he was sorry but it was impossible. He went on to say how cramped the conditions on the boat were. 'Your friends would be extremely uncomfortable,' he whined. His foxy eyes rested on Marcia. 'I'm sure the beautiful lady deserves something better than that.' It was apparent he had something to hide.

Joe responded with an icy glare. 'Have you forgotten you owe me one?'

That did the trick. Shamed into defeat, O'Riley grudgingly agreed to take them on board.

Webster flashed Joe a look of gratitude and thanked O'Riley, assuring him that he and Marcia would willingly squeeze in anywhere, and they wouldn't cause him any bother. The fishermen could get on with their fishing and forget they were there.

O'Riley nodded without conviction. For some reason he seemed perturbed. He drew out a pocket-watch and peered closely at its dial. 'We'll be ready to sail in an hour,' he said sullenly.

The three expectant faces opposite him lit up with relief and thankfulness. Joe grabbed his hand and shook it furiously. 'You're a good man, O'Riley,' he said. 'Consider the debt paid. And don't you be worrying yourself — my friends here will be glad to keep to themselves, you can be sure of that!'

O'Riley gave only an unintelligible grunt, but the expression in his eyes was clear enough. He could well have done without their company.

It was almost midnight and a chill breeze was blowing across the open wharf. Inside Fitzwilliam's they had enjoyed its warmth and comfort, but now Marcia shivered and clutched her coat tighter to her body as she and Webster hurried along behind O'Riley and his mate to board the *Megan*. After thanking Joe profusely for all his help, they had parted company for the ten-minute walk to O'Riley's boat which was moored, along with several others of its own type, in a small harbour some distance away from *The Lady of Killarney*. O'Riley and his partner kept two or three yards ahead of them, still deep in muttered conversation, and clearly discussing matters which they intended to keep to themselves. The gentle chopping of the waves and the squeaking timbers of the bobbing boats could be heard as finally the two fishermen stopped and beckoned them to come closer.

Lying in wait in the water before them was the *Megan*. She wasn't very big – maybe sixty feet long on the waterline – but to Marcia and Webster she was magnificent.

'Arnie!'

O'Riley's shout brought an oilskinned figure popping out from behind the wheel-house. As he hurried over across the deck towards them, they saw that he was a much younger man than the other two fishermen. They followed O'Riley and his mate in single file down half-a-dozen slippery stone steps till O'Riley, who was leading, stepped from the last one directly down into the *Megan*. As his elderly mate nimbly followed after him, Arnie stood motionless on the deck, regarding Webster and Marcia with puzzlement and suspicion.

'Give 'em a hand!' O'Riley barked.

For several seconds, Arnie remained transfixed, clearly not understanding his skipper's uncharacteristic wish to have two strangers come aboard.

O'Riley, noting his confusion, spoke up quickly: 'It's a favour for oily Joe – I owed him one. *The Lady*'s in dock. His friends here are sailing with us across to Cornwall.'

Satisfied, Arnie nodded and held out his arm to help them aboard the swaying vessel.

'Take 'em down below to the galley,' O'Riley called back as he and his mate stepped into the wheel-house.

At first sight the galley seemed quite small and bare, but it was lovely and warm; the heat generated from a small, black, coal-fired stove. The fire inside glowed redly, and a battered kettle hissed contentedly on the top. Close by was a small, chipped, enamel sink and a table which was bolted to the wall. Next to it

j

was a cupboard. There was another table with a bench either side, all firmly fixed to the deck. There was an open doorway in the wood panelling opposite. Inside, all that could be seen were two bunks covered by an untidy heap of blankets.

Arnie gave them a friendly grin and told them to sit down while he made them all some tea. With the aid of a soiled and crumpled tea towel, he lifted the hot kettle and proceeded to pour the spluttering water into what looked like a small watering-can with a lid on top. 'By the way,' he said, not looking up from his task, 'the heads are up on deck . . . door next to the wheel-house.'

Chapter Thirty

The weather at daybreak was lovely. Summer had started early and the sea all around them was as calm as a mill pond. Webster and Marcia had had the cabin to themselves. Arnie had picked up an armful of blankets, and after wishing them 'pleasant dreams' had closed the door and bedded down on the floor of the galley. The others must have done the same when they came off watch because the quietness of the calm night was frequently punctuated by a variety of shuffling and muttering noises, but neither O'Riley or his mate disturbed their nocturnal privacy.

This morning though, they had seen them up on deck. He had been busy with his mate casting out the lines to catch some fish. Thinking it wise not to interfere, Webster had given them a wave and had left them to it. Feeling fat and full after the bacon and eggs that Arnie had cooked them for breakfast, he decided to move around the deck a little to enjoy the sunshine with Marcy. For a while they rested their arms on the side of the boat and idly watched the widening V of white foam as the Megan smoothly sliced through the blue velvet water. But the continuous rippling of the water eventually affected Marcia and, feeling somewhat embarrassed at being the only woman on board, she asked Webster to come with her and wait outside while she used the lavatory.

He laughed and escorted her to the heads.

While he waited for her outside he watched the men, still busy near the bow of the boat. Arnie had joined them now and they all seemed unaware of his watching eyes, intent only on making their living. Between Webster and the fishermen was a small hold. He saw that the hatches had been opened and presumed this would be where the boxes of fresh fish would be stored for their journey back to Rosslare.

When Marcia rejoined him they strolled together along the deck and stopped to look down into the gaping cavity of the hold. It wasn't very interesting – just a few wooden fish boxes stacked up at one end, with a roll of fishing net squeezed in behind them. They were about to walk away when Marcia gasped and pointed in the direction of the fish boxes. She dropped to her knee for a closer look.

'What is it?' Webster asked, stooping down beside her.

'Keep away from there!' The stern tone of O'Riley's shout put a sharp stop to her curious scrutiny. They both straightened up awkwardly, and with their tails between their legs walked hand in hand back to the relative tranquillity of the stern.

Safely out of earshot of the others, Marcia regarded Webster with open amusement. 'I think our captain's a smuggler!' she said simply.

Something had caught her eye when she had glanced down into the hold. A corner of the netting had been accidentally disturbed to reveal more boxes tucked away behind it. And they weren't fish boxes either. In fact, to Marcia, they looked suspiciously identical to those which Reuben had silently collected from the mysterious van that had visited Tolcarne Merock late that night.

Webster grinned now. 'That would explain his reluctance to have us as passengers,' he said. 'The sly old devil.'

They both agreed to keep well away from the hold and to let O'Riley think his secret was still safe. There was no telling how the old sea-dog would react if he found out that his illicit supplies were common knowledge. They spent the rest of the day on their own, lazily stretched out on the warm deck enjoying the sunshine. Arnie, who seemed to be the main cook and bottle washer, brought up their meals which were devoured greedily, their appetites whetted by the pure, salty air. O'Riley and his mate remained aloof.

Webster and Marcia watched the sun as it slowly slid down below the horizon. In an instant the air held a penetrating chill, so without more ado they hurried down to the warmth of the galley. It was a relief to find just Arnie down there; they didn't feel quite so unwanted in his friendlier presence. He was dressed up warm to go on deck. On the table was a tray with five steaming hot mugs of cocoa. 'I was just about to bring yours up to you,' he told them with a smile. He took two mugs off the tray and placed them on the table for them. 'I'd better be going,' he said, pulling a thick woolly hat down over his ears. 'Skip likes to have his cocoa on time.' In two long strides he mounted the wooden stairs and was gone. The cheerful tune he was whistling faded into the distance as his footsteps reverberated over the deck.

Webster awoke with a start. The cabin was in complete darkness. Marcia had her back to him, but by her soft and regular breathing he guessed she must still be asleep. Careful not to wake her, he felt for his torch. The feeble beam picked out the hands on his watch. 'Just after one,' he muttered softly to himself. Propping himself up on one elbow, he strained his ears to listen. Something felt different. The boat seemed to be shrouded in silence; he was sure they weren't moving. Suddenly, the sound of urgent muffled voices reached his ears. Fully alert now, he swung his feet to the ground and sat on the side of the bunk, listening. He could hear the gentle slapping of the water against the *Megan*'s hull eerily resounding around the dark cabin. Levering his tensed body off the bunk, he crept over to the door and opened it just enough for him to peer into the galley. A dull light showed him that it was empty. Curious, and venturing out in his bare feet, he mounted the few wooden treads that would allow him to look out and see the upper deck. For a moment he could see nothing. Even the sky held a strange blackness, utterly devoid of stars. A dull clatter, followed by an angry retort, directed his gaze to the hold. As his eyes grew accustomed to the gloom, he saw that the hatches over the hold had been removed. Reflected light from within the hold shimmered upwards to reveal O'Riley's mate crouched on the deck beside them. His attention was riveted to whatever was going on in the depths of the hold.

Webster gripped the hand-rail with excitement. He now noticed that a thick rope was suspended over the hold itself. His eyes wandered part way up the rope until it disappeared completely into the darkness. Suddenly the rope started to sway to and fro as if it held a heavy weight of some kind. Webster watched as the fisherman grabbed at the rope, seemingly to steady its upward progress. Then a large basket came into view and in a flash it all became clear to him. Marcia had been right. That was illicit booze being hoisted from the hold. He wondered why he hadn't figured it out before. The heavy darkness and the echoing sounds meant they were anchored in a large cave. The rope and basket was being manipulated from somewhere up on the cliff. Although he could not see it, Webster knew there had to be an opening of some kind in the cave roof. He had seen enough. Slowly backing down the stairs, he hurried back to the cabin.

Marcia stirred as he lay down beside her. 'Your feet are cold,' she complained sleepily.

'I've been watching our friends up on deck,' he said, cuddling into her warm body.

'Why? — it's the middle of the night for goodness sake.' She sounded more awake now and Webster told her about the goings-on up on deck. When he had done Marcia couldn't help smiling to herself as she thought of Reuben and his plentiful supplies back home. 'We seem to be surrounded by black-marketeers,' she said. Thinking about her old boss made her long to be home in the safety of the farmhouse. She asked Webster if he had any idea of where they were.

'We can't be far off — '

A loud banging on the cabin door, accompanied by Arnie's shout telling them they were wanted in the galley stopped him in mid sentence.

'Do you think O'Riley saw you?' Marcia whispered anxiously.

More loud banging followed by Arnie's urgent shouting of 'Are you awake in there?' galvanised Webster into action.

'We'll be right there,' he shouted back.

When he opened the cabin door he saw that Arnie had company. O'Riley was sat at the table, and as soon as they both emerged he beckoned them over to join him.

Giving Arnie a sheepish grin, they settled themselves down at the table opposite the skipper and waited for the onslaught. They were both knocked completely off-balance when he told them it was time for them to go ashore. Webster squeezed Marcia's hand firmly under the table to stop her from speaking, thinking it was best to hear O'Riley out first. Long seconds dragged by, and they began to feel uncomfortable as the skipper just stared at them. It seemed that he was weighing things up in his mind before committing himself. Suddenly, as if pleased that his mind had come up with the right solution, his hard expression changed into the semblance of a smile and he told them they were about to reach Mawgan Porth in a basket.

Webster laughed. 'In a basket!' he said in mock disbelief for O'Riley's benefit.

As if taking them into his confidence, the cunning old skipper leaned forward and told them he had friends in these parts who sadly were unable to fish for themselves. 'Whenever we sail along the north Cornish coast,' he said, 'I drop off a few boxes for them . . . out of the goodness of me heart, you understand. The thing is,' he went on, 'one of moi friends knew of a shortcut — takes time and money to find a suitable harbour, that it does.' He looked towards them, hoping to find they were sympathetic to his cause.

Webster nodded understandingly.

Satisfied, O'Riley continued in a sterner tone: 'Not many others know about this shortcut — it's a secret — and for my friend's sake I must ask you to keep it to yourselves.'

They both nodded furiously but the skipper still felt uneasy.

'Would ye be prepared to swear on the Holy Bible that our secret will be safe with you?'

This time Webster and Marcia put their hands on their hearts and told him they would never ever tell another soul. 'We are so grateful for your kindness,' Webster added sincerely.

That did the trick. O'Riley was at last convinced. 'Follow me,' he told them, grunting with the effort as he extracted himself from the chair. 'You too, Arnie.'

They all ascended the galley steps.

O'Riley's mate was standing by the hold. This time Webster noted the doors had been closed and the rope and basket rested loosely on the deck.

'Jimmy Trezaize will be waiting at the top for ye,' O'Riley said. He caught hold of Marcia's arm saying, 'I think the basket will hold one at a time . . . best if you go first, young lady.'

She looked nervously back at Webster.

'It will be okay,' he said. 'I'll be right behind you.'

The mate steadied the basket while the others helped her in. Arnie told her not to worry as it was as safe as houses. He should know, he added cheerfully, because he'd had many a ride in it himself.

Marcia crouched down inside and gripped the sides of the basket as the mate tugged on the rope and looked upwards to shout in a powerful voice, 'Ready . . . Pull!'

Guided by the mate's hand, the basket ascended steadily until he had to let go. Webster watched with concern as the swaying basket continued on its own to eventually disappear into the heavy blackness of the cave's roof. He wished he could have gone with her; she had looked terrified.

'I'll be up there with you soon, my darling,' he mouthed softly. Wiping his hand across his brow, he realised he had broken out in a cold sweat.

Nobody spoke as they waited on the deck for the basket to return. Webster couldn't stop himself from staring up into the blackness. It seemed ages since she went up; he was beginning to wonder what was going on up there. Then, without warning, the empty basket, swaying like mad, dropped like a stone before his eyes.

Before the mate could steady the rope he had leapt in and tugged on the rope himself.

'Ready!' Arnie shouted up.

Webster threw him a look of gratitude for his cheerful hospitality and gave his thanks to them all. Before he was lost from their view he called back down to O'Riley's upturned face, 'Don't worry, skip, we won't forget our promise!'

The shaft up from the cave narrowed as he neared the top. From time to time the basket bumped against the unyielding, dank-smelling rock, and he imagined how frightened Marcia must have been, because he felt bad enough about it himself. Give me a bomber any day, he thought wryly.

A fresh wave of cool salty air filled his nostrils, and he looked up to see that the blackness was relieved by a dark grey circle of light. He was almost there. He could see now that the rope holding his basket was suspended from a tripod which bridged the opening. In its centre was a squeaking pulley which fed the rope through to its other end and the source of its pulling power which as yet remained out of sight. Suddenly a voice yelled, 'Whoa!' and a strong pair of arms helped him out onto the tufted greenery of the cliff-top. In an instant Marcia was beside him and cuddled safely in his arms.

'O'Riley said to drop ee off outside the aerodrome. Is that what you be wantin'?' The speaker's gruff Cornish burr was evident, but his anonymity was preserved by his dark clothes and a black balaclava helmet which left only a narrow gap for his eyes.

Webster guessed rightly that this was the skipper's friend, Jimmy Trezaize. 'If it's no trouble,' he answered, as both he and Marcia quickly became aware of the steady clopping of hooves. Another man dressed in the same way as Jimmy and leading a heavy shire horse drew up alongside them. They could see clearly now that this was the pulling power behind the basket's rope. It had been securely fastened to a halter around its neck. Without a word the two men swiftly dismantled the rope and gantry and flung it into the cart behind the horse.

After a whispered discussion between themselves, Jimmy told Webster and Marcia to get up in the cart. He explained to them that they were to ride back to the aerodrome with his mate as he himself had other transport.

His mate jumped in first and seized the reins, clearly anxious to be on his way. Webster jumped in and helped Marcia up, and they settled themselves on the floor at the back. They swiftly realised their driver was a man of few words but it didn't bother them in the slightest. They were so happy to be on the last leg of their long and arduous journey. They held on tightly to the sides of the cart as it swayed and lurched over the narrow bumpy track. Somewhere away in the distance could be heard the sound of a motor purring into life, and they guessed it was Jimmy's vehicular transport. Marcia giggled. 'I wonder if it's a van?' she whispered.

On the journey back, Webster had used the time to tactfully explain what could happen when they stood in front of his superiors. Marcia tried to remain calm while she listened but her insides were twisted into a writhing bunch of nerves. 'Just tell the truth,' he told her. 'You have nothing to hide.' They agreed not to mention O'Riley's escape tunnel, but to say that he had delivered them to the small fishing harbour at Newquay. It was a small white lie, but as it was of no consequence to the RAF Webster felt justified in keeping his promise to the old sea-dog.

With no more than a cursory glance behind, Jimmy's mate drew up the reins and stopped the cart just a few yards off from the main gates of the aerodrome. Webster helped Marcia down and called out his thanks as the cart began once again to trundle on its way. Webster could see the shadowy figures of the sentries as he walked towards the gates. Gripping Marcia's hand, he approached them purposefully. 'I'm sergeant Toddman. I wish to see the guard commander.'

'Do you have any identification, sergeant?'

'I do.' Webster flashed his identity disc.

'This way please.' One of the sentries escorted them to a building just inside the gates. Marcia felt sick as she stepped into the harsh glare of the guardroom and the door was slammed behind her.

Chapter Thirty-one

Reuben was grumbling to himself as his tired feet shuffled down the front path of the farmhouse. Jimmy was due to arrive more than an hour since, and he had been on the point of going to bed when he at last heard the van stop quietly outside his front gate. 'Where on earth 'ave ee bin,' he growled as he waited for Jimmy to open the doors in the back of the van. 'Bin 'angin' around waiting fer ee fer ages.'

Jimmy reached into the back of the van and dragged two of the boxes towards the edge for Reuben to pick up. 'O'Riley had another package for us to deliver tonight,' he explained nonchalantly.

'Trust O'Riley to take advantage,' Reuben said irritably, as he moved to retrieve the first of the boxes.

Jimmy could hold out no longer. The village had been buzzing with gossip for weeks now about Reuben's Land Army girl and the airman. And Reuben, who was considered to be a hard nut by all accounts, had taken it very badly. Some had even gone as far as to say he had aged a good ten years since her disappearance. Jimmy rested his hand on the old farmer's arm, and told him to wait as he had something of importance to tell him.

'It better be good,' Reuben replied impatiently, only thinking now of the warm bed that awaited him.

Jimmy explained how the boy Arnie had rode up first in the basket with a message for him from O'Riley.

Reuben tutted disinterestedly.

Jimmy went on: 'We were then told about a special package which would be sent up as soon as the boxes of booze were safely stowed away in the van. This special package was to be taken by horse and cart and dropped off up by the aerodrome.' Jimmy smiled to himself as Reuben yawned loudly, signifying his boredom. He was enjoying this, it wasn't often he could claim he was one up on the old blighter. He moved his face closer to Reuben's. 'You'll never guess what it was.'

Reuben had had enough. 'Git on with it, man,' he rasped. 'Why dun't ee 'urry up an spit it out . . . I can see you be dying to tell me.'

Jimmy could hold out no longer. 'Our special package came in the shape of a certain Land Army girl and her RAF boyfriend!'

The colour drained from Reuben's weathered face. 'Are ee sure of this?' His words were softly measured. 'Is it really our Marcia?'

'Aye, yer can be sure of that, Reuben.'

'Thank God . . . . and you too Jimmy,' Reuben added almost as an afterthought.

Jimmy quietly closed the doors of the van, and watched Reuben as he walked back up the path to the farmhouse. Even with the weight of a clinking box tucked under each arm, his step held a newfound spring. There's one old bugger who won't be getting his beauty sleep tonight — Jimmy chuckled aloud at the thought as he slid himself into the driver's seat.

Chapter Thirty-two

Jimmy had been correct in assuming Reuben would have no sleep. As soon as he had concealed his boxes in his bedroom he came back downstairs and poured himself a large whiskey. He sat down in his chair and sipped the reviving liquid as he let his thoughts dwell upon the unexpected wonderful news. William, sensing a change in his master's mood sidled over from his spot near the door and rested himself down beside him. He looked up contentedly as Reuben gently massaged his ears and told him their Marcia would soon be home with them.

The clock chimed four times. Reuben glanced across at it, then, sizing up how much of the whiskey remained in the glass, tilted it up to his lips and drained it in one gulp. With an agility that belied his years, he leapt from his chair — frightening poor William to the extent of sending him retreating to his place by the door with his tail between his legs — and dashed out to the hall. 'I know 'tiz early,' he said, talking to the bewildered dog, 'but I can't keep it to meself no longer!'

The collie grunted and put his paws over his eyes as, almost at once, he heard loud banging, followed by his master's excited cries of, 'Ruby! Norman! Wake up! 'Tiz good news!'

Reuben had the good news verified later on in the day by an airman from the RAF camp. He did not let on that he already knew. Mindful of the possible implications, he preferred to keep his private life out of it.

However, the household had to wait several long hours before they were to be united with their beloved friends. It wasn't until sometime after tea that William's bark heralded their arrival.

Reuben, Norman and a well rounded Ruby rushed out into the yard to greet them. ' 'Bout time too,' Reuben said gruffly as

Marcia flung her arms around him, clinging to him while she laughed and cried at the same time. Self-consciously, he brushed away the tears that spilled uncontrollably down over his own cheeks and said sadly, 'You'm looking some thin, m'dear.'

Webster embraced him joyfully. 'What we both need is some of your pork and potatoes,' he laughed.

Chapter Thirty-three

Those next few days at Tolcarne Merock saw a couple of unforeseen changes. One was happy, but the other was extremely sad.

But first, to go back to the couple's homecoming. The time they had spent confined to the aerodrome had turned out to be less of an ordeal than they had imagined. It was confirmed that their plane had indeed crashed, and all the crew had been reported missing, Gerry amongst them. They prayed that he and the others had made it and were only prisoners of war. At least then there was a good chance of them returning when the war was over.

When Marcia had stood frightened and alone in front of the station's commanding officer, he had asked her to tell him truthfully the whole story. This she did, whereupon his expression had softened a little and he had simply dismissed her with a sharp warning never to do such a foolhardy thing again. As she was led out from his room she clearly heard him say, 'At least she has brought one of them back safely.' And as she glanced over her shoulder she saw that he was smiling.

When Webster came out of the debriefing room he, too, had been smiling. He had been ordered to take a week's leave.

Later, back at the farmhouse, when once again they had given a detailed account of their recent ordeal, albeit omitting any mention of O'Riley's illegal activities, Webster mentioned his wish to visit his parents in Scotland while he was on leave. Reuben noticed the look of longing that flashed across Marcia's countenance at his words and reluctantly told her he would give her a week off to see her parents if she so wished. Adding grumpily afterwards, 'We've 'ad to manage without ee fer this long – another week wunt make much difference.'

So Webster and Marcia had departed for Scotland the next day, and for the rest of the week things had gone on as normal – that is until the day before they were due to arrive home. That was when Ruby lost her baby.

Only the day before, she and Norman had gone to stay with Norman's mum to await their happy event. But first, Ruby had worked hard spring-cleaning the farmhouse so that everything would be in order by the time Marcia came back from her week-long break. Sadly, Ruby had felt slightly unwell that evening and had lost her appetite. The nice tea that Norman's mum had prepared for her was left untouched. When she complained that she felt really tired, Norman advised her to go to bed early, thinking she would be right as rain after a good night's rest. He thought she must have overdone it at the farmhouse. When, just a few hours' later, she awoke in considerable pain, he rushed to the nearest telephone and summoned the doctor.

Less than an hour after arriving, the doctor had slowly descended the cottage's narrow staircase to declare sadly that the baby – a girl – had been stillborn.

Norman was distraught. His grief-stricken eyes bored imploringly into those of the doctor. 'How is Ruby?'

'She will be fine after some rest,' the doctor told him.

The following morning Norman had gone over to Gluvian Flamank farm to see if the twins would give Reuben a hand for a few days. He could not face his work right now; his place was with Ruby. Joe Trevains had offered the boys' services for as long as they were needed, saying sympathetically how he and Mrs Trevains knew how he must be feeling because they too had lost their first child. Joe tried to cheer him up a little by telling him how after a little while they tried again to start a family. 'Everything turned out all right in the end,' he said. 'You can see for yourself because we were blessed with the arrival of the terrible twins.'

When Webster and Marcia arrived back at the farm they were surprised to find Will and Fred working busily alongside Reuben, and Marcia wondered for a fleeting moment if anything was wrong. She gripped Webster's hand excitedly as Reuben walked over to greet them. She knew that the news they were about to impart would cheer him up immensely.

He was still a few steps away from them when Marcia, her excitement bubbling over, said, 'Boss, we're married!'

For a second he looked stunned by the news, then his face lit up with a score of leathery creases. 'You be dark 'orses, the pair of ee. But I'm glad.'

Marcia nearly knocked him off his feet as she fell on him to give him a hug. Her shining eyes looked back to her husband. 'We were married by special licence in our little chapel back home in Wales. It was only a small do — just Webster's folks and mine — but oh boss, it was beautiful!'

Suddenly Reuben clasped her upper arms and drew her back from him. Looking very grave, he told her there was something they should know.

Webster, realising that something very serious must have happened, moved to Marcia's side.

'Norman an Ruby's baby . . . 'tiz dead!' Reuben said brokenly.

Chapter Thirty-four

The hectic long days of summer soon melted swiftly into weeks, and autumn was lying in wait just round the corner. The dark cloud that had hung over Tolcarne Merock gradually lifted as the farmers slowly came to terms with their loss, and even Norman had started to smile again as he realised they had to look to the future now. Only Ruby remained withdrawn and seemed to prefer her own company. Marcia had tried to bring her out of herself, but to no avail. Even when she spoke of her dreadful experience in Germany, and told her confidential little tit-bits concerning their wedding, she had listened with apathy. She just wasn't the same old Ruby. Marcia understood but longed for the day when she could have her good friend back. Webster had joined the crew of another bomber as navigator and was again flying on night bombing raids over Germany. At these times Marcia would put on a brave face, but inside she was numb with worry. She knew now what awaited him and was terrified he might be shot down again. She had even stopped listening to the news, afraid of what she might hear. During their precious times together she would cling to him tenaciously, reluctant to let him out of her sight. They both knew that every moment together was very special as it could so easily be the last. At times, during the days when she had been absorbed in her farm work, her mind would suddenly switch back to the night when she had that terrifying dream. The dream itself didn't effect her so much now, but it made her think of the nun and of her strange warning. She felt a compelling urge to go back to the convent with Webster to speak to her again. Webster realised it was important to her, and as soon as his next weekend leave came up, they retraced their steps to the convent.

Marcia felt apprehensive as Webster again held the rusty ring door handle in his hand and pushed open the door in the high wall. As they stepped inside and the door slowly creaked and closed behind them, the same feeling of déjà vu, of entering into a forbidden paradise, swept over them. They were amazed to see how all the plants and bushes had grown. Without really thinking, they had foolishly imagined it to look as it did before. If anything it appeared more beautiful. Hard working bees droned lazily amongst the violets and lavender as they walked along the path towards the potting shed. Marcia kept turning her head hoping to see the nun, but the garden seemed to be deserted.

A sudden noise from the far side of the garden stopped them in their tracks. But nothing stirred down by the high boundary wall, almost covered now by the branches of several fruit trees spread-eagled over its surface. They lowered their eyes to scan the profusion of fruit bushes which flourished just below, and Webster was sure he saw one of the bushes give a wild shudder. Taking Marcia's hand, he said, 'Come on, we'll go down there and take a look.'

Marcia felt disappointment when the surprised face of a man wearing a soiled and faded cap peered out at them from behind a blackcurrant bush. He dropped his handful of freshly-picked currants into the half-filled basket on the ground beside him and, giving the impression that it was an effort to do so, rose up from his knees and squeezed past the prickly bushes to meet them.

He brushed his fingers across the sacking apron tied round his middle and after a swift glance at his red stained fingers clearly felt that a handshake would be out of the question. Instead, his tanned and weathered face blossomed into a friendly smile and he asked them if they needed any help.

He reminded Marcia somewhat of Reuben, and with that knowledge she felt it easier to confide in him. She told him how they had chanced to meet the nun here in this garden back in March, and how she had spoken to them.

He listened intently as she went on to tell him about her strange dream and of the events which followed. From time to time the gardener looked to Webster for his nod of confirmation that indeed this is what truly happened. Then, as if satisfied, he would turn back to Marcia to hear the rest of her story. She told him how, since their remarkable escape from Germany, she had thought of the nun a great deal. 'I felt I had to see her,' she explained, 'to tell her about the things that have happened to us.' She looked earnestly into the gardener's eyes. 'Is that possible?'

The old gardener looked down at his feet for a few seconds, as if searching for an answer. Then, slowly raising his eyes to meet Marcia's, he said, 'What I have to tell ee, you might not want to hear.' Noting the look of concern on the faces before him, he quickly added, ' 'Tiz nothing to worry about, but before I tells ee the tale I need to wet me throat, I be fair parched.'

They followed him back to the potting shed, where a flask of tea evidently awaited him, and sat down on a rustic bench while he went inside to fetch it.

Marcia shuffled closer to Webster to make room as the gardener came out carrying a mug in each hand. He handed one to Marcia, apologising for having no more mugs and telling them they would have to share. Watchful of the scalding hot tea, he carefully sat down beside her and sighed gratefully as he raised the mug to his lips. They waited patiently as he sipped the hot tea almost continuously, clearly intent on draining every last drop before proceeding with the tale he had promised them.

At long last he flung the dregs over the garden and placed his mug down on the ground between his feet. Turning his head sideways to look at them, he asked, 'How old was the nun?'

Marcia was surprised at his question but told him she thought she looked roughly about her own age. 'Very pale,' she told him. 'But with large dark eyes — very penetrating.'

The gardener bit his lip and nodded as if expecting the answer she gave. From above them a quivering dark cloud of swallows suddenly swooped down over the garden. Distracted, they watched for a moment or two as the birds gracefully dipped and dived over the bushes to feast upon unwary insects that could not escape their eagle eyes. The gardener's next words sent a shiver down their spines. Still intent on watching the antics of the swallows, he muttered softly: 'You've seen a ghost!'

The initial shock of being told their nun was a ghost quickly dissipated, and when he turned to them and gravely repeated the statement, their faces registered only incredulous disbelief.

'She couldn't have been,' came Marcia's faltering reply, ' . . . could she?' She looked at Webster, hoping for a reassuring

212

answer.

'All I know,' Webster said, 'is that she looked as real as you or I.'

'Ah, that may as be,' the gardener said. 'But I think t'would be for the best if ee listens to what I 'ave to say — then the two of ee can make up yer own minds.' He pondered for a moment, then he said, 'This is my garden. I've rented it from the convent for many years and in all that time I can honestly tell ee, I have never seen a nun.' He went on to tell them that the nuns had a garden of their own which was inaccessible to the outside world, as the nuns belonged to a closed order. And as far as he knew, no one had ever set eyes upon them. He told them that when he had cause to speak with the reverend mother over matters of the garden, he would enter the convent by means of a door which was for the sole use of visitors. Inside was a small room, bare except for two tables. One table was long and narrow and arrayed with little holy items which the nuns had lovingly made. Each item bore a neat price tag, and a crude wooden box with a slit in the top waited alongside for honest people to drop in their money. The other table was round and smaller. On it was a visitors' book, a hand bell, a pencil, and a neat little pile of notepaper. In the wall behind the table was a window. 'This window is heavily grilled so that nothing on the other side can be seen,' he told them. 'When I needs her, I rings the little bell and wait. If 'tiz convenient, then the next thing I hear will be her voice. It sounds to me as if she's getting on in years,' he said. 'I reckon there's only a handful of 'em left in there now, and from what I can gather, all of 'em are getting on a bit.' He waited for a moment for his words to sink in, then he said, 'Now to get back to your nun . . . '

Marcia shifted her position on the hard seat and excitedly squeezed Webster's fingers. This is what they most wanted to hear.

He said, 'Legend has it that many years ago a young nun died in the convent of a broken heart. The story goes that she was the only daughter of a well-to-do family and that she fell madly in love with a handsome young fellow who her parents considered was beneath her. The lovers planned to run away together, but somehow her parents found out and as a punishment she was banished to this convent. But the young lovers somehow managed to plan her escape before she entered the convent. They knew there was no way the young man could get inside the

213

convent, so she would have to find a way to get out. They planned that in the afternoon of the twentieth of March she would meet her lover here in this garden. His horse would be waiting for them outside the high wall, and they would ride off to spend their lives together in some far-off place. But it wasn't to be.' The gardener stole a glance at his audience and could tell by their faces that his story was beginning to take effect. He went on, 'It was quite late in the afternoon before she was able to slip away, but when she reached this garden her lover wasn't here. She waited, at first thinking that something unforeseen must have happened for him to be so late. Then, as the hours drew on and he still hadn't come for her, she knew that something terrible must have happened to him. Heartbroken, she dragged herself back to the convent and wished only for death – she could not live without him. From that day hence, she neither ate nor drank, and before long her wish was granted. But just before she died she opened her large dark eyes and they were shining with happiness. Her pale, thin face lit up with a smile as she whispered her last words – "*We are together at last*" she said.'

The heavy silence that followed was broken by Marcia who quietly asked, 'What had happened to her lover?'

'Ah, 'tiz a sad story, m'dear,' came the low reply. 'On the morning of the twentieth of March he was found at the bottom of the cliff with his neck broken. 'Twuz said her parents found out what they had planned so 'ad him conveniently removed, so to speak. Nobody knows fer sure what really happened. Verdict wuz he slipped and fell, but the people from round here all thought twuz no accident.'

'That's awful!' Marcia cried.

Webster was lost for words and could only put an arm round her shoulders to comfort her.

She looked at him with troubled eyes. 'In a way it all makes sense now, doesn't it?' she said sadly. They thanked the gardener for his time and left the garden.

Marcia was sure, now, that fate had led them to the garden on the day of Ruby's wedding. Later, when she shared the tale with Reuben, he listened to her without surprise. 'Why didn't ee tell me this in the beginning,' he said irritably, feeling put out that she hadn't taken him into her confidence earlier. 'I knows the story – 'tiz common knowledge to the old folks round here. I could 'ave 'elped ee. But then again . . . ' he grinned at her impishly, ' . . . I probably would 'ave said 'twuz a cock-n-bull story anyways. After all's said an' done, who in their right mind would believe in ghosts?'

Chapter Thirty-five

Throughout 1944 the war raged on, but life at Tolcarne Merock had brought little change. Each season had delivered its certain toil to keep the hands and minds of the farmers busy, leaving little time to dwell on the serious matters around them. In Marcia's case, the hard work kept her sane as she lived with the knowledge that her new husband was dicing with death almost every day. Ruby had eventually resumed her farm duties, but it was obvious to those closest to her that she was far from being her old self; she had lost her usual sparkle. Although she never said so, the others felt that each job she tackled had become a chore to her. Her demeanour had affected the normally happy-go-lucky Norman, and Marcia for one missed his usual light-hearted banter.

Oscar Grenville still visited them from time to time, using his remarkable sixth sense to ensure his visits coincided with ample quantities of home-cooked food and illicit booze, which Reuben, blissfully unaware that it was no longer a secret, still furtively collected in the dead of night.

By the end of the year, Marcia was glad to see the farmhouse adorned once more for Christmas with its festive finery. The war was dragging on too long and people were becoming more and more depressed. At least the cosy twinkle of the decorations helped a little to lift their spirits. The month of December had sped by so quickly that 1945 seemed to have crept in when no one was looking. The first few weeks found the workers busy with the many routine but humdrum jobs that needed to be done in the first cycle of the farming year.

When March arrived and it came around to Norman and Ruby's first wedding anniversary, Oscar had turned up, unannounced, just before tea. This time his sixth sense had let him down badly. The pair had stressed neither of them wanted any fuss so the day took its natural course. When Marcia offered him a half of her pasty, he graciously declined and said he had an urgent appointment elsewhere. He was gone in a flash. As the door slammed shut behind him, Reuben muttered under his breath, 'Sly old bugger, gone off to foist 'imself on some other unsuspecting poor ole sod, I 'specs.'

When Marcia looked across the table at Reuben, the old rogue's face wore such a look of superior indignation that she couldn't stop herself from laughing and almost choked on a mouthful of pastry.

After tea she told Reuben she was going out for a walk. Webster was on one of his long spells of duty, and she felt that a walk would help her pass away the time.

When, after an hour or so, she returned, Reuben asked her if her walk had taken her anywhere near the convent. When she answered yes, he just said quietly, 'I thought so.'

On May the eighth, when Reuben bustled out into the yard to tell them he had just heard over the wireless that the war was over, Marcia sank to her knees and burst into tears of joyous relief. Norman grabbed Ruby and they danced a wild jig around the tractor, while William looked from one to another as if they had taken leave of their senses.

That evening when Oscar Grenville happened to call, he found that most of the villagers had beaten him to it and were already enjoying the old farmer's hospitality. However, it didn't take him long to make himself at home. After sampling a good deal of the mouth-watering goodies from the heavily-laden kitchen table, he sidled over to Reuben and the pair of them, like bosom buddies, slunk off to the comfort of the parlour, where no doubt a special bottle of the old farmer's best awaited them. Even Ruby had come out of her shell after a few glasses of port. And Norman, so happy to have her back, did as everyone requested, and sang for them.

The next morning, when all the light hearts and heavy heads rallied themselves for their particular work of the day, they all agreed they would never forget the wonderful celebration they had shared. It certainly had been a night to remember.

By the end of the year Webster had been demobbed and by a stroke of luck was offered a partnership in a veterinary practice in his home town of Dundee. Although very excited about the prospect of moving to Scotland, Marcia had mixed feelings. She had grown to love Tolcarne Merock, and if she was honest with herself, old Reuben as well. But her main priority now was her husband, and wherever he went, she would be with him.

When finally they bucked up enough courage to tell Reuben of their plans, he went quiet for a moment and looked down at his feet. Then his head snapped back up to face them. 'Best place for ee!' he growled, before stomping off to be on his own.

Epilogue

Shouting voices startle me. Suddenly I become aware of the flowing river before me, and the cold, unlit pipe in my hand. I force my mind to think as I grimace with the effort of stretching my stiffened joints. Ah yes, my mind has been wandering back over the past again. It never ceases to amaze me just how vividly I remember the things which happened more than forty years ago, and yet I often fail to recall certain details which perhaps occurred only yesterday.

The yelling voices are closer now. I raise a hand to shade my eyes from the shiny glare of the water and see that the voices have materialised into Jeremy and Andrew, Marcia's two grown-up sons. They are in one of the nearby fields that belong to Tolcarne Merock.

Gliding swiftly towards them, and being guided by two excitable black and white collie dogs, is a pulsating creamy-white pancake of sheep. They are probably being moved to a more suitable field. The two men have spotted me now and they wave their hands in greeting. I smile, although they are too far away to see, then I wave back. If only Reuben could see them now, I think to myself sadly.

He did see them once just before he died. It was back in forty-nine; Jeremy was just three, and Andrew was little more than a baby. Reuben's health had started to fail soon after Marcia had left for Scotland. Although he didn't say much, you could tell he missed her dreadfully. Norman and Ruby came back to live in the farmhouse to keep him company, and in the ensuing three years he gradually left the running of the farm to Norman. It was as if he had lost all interest and preferred to spend his days sat in his chair by the fire. Even William couldn't be persuaded to help

219

Norman, preferring to stay close to his master's side, and nothing would budge him.

Near the end, Ruby could see he wouldn't be with them for much longer. She wrote to Marcia, informing her of her fears for him. Leaving Webster behind with his busy practice, Marcia and the two boys — Jeremy who was three, and Andrew little more than a baby — came back to Tolcarne Merock to stay for a few days. Reuben loved the boys and with Marcia fussing over him like old times, he seemed to have taken a turn for the better. By the time she had to leave she had high hopes that her tough old boss was going to make it, and she promised him another visit as soon as she could get away. As soon as her back was turned, he quickly slipped back into his ailing state and before the week was over he had passed away quietly in his sleep. He left Tolcarne Merock to Norman.

At first everywhere on the farm seemed empty without him. But the weight of new responsibilities on Norman's shoulders soon helped him to concentrate on the present. Just a few times he caught himself thinking he must tell boss about something or other, only to realise he couldn't; he was on his own now.

Life could have been perfect for Norman, but his relationship with Ruby was far from happy. Looking back, she was never really the same after losing her baby, and one day she just upped and left. She went back to London, saying she missed its bright lights and bustle. She was never cut out to be a farmer's wife, and their marriage was over.

Norman was devastated, but no amount of pleading would change her mind. He carried on at Tolcarne Merock alone and ruthlessly buried himself in his work. But life, as we know, is far from predictable, and it's strange how things worked out in the end.

Apart from keeping in touch with an occasional note or the usual birthday and Christmas cards, six years were to pass before Norman saw Marcia and the boys again, and it was under very sad circumstances. Webster had been killed outright in a car crash. He had gone out one bitterly cold night to attend to a sick animal. A car coming towards him at a ridiculous speed skidded on a patch of black ice and crashed headlong into him. Neither driver survived.

When Marcia was able to think more clearly, she felt she had to move away from Scotland. Without Webster, she felt so alone. Her thoughts turned to Cornwall and Tolcarne Merock, and she realised she longed to get back there.

When Norman received her letter asking if he would like a housekeeper and two lively boys, he gladly agreed to the arrangement.

The lonely and neglected farmhouse suddenly burst into life again with the boy's energetic zest for life and learning. The house again shone from top to bottom, and homely cooking smells wafted out of the kitchen window.

Marcia was back to care for it. The house was happy.

From behind me a gentle hand rests on my shoulder and startles me back to the present day. A soft kiss is planted on my cheek and loving words are whispered in my ear. I look back into the loving eyes of the woman I married twenty happy years ago. Her hair is grey now, but she is still beautiful. Together we watch as the sun slowly sinks down into the ocean. She takes my hand. 'It's getting cold, Norman,' she says.

I take one more look over the land I know so well and sigh. I turn to her and smile.

'Let's go home, Marcy.'